RICHARD MALMED

DEATH OF A PEOPLE

The Cathars

WORKBOOK PRESS LLC
187 E Warm Springs Rd,
Suite B285, Las Vegas, NV 89119, USA

Website:	https://workbookpress.com/
Hotline:	1-888-818-4856
Email:	admin@workbookpress.com

Ordering Information:
Quantity sales. Special discounts are available on quantity purchases by corporations, associations, and others.
For details, contact the publisher at the address above.

Library of Congress Control Number:
ISBN-13:   978-1-954753-20-4 (Paperback Version)
             978-1-954753-21-1 (Digital Version)

REV. DATE: 17/02/2021

At Tomb

Miriamne began to shout and cry wildly at Golgotha to the west of Jerusalem. "His body is gone, his body is gone, what have they done with him, with… it." Since running from Golgotha and the family tomb of Yusuf of Arimathea, she had been followed by several men in gleaming white robes, but she was oblivious to them in her grief. Finally she fell to her knees by the side of the dusty road. The men approached her cautiously. "Miriamne, Miriamne, be calm. He is with us," They whispered. She looked up with disbelief. She had waited the days from the crucifixion until the third day. As his wife – even a secret one – it had fallen on her to scrub the body with herbs and let the flesh melt off the bones for a year until his remains could be collected in an ossuary for permanent burial. But they weren't there. None of him was there, only his shroud folded neatly on the shelf. She looked up through tear-stained eyes, disbelieving. "Who… Who are you?"

"We are Essenes, we have collected Yeshua and taken him with us."

"To where?"

"To the wilderness."

"What will you do with him there?"

"Heal him." By now Yusuf of Arimathea had come upon them. He had been summoned by one of the Essenes.

"Miriamne, Miriamne, calm yourself." With Yusuf's presence,

her percussive breathing began to slow and she looked up at him. He was a friend, a good friend and a follower of Yeshua and his teachings.

"What is happening, Yusuf?"

"We have taken him to safety in the wilderness."

"To bury him?"

"No, no, he is alive but in pain and suffering."

"You mean, he lives?"

"Yes, yes… Come with me." She rose, looked at the men in white robes around her with some wonder and followed Yusuf to where several donkeys stood, tethered to an Acacia bush.

"Please," he gestured. She mounted one of the little animals and followed as Yusuf clucked to his donkey.

"But Yusuf. The stone… the Roman guards… What?"

"Miriamne, don't ask, just follow."

"But I saw him die."

"Please, no more questions."

They rode for several miles along an old path. As they reached a small cliff in the pinkish brown hill by the wayside, Yusuf pulled a small instrument from his pack and blew, emitting bird-like sounds. From the top of a hill, a teenage boy emerged and began to make bird whistles. The boy descended the hill and led them around a curve in the road where two men in white robes came to greet them.

"Ah, Yusuf. Come! Come!"

Soon they crouched into the entrance of a small cave and followed the trail into a larger cavern. There lay Yeshua on a bed of rock, administered by several women in white robes. His body was covered with wounds which had herbs and grasses clinging to them.

Miriamne broke into a run. "Yeshua… Yeshua. You are alive." He smiled, "Yes, it would seem so." He smiled weakly.

"But how… I saw you die… and the Roman guards, the stone over the tomb…"

"Miriamne, please, don't ask. It is dangerous." He turned his head to Yusuf and nodded. Yusuf touched Miriamne on the shoulder. "He is recovering from his wounds. His back has many scourges, and his side was pierced."

"Yes, yes, I saw that. But then he was hung on the cross for hours." "Fortunately, his legs were never broken and he was only bound with ropes."

"Do you have something to do with this, Yusuf?"

"Please, Mariamne, accept that he is with us."

"Yes, yes, of course. But the men, our disciples."

"Some will hear from us in the future, but not now. Most have fled."

"What will we do?"

"As soon as he is well enough for the journey, we will go to Alexandria."

"What can I do now?"

"Help the women with his healing and pray." And so Yusuf left Mariamne in the cavern and rode back to Jerusalem.

Days followed as Yeshua began to improve, soon he was walking and eating regular food, but he had yet to see the light of day.

"You know, Mariamne, I must address the disciples and tell them what happened."

"Yeshua, I must respect your safety. Many of them have fled and some have gone north to Syria. They fear the Romans."

"Then, bring Peter to see me." At this, one of the Essenes spoke.

"Yeshua, he cannot come here. This place must remain secret."

"Yes, yes, I understand. Can we meet in Alexandria?"

"How do you feel? Can you travel?"
"I think so. Am I safe in Alexandria?"
"Yes, we can protect you there."
"Give me a few more days, then I want to go to Alexandria."

To Alexandria and On

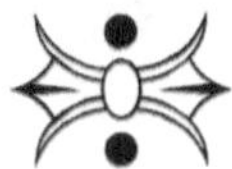

"A few more days" was optimistic, but some more recuperation and Yeshua was ready to go to Alexandria. The Essenes stocked a small cart drawn by donkey with enough provisions for the trip. They joined a caravan going across the Sinai from Jerusalem. Miriamne drove most of the way as Yeshua was shielded from the sun under a sheet, kept cool with a few cups of water splashed on the sheet. After a few arduous days, they veered off on the road to Ramses, the Jewish village just east of Alexandria and were welcomed by some locals. There had for many years been this Jewish settlement in Alexandria. There were those who looked to Jerusalem and the Temple there, and those who looked to the Alexandrian Temple. The priests at the Alexandrian Temple were not of the hereditary Sadducee line, but were independent. It was these that Yeshua had visited and befriended in his early wandering years before he sought out John the Baptist and then began his own ministry. These priests had become senior officials at their Temple now. As they came out to greet Yeshua, they were shocked to see this frail creature standing with the help of the donkey cart in their street. He was not like the days of his youth when he was an itinerant scholar staying with them.

"Egad, Yeshua what has happened to you. We have heard rumors of your arrest by the Romans, but nothing further."

"Alas, my brothers, I have survived a crucifixion and flee the

Romans. But…"

A dozen voices broke out. "What?" "Survived a…" "Flee the Romans." Miramme now spoke up.

"Good men, I must ask for your silence and your help. What you see now is a secret. You must know nothing of this and you must help us. Even now, the Romans seek us. If it were to come out that he had escaped, there would be trouble for all. Including yourselves."

The Alexandria Jews being a minority were permitted a freedom and an autonomy from the Romans. In Jerusalem, the Jews and their many factions were a rebellious bunch, always causing trouble; here, they kept to themselves and were neither taxed more than the Egyptians, nor harassed in their religious practices. These priests had heard of the troubles in Jerusalem, but had not experienced them.

Yeshua handed them a letter from Yusuf of Arimathea which explained their history and asked for help.

"Ah, Yusuf. A wise man. Yes. We will help, what can we do?"

"Hide us for now, and then let us escape to Hispania."

"Hispania, you say. You must travel along the desert of Numidia and get a boat to cross the Great Sea."

By now, Lazarus and another one of Yeshua's followers had joined them in Alexandria in the company of a few Essenes. They greeted Yeshua and Miriamne warmly and sat around the cooking fire looking at the embers.

Lazarus spoke. "Yeshua, I thought you were dead. You were on the cross for hours and then you died."

Yeshua laughed softly. "Did not you, Lazarus, take the mandrake and 'die' in Bethany? They had me summoned to raise you from the dead."

"But, Yeshua, you told me it was too dangerous and never to try it again. You were angry with me."

"Yes, but the times called for desperate measures." Lazarus and the rest fell silent and sipped the lentil soup until it cooled.

"So what will we do now?"

"Miriamne and I had decided to flee to Hispania and begin to preach there."

"We must join you. We will help however we can." After some thought and a few nods from Miriamne, Yeshua assented. They would come, too.

Lazarus had brought with him in a large cart a number of things which Yusuf had supplied them. There were many sacred scrolls along with the Torah as well as many Greek scrolls. There was also a large purse to pay for their journey.

"Yes… Yes. Exactly. Can you help us?"

"Of course, many of our people send vessels for trade, but to Rome not to the West. But the currents are bad. Here they push the ship back to the east. Only from Numidia, they go north and then along the coast to the west and Hispania. You must first travel to Numidia."

Numidia as it was now called had been Carthage until it was conquered by Rome years ago. After the conquest, it had been leveled and was only farmland. Now, it was a vast wheat field that grew grain which was shipped to Rome. The road was easily traveled, but only by caravan. Bandits lurked among the hills and preyed on solitary travelers. Yes. They must join a caravan. But now, they would not be among friends, so they would need protection even in the caravan from inquisitive eyes.

And so, after a few days rest in Ramses village, they hitched the donkey back to the cart and prepared to join the caravan. As they were about to leave, the priests came out to join them.

Several of the Essenes carried armfuls of scrolls as well.

"Master, we must give you some things for your journey."

With that, some of the younger priests came out bearing religious scrolls. Of course, there was a Torah in the Aramaic of Yeshua's Galilean village but also scrolls of the prophets, and texts in Greek.

By now, the Greek wisdom spread by Alexander had begun to make inroads in the Jewish culture. These priests envisioned Yeshua and Mariamne establishing a congregation in Hispania. They would need these works to educate their new neighbors. Yeshua was most grateful and laid the case carefully in the cart under the canvas sheet.

And so they left.

The wait for the caravan was not long as they joined in the long line. Their payments were duly accepted by the outriders who would guard the caravan as they galloped back and forth along the line of travelers to the west. These men were of all sorts and bore the scars of many battles in many places fighting for many realms. Some wore scarves to cover their old wounds, but all bore their weapons of choice, mostly spears and swords which they brandished as they rode.

They went south of the Nile delta and then west along the Roman road to what had been Carthage. From time to time as they mounted the ridges, they could see the Great Sea on their right. A few cool breezes blew from the trade winds blowing east, but the sun beat down on them. Yeshua was still weak and lay under the sheet which was soaked with water from time to time. The others rode the large cart Yusuf had supplied. Lazarus drew a map on large leaves and a boat. He drew the Great Sea and a distant shore to show fishermen where they wanted to go.

On occasion, they would sing or chant songs and hymns as the cart rocked along slowly in line. It was several days journey to Numidia. At night, they camped under a large tent. The nights were cool and large fires were set along the line of the caravan to keep warm. For his safety, Yeshua stayed under the sheet at night and was covered with animal skins. As the caravan proceeded, some of the travelers would turn off and go to the coastal towns. By the time it reached Numidia, only a few carts and camels were left. Soon they would reach the town of Girta just a few miles from a small bay of fishing villages on the Great Sea.

Outside Girta, they pulled off from the caravan and pitched tents and set a cooking fire. After several days on his back in the cart, Yeshua was happy to get out and walk around the area. He had been composing some sermons in his head and jotting notes down as they went.

Lazarus was dispatched to the fishing village in the bay to secure a boat to take them north to Hispania. Maximinus, one of Yeshua's followers, came with him. He had been a fisherman at Capernaum. It was thought he could help in speaking to these coastal fisherman.

None in their group had navigated the Great Sea, so they must rely on those who did. He had a nice purse hidden back in the cart as he drew up to the huts scattered along the shore.

As they approached the shacks of the fishermen, they tried to speak with them, but could only communicate in rough forms of Latin. Lazarus had some schooling in an educated form of Greek, while the fisherman only had a few words of street slang. Lazarus showed them his hand drawn map and had to make do with sign language and acting out his questions.

Eventually with much improvisation, the fisherman began to understand that Lazarus and five people wished to sail by boat north to the Roman province of Hispania by sailing along the west coast of Sardinia. The fishermen shrugged and seemed to say that they only fished a short distance from the shore and that the Great Sea was very rough and dangerous at times with big winds and big waves. As they drew in the sand a rough map of northern Africa and the sea, they included a blob which they seemed to call an island. Eliezer took this to be Sardinia as he could see on a map he had from Alexandria. The fishermen nodded enthusiastically on recognizing the island on the map. But then, one – maybe their leader – puffed up his cheeks and blew as he pointed to the passage to Sardinia and made great sweeping movements with his hands to show big waves. Maximinus asked if the waves were big all year long or just in certain times. He mimicked shivering in winter or wiping sweat from his brow in summer. As he knew from the Sea of Galilee winter was dangerous, summer not. Finally, the fishermen agreed they went further out and even to Sardinia in the summer. So now a deal could be struck. The fishermen would for much silver take the five in two boats across the Great Sea. Eliezer said he would be back with the silver and the passengers in a day and so it was agreed.

Miriamne was very grateful to Lazarus for arranging this passage and ran to tell Yeshua. But he was skeptical. In his travels he had experienced the severity of the squalls which could blow up without warning on the Great Sea. The Sea of Galilee was bad enough. But it was now late spring and the threat of such storms was diminished. So he nodded. It must be done. And so they prayed. At the back of everyone's mind was Noah who had been spewed by a great fish onto land after his boat had been buffeted by waves. Would Yeshua and Miriamne be spewed on land and commanded to preach as had Noah. Let it be so.

To the Great Sea

Lazarus arranged for the sale of the donkeys and cart in Girta so long as the buyer would take them and their belongings to the bay. With a shrug the buyer agreed. So Yeshua, Miriamne and the rest loaded the cart and drove to the bay. The fishermen greeted them, but eyed the women suspiciously. Women were generally not welcome on boats. Nonetheless, the fishermen helped to load the bundles on the two boats, but seemed to inspect each parcel with great attention. Yeshua who sat by the side became wary of this scrutiny and called Lazarus to him.

"Lazarus, be careful with these men. They are not to be trusted." "Yes, Yeshua, I see. They smile and greet us, but I feel too warmly. We must be careful."

And so they slept by the bay that night and prepared at first light to embark on the passage. The group was divided between the two boats as they pushed off. A light easterly breeze filled the sail and the boats crested the incoming surf and soon were cruising at a nice pace northward. While the boats rocked somewhat, the journey would hopefully be as smooth as this the entire way. Nonetheless, several of the group were sea sick; the constant rising and falling was not something they were used to. They traveled by camel, not by sea.

At last, land began to appear on the starboard side and a cheer rose among the group. Even the fishermen were relieved to see this landfall as they had never been this far off shore. And so they pulled into a rocky cove and drifted until they could see a beach where they could beach the boats and find fresh water. A night was spent in the safety of the land.

As morning first rose over the hills to the east, a storm with thunder and lightning blew in from the north and west. The fishermen drew into a tight huddle and began to gesture and speak in excited tones. Yeshua and Lazarus knew this was not a welcome sight. Their fears were justified when the fishermen turned with large hooks and knives and forced Yeshua's group to stand to one side. They then began to unload bundles from one boat and place them all in the other boat. Lazarus and Maximinus implored them to leave some food and water, but the fishermen began to open the bundles and scatter them on the ground looking for valuables. Mercifully, they did leave some food, and the large bundle of scrolls wrapped in leather. They pushed the loaded boat into the mounting surf and set sail under the now gathering wind from the north heading back to Numidia.

As they left, Miriamne looked bewildered at Yeshua who stood looking at the departing boat. After a few moments of reflection, Yeshua said, "We had always feared this and now it has happened. I have been assured that the current will carry us to the north and Hispania. We must let the storm pass, gather water and push off when it is calm." His presence seemed to reassure everyone. They turned the boat over and crept underneath. They lit a small fire and began to cook a lentil soup and churn a hummus. Miriamne began to sing a hymn from the Psalms and everyone murmured the words while grasping the warm cup in their hands. It was to be an obstacle – this betrayal but not the first they had faced, and it would not result in death. Yeshua had said so.

The storm lasted until the early evening and then tailed off into a light drizzle. Lazarus and Maximinus went out into the now calm water and began to feel for the current. Sure enough it was drifting north again. They returned and told Yeshua.

"We have little food and water. We cannot waste time here. We must travel both by night and day and drift as long as we can with the current." So they flipped the boat over and dragged it back to the sea, threw in the few remaining bundles and jumped back into the boat. The North Star was now visible in the clearing sky and so Maximinus held the rudder steady for that direction.

The wind was still from a northerly direction. Without any experienced sailors to figure how to use the headwind to their advantage, the boat drifted freely and slowly northward on the current. The next few days, the sun came out in full force, the sea was not calm but manageable, and so the boat drifted with little difficulty.

Suddenly, a new current began to push the boat in a westward direction. Maximinus fought to continue northward, but the boat now was headed north and west, somewhat buffeted by the westward current hitting the boat midships.

The food and water had dwindled very low and the sun was hot. Where were they? Could they continue on? Prayers were said, hymns sung. But they knew something must happen. They were drifting further west, and not making much headway north.

And then, land. Yes. A cliff was visible now off the starboard side. Maximinus fought with the rudder to head north, but the land did not seem to come any closer and a new current from the east seemed to fight the current from the north. This current was darker and colder. Maybe a river pouring out into the sea. Yes, it was colder and darker.

They seemed to be drifting faster and now land was spotted to the west, ahead of the boat, and coming on at a fast rate.

Yes, they were nearing this new land. The cool current was now pushing behind it and the boat was moving in surf coming from the sea as well. Yes. It was land. Within an hour they were carried by the surf towards a growth of greenery off a small beach. As they drew with 100 feet, Maximinus and Lazarus jumped into the water and began to pull the boat ashore. And soon, they landed. They hefted the boat onto the beach and turned it over for shelter.

They spread their things out on the beach to dry and calmly ate hummus and dried fruit. And then they heard a tinkling. The sound of goat bells. Soon, a young boy and a few goats wandered out of the foliage. Lazarus came up to him. Could he speak Latin? Yes, the boy spoke a form of Latin, and so they talked back and forth.

It seemed there was a small village where the boy lived with his parents. They were Gauls who had now come under Roman rule. They were not far from the Via Domitia, the large Roman road which ran from Rome along the north coast to Cadizá, Spain. They were in a civilization of some sort. They were pagans, and rarely saw their Roman overlords, but lived in peace in their small village rarely bothered by anyone except the greedy tax collector.

The group kneeled and prayed. Miriamne led the hymn in a low voice. Yeshua sat by the side, weak from his wounds and now this debilitating sea voyage, but he blessed everyone. It was hard to tell what God had intended by all this. The arrest, the crucifixion. He was still mystified as he had awakened in a cave with ossuaries on the shelves near him. And then men had come in at night to spirit him away in an open cart. The trip in the sun down the Sinai coast to Alexandria. The events were mounting in montages in his head. But he was here now. Beside Miriamne who intoned hymns from the Psalms. With all this misfortune, they were still alive. Had they been spewed on the shore like Noah?

Soon they gathered up their bundles and followed the boy and the goats back to his village. As this strange and ragged assemblage neared the town, a few of the women came out to see what this boy and his goats had brought them. It was clear that they were hungry. Lazarus made do the best he could with his meager Latin and the women brought out eggs and fruit for the group. As the women began to ask who they were and where they were from, Yeshua cast a wary glance at Lazarus and motioned him to the side as the rest ate.

"Lazarus, you know we are still in Roman lands, and I am wanted for some Roman crime. No one must know who I am or they will surely arrest me again."

"Quite so, master. What shall we do?"

"I think we must speak Greek from now on and say that we are from Egypt. That our boat went adrift. That is all. We are Egyptians."

"Yes. We are not light-skinned like they are. They cannot know the difference between Jews and Egyptians. Maybe they can speak Greek. Try!"

While concealing Yeshua, Lazarus introduced Yeshua as Jesus and Miramne as Maria as their names were in Latin. Lazarus made a few attempts at Greek, but got little recognition and so reverted to Latin. The women were satisfied. The Egyptians were well known in southern Gaul and much appreciated because they supplied the north with grain. And so, the identity of the group remained a secret and, from now on, they were merely ship-wrecked Egyptians. Ship wrecks frequently washed up on these southern shores.

The group was told that they had landed at the mouth of the Rhone River. They were not in Hispania, but were in southern

Gaul, in an area called "Oppidum Ra" at the mouth of the Rhone.

The people living there were peasants and held a confusion of beliefs in the gods. Their old temples and places of worship had been taken over by Roman priests of the various Roman gods – pallid imitations of the Greek ones. So the enthusiasm for worship was lukewarm, at best, but still the sacrifices for good harvests, fertile farm animals and fertile wives must be observed or who knows what might happen. Yeshua toured a few of the temples on worship days but kept his peace. To say temples was inaccurate, they were large mud huts with wooden figures daubed with earthen colors. Some were hand formed from clay. But it was striking how similar the devotions of the pagans were like those of the philistines and other pagans of Palestine. Had he been wrong? Had the Jews been wrong to worship the one God, and be guided by the Torah? Had he been punished by fate for his arrogance that he might lead people to a kingdom of heaven? And now, he was a sickly broken man – not dead, but the religious fervor was difficult to summon up. As was his way, he walked out to a rock and sat to brood, and pray for guidance. Was this the end?

Nonetheless, the group continued to gather at sundown on Friday to light candles and say the prayers they had prayed for generations back. There were not enough for a minion – ten men to attend the service and read the Torah. It should have fallen to Yeshua to read the weekly portion of the Torah, but this was a miraculous landing on a new coast and a time for new beginnings. It fell to Miriamne, now to be known as Mary, to read the Torah portion – and she added her own postscript. She read as well the portion about Noah, spewed from the belly of a large fish and directed by God to preach. Only this time, not in Nineveh but in Oppidum Ra. So the travelers retired to the Sabbath meal and once again to praise God for their rescue from the Great Sea for some as yet unknown purpose.

Limoux – 1,200 Years Later

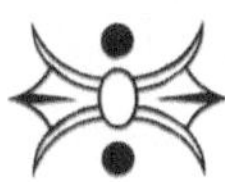

The two women joined the caravan at Limoux bound for Carcassonne. For most people the only safe way to travel over these country roads was by caravan. Bandits lurked, and so did itinerant knights. When not engaged in actual battle for their liege lords, knights equipped as they were with horse, armor and weapons were free to pursue other interests. Robbing and pillaging as well as the occasional rape was a diversion to be pursued in between bouts of heavy drinking. So Zastra and Chloe, daughter and mother, were waiting early that morning to join the caravan. The air of early spring was warm and carried the scent of flowers and budding leaves, and the attitudes of their fellow travelers were cheerful and buoyant. The constant thrum of the cicadas filled the air. The guards of the caravan trotted up and down the lengthy train moving ponderously through the forest. Occasionally, some part of the old Roman road remained and the pace picked up, but mostly the carts, and carriages sloshed through the mud of recent rain showers. Zastra, now a woman at 17, and her mother, Chloe, mother at 34, rode behind two donkeys pulling their cart on the way to market at Carcassonne. The cart was filled with sacks, and chests of medicinal herbs for their stall where they purveyed remedies of all sorts. They were healers and their family and many in their village were healers. Generations had passed down the properties of plants for the cure of many human maladies.

Some in the village claim to have gotten the source of their cures from back in the ancient Greek manuscripts brought along with Mary Magdalene centuries earlier. Now, the knowledge passed by word of mouth. The village of Limoux had not preserved the literacy that the elders claimed once to have been the ability of all town residents. The Romans had not been kind, nor had the Arabs who controlled the region. Travel and learning were not pursuits encouraged by the authoritarian rulers. Only the Visigoths had left the town in peace, but now since Pepin the Short had chased the Arabs back over Pyrenes to Iberia, the Christian monks and bishop had kept a close eye on all activities in the realm. Since Charles the Hammer had accepted the crown from the Roman pope, monks and priests fanned out to spread their official religion of the King and the Pope. The church and the French king sought to consolidate their power by having the church control illiterate peasants by the myths their priests taught.

For it all, the caravan was in a cheerful mood. Some had broken out lutes and drums and were playing happy tunes as those near them sang the familiar lyrics. The scents of new spring filled the air and the sun shone brightly. From time to time, the caravan guards trotted by. The women had paid their fare to join the caravan which traveled different roads on different days.

The women sat in the cart behind a small donkey. Their cart was filled with bags and boxes of herbs. The two would take the caravan on the main road to Carcassonne for market day. They would stay at a widow's hut outside town on the day before the market and then rise at dawn to claim the booth they had purchased several years ago. The market would last two days, and the market would be flooded with townspeople and other visitors who would stroll the aisles. Goods of all sorts were on offer: Mostly food – butchers' stalls hung with fresh cut beef or pork, rabbits, chickens, ducks, and even squirrels, fish lay in the open air mouths agape, fresh fruits and vegetables stacked neatly, spices, olive oil. Further from the fetid smells of the food were vendors hawking clothing: shifts, pelts, sandals, and even a few selling finery in silk and fine blue and purple dyed cotton. Chloe had selected a booth with a tent-like covering in this area. At the rear of their booth was a chest containing many medicinal herbs, now under a locking hasp, but soon to be opened and replenished with new stock the women had brought from home.

Leaving their cart at the widow's house, the women hired a porter to take their bundles from the cart to their booth on his hand cart. Already the aisles were in pools of mud as the vendors and customers tromped through the aisles. The porter wheeled his cart up to the high level which was drier, and quieter. Slowly the boxes were offloaded and the herbs stowed in compartments in the chest at the rear of the booth, or laid carefully on low tables around the edges of the booth. The women brought out their stools, smoothed out their shifts and began to prepare for their trade.

As the sun rose over the top of the buildings lining the square, a multitude began to drift in and stroll the aisles. Zastra and Chloe were by now well-known and were greeted warmly by the passersby. While Chloe had pulled her headscarf over her now graying hair, Zastra sat with cascades of chestnut curls falling about her shoulders to her waist. Her gray-green eyes searched intelligently among those who stepped under the roof of their tent. Each customer would whisper their maladies as they bent forward, the women would ask a few questions, demand a fee and then turn to root among their chests and bundles until they found the right cure. There was no doctor about, and besides, most people dismissed them as quacks. They were however, familiar with how diligent and respected these purveyors of herbs could be.

Boils were a common complaint since few people bathed. For this, she lanced the boil and applied garlic directly. Constipation was often a result of poor eating habits; for this, psyllium seed was doled out; the opposite, diarrhea was healed with bilberry. The older women whispered their complaint of hot flashes; for this: red clover. For an assortment of pains of the back, chest, limbs and whatnot, crushed willow bark. For the recently pregnant suffering, morning sickness, ginger in tea form or mashed into food. Menstrual cramps begot kava, shingles capsicum, and yeast infections – garlic or goldenseal. Soon the line was down the aisle. People stood with coins in their hands ready for Zastra and Chloe who bustled around their little stall. Since the Jews had been chased from the area, there had been no reliable doctors and the two women were now the only welcome practitioners of the healing arts.

Osric

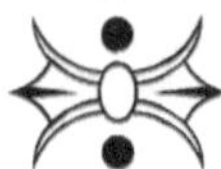

Towards midday, there was a bustling and a hubbub from outside the booth. Those in line began to draw back from the booth as a young lord and his two retainers swaggered up the aisle. Young Osric was dressed resplendently in a hand embossed leather doublet with his family's seal of a stag rampant in a field of gold. He wore tights with one red and one green leg with a large cod piece. From his waist, a broadsword dangled. His retainers also had broadswords strung over their backs, and dressed in heavy leather shifts.

"Oh, ho, little wren," Osric chirped at Zastra as she turned from the chest at the rear of the booth. By now she had been working for about six hours, and a damp ringlet of chestnut curls hung down her forehead. "What brings you to our fair city?"

Realizing she was being addressed by an important personage, she curtsied. "Purveying medication, your grace."

"I had heard we had a pretty little sparrow up here. You are refreshing, my dear." He addressed her in terms reserved for low and menial servants – "tu" – and not the formal or polite – vas – as most reputable people deserved. It was an insult.

Chloe flashed a look at Zastra – a mother's warning to mind her manners. A lord could – at a whim – bring the law down on any commoner in his realm, and, now with the support of the church, his power was even greater.

"Can I get you something, my Lord?" Zastra asked with her

eyes cast downward, avoiding and ignoring the insult. A crowd had gathered outside the booth to watch the interplay.

"Yes, my pretty sparrow. Something for my heart. It races when I look at you." A chuckle rose from the assembled onlookers.

"Your heart, good sir. Ah! I see. Perhaps you need a purgative to rid you of your bad manners." The glare from Chloe grew more intense, this was now a dangerous time. The Lord could exact revenge for a minor insult, especially in front of his subjects. Osric was not the lord, only the teenage step son of the Lord, Alphonso, who, it was rumored, was in ill health. The son could not order revenge, but he might seek his stepfather's aid. But now, Alphonso was, it was said, not exerting his power.

"Might I know your name, my sparrow?"

"It's Zastra, my Lord." She could not refuse or ignore this request.

"Where are you from?"

Again. "Limoux, my Lord," with a curtsey this time.

"Ah, I see. A country mouse."

"Are you a Christian?" This was a threat, an ominous incursion for the time. Many heresies abounded and were being rooted and by the priests now at the direction of the Pope. A wrong answer could mean endless interrogation as well as torture or death.

"Yes, my Lord." Again, her eyes were lowered and avoided contact.

Apparently, having regained his stature and command over this impudent subject, Osric seemed satisfied and swaggered off trailed by his retainers. The line of customers reformed as Chloe and Zastra again began bustling back and forth between their customers and their stores at the rear of the booth. Around 1:00 p.m., the crowd had thinned, so the women took a short rest and went to a small stand to sit and have some fresh tea.

"You know, Zastra, how dangerous that is!" Chloe barked at her daughter.

"Yes, Mother," Zastra groaned. "I know who we are." She had lowered her voice. The women came from a Cathar community - closely scrutinized sect whose beliefs differed from the demanding friars – anxious to find someone to persecute.

Yes, Zastra knew. She was working to become "perfect" and take the vow of "consolamentum." She was a Cathar – now considered a heretic, and, thus, a permitted victim of robbery, rape and even slavery. As yet the village of Limoux was not known to be a Cathar enclosure. Friars, as these men were known, were not priests, or even educated, but the Pope had authorized them to roam freely and sort out those whose doctrines differed from the Orthodox. As a result, they were called Cath-ars, not Cath-olics, to show that they were Arians – a sect which did not accept the trinity; and questioned the divinity of Jesus. Instead, they looked to Mary Magdalene – who was reported to be their founder. They considered John the Baptist to be Jesus' superior. Cathars from this region spoke a different dialect from their Frankish overlords and this might be singled out by their accent alone. They said "Oc" instead of the Frankish "oui" for yes, and so the region was called "Langue D'oc" or language of the Oc. So Chloe and Zastra were careful to speak the prevailing dialect. For this reason, Osric's questions had a barely concealed threat – a careful ear might hear the "Oc" tones, and entitle Osric to make them his prisoners at will. The seemly innocent scene was fraught with danger and the onlookers, at least some, were anxious to observe the drama. Alas, there had been none. But the two women where still shaken, nonetheless. Zastra's impudence had been accepted as a young girl's sauciness, hopefully and Osric would be seen no more. His kind could only marry other nobility and not lowly commoners. That did not prevent the young lords from frequent dalliances. But Zastra had begun the vow of holiness and any such liaison with Osric would be a disaster – even if unwilling. Cathars viewed the body as a material burden, used only to encase their spirit which was holy. Defilement of the body could have a debilitating and permanent stigma on their soul. Certainly Osric could know little of the harm he had threatened. Chloe well knew the ways of this so-called nobility, who could treat any in their domain as personal property. The women were still shaking as they sat at their tea and nibbled on the raw vegetables they had brought from home. Yet, these fair days were an important source of money for their village and they would have to return to their booth. Even now, their customers waited patiently by the booth for their return and so, with reluctance, they heaved themselves up and trudged back to their fair and their trade.

As the sun began to settle on the horizon, the air again became chilly. The women packed up their wares carefully and signaled the porter to escort them back to the women's house where they were boarding. The porter while not an imposing figure would nonetheless discourage any thievery of the day's proceeds. Early the next morning, the women would join the caravan back from Carcassonne and safety.

Back in Limoux

The cart was packed and ready before dawn. Chloe had hidden the proceeds from yesterday's market carefully in a sliding niche in the floorboard. The donkey was still sleepy as they clucked and gave his rear some slaps until he wriggled into his harness and pulled the cart up to the roadway to join the caravan west. As the long train approached, Zastra handed one of the outriders a few coins and pulled the cart into line. The women had brought some goat's milk, and a few handfuls of nuts and fruits as the caravan stretched out over the old Roman road. The outriders cantered and galloped up and down the line at intervals. As the sun rose in the midmorning sky, Chloe took the first nap on the sacks in the rear of the cart which had been much depleted by their sales, while Zastra gave the reins a few slaps on the donkey.

Outside Carcassonne, the cart pulled out to attach itself to another caravan to the south and Limoux. As they waited in the cleared area off to the side, several riders on large horses rode up. And no! It was that pest Osric again. Zastra tried to turn aside, but he had caught sight of her and pulled up along with his two retainers.

"Ah, my little sparrow. I knew we'd find you here on this pleasant day."

Chloe was still in a light sleep on the sacks. Zastra would have to handle this on her own. "Yes, sire. Have you need of any medication?"

"Ah, my wren. Tis you I've come to see."

"Good sire, I am a commoner and you a noble. There is nothing you could want with me." She spoke the truth. At his father's castle, there were sure to be a flock of ladies in waiting – all noblewomen hoping for advantageous marriages while they tended to the queen and other matters of court. It was widely rumored and often observed that doings in the castle between the knights and those ladies were lascivious. A commoner could only serve as a concubine for a noble, and, when the attraction was gone, she would become a scullery maid at the lowest level in the castle. "Good sir, I look to take the holy vows. I have sought a life of celibacy." In fact, she spoke the truth. Her ambition was to become a "perfect" among the Cathars and preach as her mother did among the Cathar faithful. While not necessarily a celibate profession, it was a holy one, highly regarded among her people. Of course, she would mislead him. In the true Catholic Church, the young novitiates were expected to be virgins. Even a rape might disqualify them from the holy orders. Forcible and unwanted intercourse with such a woman, even a commoner, would cause an open revolt of the lord's subjects. Zastra hoped that would end the discussion. But Osric persisted. He had been drinking though it was just past midday and he was encouraged by the guffaws of his two retainers. By now, Chloe had been awakened and rose to her feet in the rear of the cart and in a low growl, spoke to Osric with a fixed glare.

"Good lord, Osric. We know who you are. We are the Count of Toulouse's loyal subjects and entitled to his protection. Please leave us in peace lest the men of our village bring this matter to the next assizes." She was threatening to make a plea at the next month's court session where a judge appointed by the Count would sit and hear the pleas and complaints of his serfs as well as deciding disputes at law. Osric well understood the embarrassment his father and he might suffer at this very public gathering. With a sneer, he jerked his horse to the rear and cantered off.

"Oh, Mother. He is a worriment."

"Yes, dear. If he only knew how much." But the jingle and clanging of the southbound caravan was heard in the distance. It was a relief. They handed coins to the outriders and pulled in line. Neither of the women napped this time. They were still shaken by the confrontation.

They were grateful to pull off the road and into their village and safety.

Cathar Meeting

After the long caravan journey, Zastra and Chloe had come back to the village late, had a small meal by the candlelight and fell exhausted into their pallets in the small back room of their house. The sun was already well up in the sky by the time they awoke to the sound of people bustling about their chores. Zastra went out to buy some milk and fruit while Chloe lit the fire and spread some flatbread dough on the iron plate to rise into a bread. Herbal tea was also brewing on the grate.

The women sat around the fire pit and sipped their tea and nibbled at the meal.

"So, Zastra, what shall we do about this affront from Osric?" The next meeting of the village would be that evening for the weekly service and prayer meeting.

"We must tell them and see what can be done." What to many would have been a passing, insignificant macho display by a teenage boy was to this village a threat to their security.

As evening fell on that day, the villagers began to assemble around the small shrine in a field at the edge of town. The shrine was to Mary Magdalene – who, it was rumored had crossed the Mediterranean and founded this colony in the southern part of the Frankish realm. The Cathars, perhaps in fear of the evils of past history, avoided a permanent priesthood, or an organized church. They were harkening back to the Roman era when the Christian Caesars and their puppet popes ruled the surrounding land, and even to the days of the Temple when the Sadducee priests controlled the sacrifice and Jerusalem. These many years later, no one remembered. Everyone could be a "perfect," everyone could address the prayer meeting, and there were only prayers in the vernacular. Some could read and none of their Catholic neighbors could read. Since the Bible was only available in the Latin of the Roman Catholic Church, few read it. But much of it was presented orally by the few priests who had studied Latin. Mostly they were peasants, farmers who had fields outside the town, but came in at night. They raised vegetables and fruits and were mostly vegetarian except for fish and eggs and occasional deer and squirrel. Little was known about them in the surrounding areas which still had vestiges of the Visigoths who had adopted Arian theology from their neighbors, the Cathars. They did not believe in the trinity. They did not believe in the resurrection and never used the cross as a symbol. This was a worriment to the priests trained under Roman tradition and the Nicene Creed.

There was a small shrine with a statue of Mary Magdalene, their resident saint, on the hill at one end of town. To what had become the Orthodox Christian, these services would be strange. While they certainly praised and revered Jesus, there was no trinity, no wine or wafer communion. They did not observe the sacraments of baptism, marriage or communion. The Cathars kept their own counsel as to whether Jesus was divine, and they believed Mary Magdalene had founded their church just a few miles away. Some saw John the Baptist as the superior of Jesus. There was no acknowledged leader of the church and the speaker at prayer meetings rotated among the members who wished to serve as such. Chloe often served as did most of the women and this week she arranged to do so. After the ritual hymns and prayers, Chloe stood in the center of the assembly.

"My fellows, I wish to describe an event Zastra and I encountered at the fair in Carcassonne this past week. Osric, the stepson of Lord Alphonso, was making a number of crude remarks directed at our Zastra as we served customers at our booth. He seemed very taken with her and when she spurned his advances, he asked where she came from and was she Christian. Unfortunately, he now knows Zastra is from Limoux and believes her to be Orthodox Christian. I took these questions to be threats – ones he might follow up on to assert his masculine pride. We have worried about this for several days now and believe we should tell our community and ask for your advice."

After some silence and some mumbling, Anton stood to address the assembly. "While I think this might be just some adolescent horseplay on his part, I do not trust these Frankish Christians. Friars have been sent out by the Pope as well now to root out heresy. If we should be discovered we are doomed and the Frankish king, like a greedy wolf, looks at our farmlands and herds with slobber on his jowls. We cannot be complacent in the face of threats. I propose perhaps that we should waylay Osric and teach him a lesson in manners."

Again, silence and then mumblings. Sara stood. She was an elder and a perfect. "I must disagree. I accept the threat might be just a minor harassment, but believe we should not compromise our safety. If we attack Osric, we risk the discovery of our existence and retaliation in force. No. I would send a delegation to Alphonso and assert our embarrassment to our Zastra. Surely, he will understand how a community will protect its womenfolk. He will not like discontentment of his subjects over a sniveling pup's insult."

The matter was discussed back and forth, until a consensus was reached: that a delegation would be sent to Alphonso. Of course, Chloe wished to be part of the delegation. Another man who had served in Alphonso's castle and was liked by him also agreed to go. And so, a troop of five was agreed upon. The day of assizes was near and so it was decided to approach the Lord on that day.

Chloe and Anton to the Assize

The day of assizes was a Wednesday. On this day, Alphonso had decreed the existence of a local court so that petitioners could come to it and ask for help, or the judgment of a dispute. The so-called castle was a ramshackle collection of stones, wooden beams, and some mud packing the openings. Outside a number of warriors dressed in what passed for uniforms. To say uniform, however, would be inaccurate. They all wore a green cloak over a collection of mail, or leather chest pieces and under that a doublet which hung to their knees. They wore leggings of a variety of browns or tans. Some held spears, some broadswords and some no weapon at all. A line had assembled from dawn in between the lines of these warriors who shuffled uncomfortably from foot to foot. The crowd in line mumbled and ambled slowly forward as those in front had their time with Lord Alphonso's man, Geoffrey. Geoffrey was a large man with a vast amount of reddish beard and hair roughly framing a pleasant red face with an amiable smile. He had been born to a local serf and might have spent his early life as his father had in a rude hut tending a field of some sort growing whatever. But at about age seven, he was bigger than the other boys in his village and was selected by the lord to be trained as a warrior. He spent several years mastering the sword and the spear, but mainly cleaning the armor of the older men. By the time he was an adolescent, a war had broken out with a neighboring lord and Geoffrey was pushed into the line.

He did succeed in bashing a few heads with a mace all under the eye of his commander. From then on he was promoted to full soldier and trained with the men. Virtually all the men were Gauls conquered a few generations earlier by Caesar or Visigoths, recent barbarian invaders. It hadn't changed the lives of the serfs much, they still lived on the same land and grew the same things, but now they gave part of their crop to a Roman tax collector. In turn, several Roman centurions would appear for a few months at a time to train the soldiers in Roman style combat. And Geoffrey did not disappoint. A large man, he could simply swing the broadsword and lop off a limb of the enemy. Since he was now a bit older and a jolly fellow, he was made a leader of a contingent of men called a century, usually a hundred men. For this, he was allowed to marry and given several towns as a fiefdom, and the title of Lord. He chose a stout sturdy peasant woman as a wife and began to receive a share of the taxes in produce which he sold at a local fair. Life had been good for Geoffrey.

As the petitioners filed up for his counsel, he unfortunately had only been given great size and strength. Wisdom had not been one of his gifts. So he smiled genially at the people before him and consulted with a wizened elderly man at his elbow. And so, he kept the goodwill of his people. They walked away happy that he had blessed them with his presence and somewhat satisfied by common sense statements he made.

Soon Anton and Chloe came to the front of the line, and were ushered into what was usually a wooden dining hall where Geoffrey sat at a raised level on a large, ornately painted wooden chair with a few men sitting to his side – the elderly fellow he consulted, and the rest were clerks who would write down his judgments and collect the ample fees required to receive Geoffrey's wisdom, however meager.

And so they approached and knelt before him.

"I know you. You are Anton, from… from…"

"Limoux, my Lord."

"Well, Anton, what are you here for?"

"To ask your help or advice on a matter of concern to our village."

"And what might that be?"

"May we approach, Your Honor, as this is a matter which requires discretion?"

"Certainly." Geoffrey beckoned his guards aside and bade Anton and Chloe approach.

"Lord Geoffrey, my compatriot here sells herbs and medicines in county fairs in the area with her young daughter. Whenever she leaves our village for Carcassonne, she is harassed by Alphonso's stepson, Osric, the young son of Fulgencia, who makes lewd remarks to her daughter and follows them in the caravan home. So far he does not know where they live. The daughter intends to take holy orders and is embarrassed by these taunts. We wish to ask you to intervene and stop Osric from these brutish assaults. We fear he may grow more active and harm our womenfolk."

"Ah," Geoffrey turned to the wizened little man to his right and engaged in several whispers. "Good Anton. These incidents would like mere child's play by a teenage boy, meant for nothing more than a jest."

"Perhaps, Lord Geoffrey. However, he has grown more aggressive each time. A simple request to Lord Alphonso might stop this behavior once and for all." More whispers to the wizened man.

"Good Anton. I am loathe to present what Lord Alphonso may view as a trivial annoyance. We are soldiers and deal with weightier matters. May we suggest you approach Esclarmonde de Foix – a woman of knowledge and strength."

Anton turned to Chloe and whispered. "Alas, he is afraid of Lord

Alphonso and wishes to pass this matter along."

"Who is this Esclarmonde?"

"A woman who holds a nearby fiefdom at Foix. She has a good reputation."

"It seems we will get no help from this buffoon," he whispered to Chloe.

"Alas, it is time, Madame Chloe."

"Very well, on to Lady Esclarmonde." They bowed to Geoffrey, as he nibbled a chicken leg and paid a handful of coins to the clerk at the table. They trudged out to their cart at the edge of town for the trip back to Limoux .Their three guards trotted beside them. A useless trip.

Perhaps Esclarmonde would be better.

To Esclarmonde de Foix

The refusal by Geoffrey to aid her in her quest for safety and relief from Osric continued to bother Chloe. This buffoon Geoffrey who had heard her entreaty was nonetheless a survivor. He had fought beside his lord in the past and earned his small fiefdom by being a diligent sycophant afterward. He had collected a small following of former soldiers around him and given them lands and brides. They paid their tribute to Alphonso and stood ready to join him in war if necessary. They were an unruly drunken bunch when not tending their fields, pigs and goats. In winter, or midsummer, they were at leisure to conceive new children, beat their wives and hunt. But they bore fierce loyalty to Geoffrey who could dispatch them as he saw fit at will. Geoffrey might well divulge Anton's and Chloe's entreaty to Alphonso, and it could have disastrous effects. Alphonso owed his loyalty to the court at Toulouse who owned some loyalty to the King of France. He might with the aid of the Pope uncover this heresy and confiscate their land while allowing his men to plunder and rape. Information of the type Geoffrey might dispense to Alphonso could be valuable to his future. Chloe pondered this misstep. So if Osric again bothered Zastra at yet another fair day, and trotted by their caravan on the way home while drunkenly singing lewd songs, Chloe shuddered and felt a trap. She must see this Esclarmonde – what a curious name! She must get help! What was this name – a vulgarization of "Light of the World"

but a visigothic term for "Crystal Moon." Who was she?

Chloe went to the older couple in the village. Was she safe with this lady? And so she came to the bench where Henri and Elayne sat after their supper.

"Can you help me? I need to ask you some things." Chloe was well-known and respected in the village and the ancient couple were only too happy to help. They beckoned her inside their hut. "What can we do?"

"Who is the Esclarmonde de Foix?"

"Ah, a wise and noble woman. One of us."

"What do you mean?"

"Come inside, dear. This must be kept quiet," Elayne murmured. She plucked at her companion's sleeve. "Come, Henri." It was easy to see a long relationship between the two had formed over the years. She looked adoringly at her Henri. Among their villagers who were "Friends of God" as they called themselves, "Cathars" as others did, sex was an activity in the material world. They sought only the spiritual, and so material pursuits were deemed at best irrelevant, at worst harmful to the spirit. While sex was neither forbidden, nor especially sinful, it was an impediment imposed on the body. Yet, Elayne and Henri, even at this advanced age had what was an intimate relationship. They had several children and now lived in harmony with one another.

Henry gestured for Chloe and Zastra to sit at the chairs at the table indoors while Henry sat opposite at the wooden bench against the wall. Elayne made some herb tea. Henry drew in his breath and assured all present that he was about to launch into one of his longwinded explanations. It seems the elderly enjoyed these opportunities for tale telling and Henry, as one of the village elders, was in his mid-fifties.

As Elayne poured tea and sat leaning against Henry, he began.

"I believe it all starts with some Jews who landed at what was called Oppidum Ra on the sea coast way back when. It was Mary and Lazarus, and a very frail Jesus along with some of their followers who arrived weary and hungry at what is now known as Saintes Marie de la Mer but was called then Oppidum Ra. At the time, they claimed they were Egyptians because Jesus could have been captured by the Romans. Almost from the beginning, Mary and the others began to take up in Languedoc where Jesus had left off in Galilee. They healed, mostly with herbs and spices they gathered or grew, and preached. Lost over the years in this story, the message they preached was of love – the opposite of war, and good deeds to secure the favor of their God, now our God. There were no priests, no church as they had been under the spell of in Jerusalem with the priests who controlled the rites of sacrifice. Women could preach for the first time. And they sought the perfection of the spirit over the material, they believed the soul was temporarily trapped in the body. And they worshipped the Shekinah – this sacred feminine – all the female aspects of God in conjunction with the male. Sound familiar? They believed that the day of judgment would come when the male and female aspects of God were united."

Chloe and Zastra nodded as Henri drew a longer breath.

"And Mary and Lazarus began to preach throughout and gathered a large following. It later came out that they were Jews from Palestine. Mary was pregnant in that first year and gave birth to Sarah whom we now revere as well. She later preached with Mary and for many years after. Mary continued her mission until Jesus died and then her grief overcame her. She retired to live in a cave in what is now St. Baume, but Lazarus and Sarah continued on for many years traveling and preaching. We seem to have lost our story from that point since few could read or write in our area. It was not long before the Visigoths came and conquered our area and ousted the Roman overlords. So our region began to intermarry the Gauls with the Visigoths and the few Jews from Mary's days. The "Friends of God" became a separate group and we continued to follow the vision of Mary. There was a marriage between one of ours and one of the Visigoth kings and they founded what was known as the Merovingians who ruled this area for several centuries. But the Pope in Rome did not like their religion even though they claimed it was Christian. Instead, the Pope Zachary at the time and a member of the Carolingian line murdered the Merovingian king Dagobert II while he was hunting one day. This is all a tradition, it may not be true.

"Whatever the truth of this matter may be, Toulouse became a very prestigious city in its day and the capital seat of this region. It became a rich city from its site on important trade routes, but a major cultural center. The theme of this culture was the quest for the spiritual over the material. The notion of courtly love and manners was spread by troubadours who wore red cloaks with a white dove – a symbol of the hidden church. Another symbol was the "cock" because it symbolized Peter's three times' denial of Jesus on the eve of his crucifixion. So the area was always a difficult one for the Pope. We were always accused of some form of heresy. We never accepted the divinity of Jesus and snickered up our sleeves since we knew he had escaped to our coast and founded with Mary a new religion. The area had many "black madonnas" in reverence to Mary Magdalene, not Jesus' mother Mary. And even today, St. Sarah is revered as a founder of our local religion."

Henri paused, took a sip of tea, and nibbled a biscuit. He was fond of relating their origins and he had a captive audience in Chloe and Zastra. Although they had heard these stories many times growing up, they always celebrated the uniqueness of their origins, and the fact that they knew a truth that the rest of the Papacy and Europe did not.

"So what about Esclarmonde?" Zastra, her teenage years, impatient for Henri to get to the point.

"Ah!" Henri noted, now remembering the point of his story, took another deep breath. "Yes, Esclarmonde! A remarkable woman. Born a noble and a Cathar. The Cathar church was growing when she was born about 50 years ago. At the age of 12, she met the Cathar bishops and a few Knights Templar at her father's castle at Foix and would forever be engaged in the pursuit of the Divine Feminine, the Shekinah. As we all do.

"Her father, the Count de Foix, was a vassal of the Count of Toulouse, and her mother, Zebelia, was a Trencavel and a cousin of Roger Raimond Trencavel.

"She married a Roman Catholic and in their 25 year marriage she bore six children. As is our way, she asked her husband to be released from her marriage to become a "perfect" – a form of Cathar priestess even while the Catholic Papacy had condemned the Cathar heresy and began its persecution in earnest. She sought the protection of her people from the Count of Toulouse, who out of fear of the Pope and the French king remained silent.

"It may be that by referring you to Esclarmonde, Geoffrey has intended to do you a favor. Maybe something can be done to help you, but not officially through the Count of Toulouse.

"Yes. You may rely on Esclarmonde, she is one of us."

Chloe and Zastra looked at each other and nodded. This was the advice they sought and it was hopeful. They took their final sips of the herbal tea, and rose, embracing the elderly couple. It was a good chance – this meeting.

"But how do we get to Foix, where is it?"

"Near the Pyrenees, a day's ride, Lothar can show you?"

"Lothar."" He was a retired battle hardened veteran of many past wars who had become a Cathar. He would be an excellent protector. "Thank you, Henry. You have been a godsend." And they left. They would seek out Lothar tomorrow.

Lothar and on to Foix

As dawn broke over Limoux, Chloe and Zastra had already been up. They were anxious to go by Lothar's hut and ask about the route to Foix. Could he help? Lothar was a large old Visigoth – he had been on the losing side of one of the innumerable feudal battles and was severely wounded as he awoke on what had been a battlefield in the marshes of Languedoc. As he rose to his knees, several scavengers from the nearby town were picking over the dead looking for valuables. As he rose to his feet, the few children and their mothers scattered crying in fear of this large warrior who now had grasped his broadsword. He managed a warlike bellow and brandished his weapon. Then using it as a cane, he limped off into a copse of spindly trees before falling to one knee again. He knelt there for minutes as he regained his strength and his senses and rose to limp off again. He managed to find a trail leading somewhere and sat on a fallen limb in the shade. Soon, a cart with several riders came by.

"Good sir. Who are you and what are you doing here?"

He could not tell from the hoods which covered their heads whether they were male or female, so he said, "Yes, good sirs, whoever you may be. I am Lothar – a survivor of the battle of Ajeite swamp. Who may you be?"

"Sir, we are healers. We are looking for herbs and mushrooms in these parts. We come in peace. Are you injured?"

Warily, Lothar showed them a wound to his left shoulder

and a blow by a mace to his right side. These so-called healers, actually Cathars, loaded Lothar onto a cart and bore him back to their village while some climbed into the cart to dress his wounds. He recovered in the village and was amazed at how kind people were to each other. He inquired of them their reason for treating him and was slowly indoctrinated into their ways. And so he remained a loyal villager.

But now he slept, quite noisily in his hut at the edge of town as Chloe and Zastra approached with trays for breakfast. As Lothar continued to snore ponderously, the women laid out a selection of fruits and wheat cakes with cherry jam and set a pot of water boiling for tea. They chatted quietly and said their prayers several times as the morning sun rose. At last, there was some sound of movement inside the hut as Lothar lurched to his feet and appeared at the doorway, stretching and scratching his rump. As his gaze was directed at the women, he emitted a prodigious thunderclap of a fart and smiled apologetically.

"I'm sorry, this diet of yours is not good on my stomach. All these vegetables. I need meat." His gaseous release had frightened away some of the birds resting in the tree outside his door.

"Lothar, please, may we ask you something?"

"Of course, my dears." He eyed the display of breakfast they had brought him and had already reached for a wheat cake and the jam.

"If your stomach bothers you, we can give you something to fix that. Zastra, go back to the house and get us some ginger and peppermint."

As Zastra scurried back to their bins of herbs, Chloe began the story of Osric and Geoffrey's refusal to help.

"Ah, I see it." Lothar was a large bear of a man. A full head of untidy reddish hair and a full beard with pieces of food, twigs and bits of grease here and there. But he was not slow. His eyes sparkled into alertness and his mind was quickly grasping the danger she had described." This Osric is stalking your daughter like a hyena, waiting for her to be separated from the pack. This is no idle threat or some teenage buffoonery. And Geoffrey. Yes. Geoffrey protects himself. He will not trouble his liege lord over something that may be regarded as trivial. But he is not going to harm you. In politics, he is a coward and will not be a hero or choose sides. So he sent you to Esclarmonde. A wise choice. She is a Cathar and a woman. She will know the risks and she will help you." Zastra had returned by now and was pouring an infusion of herbs into Lothar's tea which he downed in a gulp and pounded down on the table for more.

"So what should we do?"

"You must go to Foix for an audience. I will take you."

"Wonderful. How can we thank you?"

"More herbs. Oh! And you must dress like men for the journey and ride astride." Chloe and Zastra looked at one another. They shrugged and nodded. It was decided. Zastra put several small napkins wrapping herbs on the table. "Here is a month's supply. Try them morning and night. But, good Lothar, I wonder could we cut your hair?"

"Ah, your vows include cleanliness, unfortunately it was not in my upbringing. Please do what you can. I seem to scare small children when I walk these streets."

Chloe and Zastra arranged with him to leave at dawn the next morning.

"Uh, dawn? I hope not. I sleep late. You can come about this time and, please, more cakes and jam," he said while downing yet another mug of tea.

The next morning, once again, the women eager for the trip had packed and repacked, consulted the meager map to Foix, and then said their prayers again. And still, the sun was not high enough in the sky to see Lothar. They prepared another sack of cures for Lothar and his various ailments. Although he did not need garlic to increase the smell he threw off copiously, they included garlic for several excrescences on his face. Finally, they could wait no longer and walked the two horses they would ride over to his hut. They had borrowed and taken in shifts and tights from Chloe's ex-husband. She had asked for a release from their marriage so she could pursue her vows of becoming a perfect in their religion. After many pleasant years of marriage, he was willing to give it and move in with one of their daughters. He was not a big man, so the tailoring necessary to have his clothes fit was not a big task. And so, they were now dressed as ordinary peasant men with large brimmed hats against the sun. They had borrowed swords as well to complete the picture of wary travelers.

Once again, they sat at the small table under the tree in front of Lothar's hut and laid out the breakfast. They were again greeted by a thunderclap as Lothar lurched to the doorway.

"I could smell the tea. Wonderful!" He scratched himself copiously and made for the wheat cakes and jam. "That stuff, what was it, ginger? It worked. My stomach didn't grumble. I still want meat, but I feel much better." In truth, he smelled better, too. The strong aroma from his breath had a definite smell of peppermint. When he finished his breakfast, he turned to look at the horses the women had brought. They were horses of the Camargue; short, white with dark skin underneath, and sturdy. These two were older and quite docile, but many of their kind still lived wild in the swamps of Languedoc. Lothar smiled. "Perfect, perfect for our journey, nimble and sturdy."

Soon, another man came up leading two horses. He was a thin young man. "Ladies," Lothar said, gesturing to his young fellow. "This is Ulf. He will come with us for a little more safety. He is one of your best fighters although he doesn't look it." Ulf nodded. Yes. He did not look it. Quite thin and with a large nose and a protruding Adam's apple. The horses were large warm bloods – very thick and powerful workhorses. Now, they too were a little long in the tooth and returned from military duty.

Soon, all mounted, and trotted lightly out to the Via Domitia, the old Roman road running along the coast from Rome all the way to Cadiz in Hispania. Parts of it needed repair here and there but for an easy journey, this would be best. The road had travelers of all sorts going to and fro so safety was not a problem. At intervals, it could be quite crowded, but it was still early in the day and traffic was light otherwise. They rode on quietly with Lothar stopping by Chloe's horse for a few more wheat cakes and an apple or two.

As they veered off the Via Domitia onto the smaller path through the foothills of the Pyrenees, Lothar barked at Ulf as they both became more alert. They quickened their pace to a trot, but the ride still seemed quiet and uneventful. They pulled off the pathway to a clearing with a small clear stream running past. Chloe and Zastra started a cooking fire and stirred some vegetable stew of beans and herbs but mostly lentils. Ulf had found a rabbit and skewered it to roast on a spit. It sent off a wonderful aroma and Lothar eyed it hungrily, but hunkered down guiltily as Chloe glared at him. Meat was forbidden to Cathars; Ulf they did not know but Lothar had no excuse. He shrugged when offered a bite by Ulf, who chuckled at his reticence in front of the women. Ulf exaggerated a smacking of lips and emitted sighs of contentment with a few glances in Lothar's direction. After dinner while there was still some twilight, Lothar sat as Zastra cut his hair and trimmed his beard. As it turned out, he was quite a handsome fellow, but Ulf was quick to remind him of Samson. Just as quick, the women remonstrated Ulf for his abuse of the Bible. He exhibited no shame.

To be on the safe side, the cooking flame was doused and the men agreed to split shifts as sentinels while the women slept. Fortunately, there were no untoward events that night and a quick breakfast was laid out. They were now but a short distance from Foix and would be there by noon.

Soon, off in the distance, sitting on a high spire of rock, the Foix castle came into view. A magnificent site of towers and walls perched on the very top of the spire with steep escarpments on the left and a small town grasping on the left in mounting rows. A wall surrounded the lower edge of the town with a high entrance gate. Even as in King Solomon's day, visitors had to negotiate two turns in a narrow gateway before entering the town proper. Guards shouted down to visitors asking their business in Foix. Lothar bellowed up that people from his village wished an audience with Esclarmonde. Lothar recognized one of the guards from battles in the distant past and was admitted along with his companions. They followed the winding road up to the castle gate. There, a messenger was dispatched to Esclarmonde for an audience. He returned shortly thereafter with a consent for the following morning. Lothar then sought out an old tavern by the river's edge he was familiar with for their night's accommodations. The horses walked carefully over the narrow cobblestone streets to the row of taverns near the east wall. Arrangements were made for rooms and Ulf lead the horses to a livery for the night.

The inns in a Cathar town were decidedly different. While wine and beer were available, few partook. Most ate quietly from bowls of greens and fruit, with steaming bowls of lentil potage. Not lewd or raucous, the women and men sat side by side. Talk mainly was the increasing so-called inquisition by rude unlettered friars who sought out heresy among the inhabitants of Languedoc. God had been good to the Cathars over the past several hundred years in the region of Toulouse, so it was difficult to see why the Kingdom of Heaven would be delayed by their so-called heresy. Yes, they doubted the divinity of Jesus, yes, they were confused by the Trinity which held that the father and his son were one and the same and there was a Holy Ghost as well. Yet without this belief, they performed good deeds and healing while seeking to unite the Sacred Feminine with the masculine God who only inspired power and war. Only recently, the call to the Crusades had ended in one disaster after another. While the Pope's promise of remission of all sins was an incentive to free Palestine of infidels – Muslim Arabs living in peace, the Crusades had slaughtered Jews in the German cities, besieged, looted and murdered in the Catholic city of Byzantium, and been defeated with disastrous results in battles with the Saracens. It was all a mystery to them, this Pope. And now, he sought to convert the Cathars. Would the use of physical force now be used? It was rumored that a monk named Dominic Guzman was inquiring as to who followed this Cathar faith.

Chloe and Zastra could feel the warmth and the comradery these discussions engendered. Surely, tomorrow this wondrous Esclarmonde would come to their aid. And so, they went to their quarters on the second floor with a full belly and a feeling of calm.

Esclarmonde

Chloe, Zastra, Lothar and Ulf climbed the circular exterior stairway of the tower on top of the large square building that served as the castle's keep – the last place of refuge in the event of an attack. At each of the stairs, there was a crenelated top of wall from which archers could fire arrows at those besieging the town. But most remarkable was the view as they rounded the north corner and could see the breathtaking westerly view of the Pyrenees stretching high to the clouds. The drop off from the west was enough to make one dizzy. It fell off precipitously several hundred feet below. The castle was perched on a hill already several hundred feet high and surrounded by walls of 50 feet. At the end of the stairway were two large oak doors leading into a throne room. The double doors were never opened, and all entrants were required to stoop and bend through a small doorway in the eastern door. They had already surrendered their weapons at the gate to the castle staircase and so stepped through into a small room. Three soldiers armed with lances in green cloaks covering their chain mail stood at attention as all four stumbled through the narrow doorway. In front of them was a beautiful older woman seated at a table with clerks seated to her left and right.

"Your excellency," said Chloe as the four all kneeled and faced the floor.

"Please, please, rise," said Esclarmonde gesturing to the four.

She was dressed in a black velvet cloak with a high collar and a white high necked blouse. The marks of age had not dulled her beauty. Exquisite wrinkles highlighted her eyes and her regal cheek bones jutted to signal a noble bone structure. Esclarmonde had been born to nobility and exposed to Cathar teaching from the age of 12. As with all nobility, she was married off to a Roman Catholic son of the neighboring nobility to ensure a feudal alliance and keep peace. After six children, she, as was the custom for Cathar wives, asked for a release from this marriage so she could start the process of becoming a Perfect in her religion. In this phase, she would pursue a hermetic life in the forest, raising herbs and medicines, caring for the sick and teaching Cathar noviates. She could now administer the rite of the consolamentum – the act of recognizing a Cathar had become a Perfect. Now, however, she pursued the responsibilities of seeing to the governing of her inherited realm. So she welcomed as a feudal lord would hear the pleas and arbitration of disputes of her Cathar subjects. She motioned to a bench in front of her table and bade the four travelers sit. Chloe and Zastra had changed into white robes of the Cathar tradition for this audience and left their masculine attire in the inn.

"What is your plea?"

Nervously, Chloe rose and unsure how to address this imposing lady, she began, "My lord…"

"Please, I am Esclarmonde."

"Please, Esclarmonde," and then she began to narrate the tale of Osric's harassment of Zastra, her trip to see Geoffrey and her trip to Foix under the protection of Lothan and Ulf. Esclarmonde nodded at various parts and glanced at her clerks who were busily making notes.

When Chloe had finished, Esclarmonde turned to Zastra, "I

see you study to be a Perfect, child."

Yes, Esclarmonde."

"Do you wish to marry and have children?"

"I believe not."

"May I suggest that, while I very much approve of your efforts at becoming a Perfect, I suggest you learn more of the world? What do you do now?"'

"I help our village raise healing herbs and travel with my mother to village markets to cure maladies and dispense herbs."

"That may be a good way to learn about life. You see, we Cathars face growing threats every day from the Pope. Local lords and the King of France look to our lands and may seek to oust us from them. It is not enough to pursue the holy life, but we may have to defend ourselves one day."

"Yes, Esclarmonde."

"As you will hear, I must practice the art of statesmanship and govern. I am not free as I would wish to be to be a simple Perfect. Now, Osric's stepfather is Alphonso. I do not know him and cannot approach him directly. He may be offended by my suggestion that his son is dangerous to you, and dismiss his acts as simple boyish pranks. He may demand something in exchange. So I cannot act overtly by a simple diplomatic request." With that, she turned to whisper to two of the clerks to her right. A whispered conversation ensued, Esclarmonde then turned and faced the two women.

"You will receive a visit from a loyal Cathar knight in your village of Limoux. He will be in disguise as a troubadour and wear a red cloak with a white dove on the shoulder. He will help you."

Chloe with tears streaming down her face, "Thank you, your most gracious highness. Surely God works through you."

"Please, Chloe, I am Esclarmonde. I value the faith you and

your daughter so piously espouse. The days of your test from bad persons are not far off. I pray that you can help in our cause."

"You may depend on us for whatever may be required." Chloe and Zastra curtsied and followed Lothar and Ulf to the door, bowing low through the narrow porthole as before. They were handed their weapons. The sun beat down on them as they descended the winding staircase. As they reached flat ground, Chloe turned to Lothar, "What do you suppose she will do?"

"I am told she works in mysterious ways. Some call her a wizard."

They went back to the inn to retrieve their packs, purchased some items at the market for the journey and went to the livery to retrieve their horses. All was in silence, as each retraced in their heads what they had just experienced. It was an unworldly moment, this audience with Esclarmonde. Mounting the stairs to this ethereal throne room, this striking beautiful woman in a black cloak, her calm demeanor and then her words of comfort. They would hold this scene in their minds forever.

As they let their horses amble along the foothills down from the Pyrenees, every so often one of the women would ask, "I wonder what she meant." These queries were met with shrugs. Ulf got out of his pack a small lute and began to strum. He sang a few of the popular troubadour songs of the day. They spoke of an unrequited love for some maiden. It was only recently that women were not married off in their early teens and consigned to a life of bearing children and being servants for their husbands at home or in the fields. Somewhere this new formed attraction to women had arisen and was spread by wandering troubadours, many of whom were Cathars spreading a subtle message of the sacred feminine. The imagery seems to unite the male and female in a holy oneness. But Ulf was just lost in some teenage lust and wanted a woman. Although he still had pimples on his face among the sparse tendrils of hairs which was a suggestion of a beard yet to come, Zastra could not let the moment pass without some gentle teasing.

"So, Ulf, do you have a particular woman in mind? In the village maybe."

A fierce blush and some dismissive noes.

"Do I know you? Aren't you Ulric's son?"

"Yes."

"So you help with the mill at the river?"

"Yes, Zastra." He rolled his eyes at her prying. She was older, very pretty and beyond his best fantasies.

"You do know that we consider celibacy a virtue and the body a source of sin." Zastra cast a glance at Chloe, who was amused and not entirely approving at Zastra's torture of Ulf. "Yes, Zastra. I know."

"Yet you harbor thoughts of romance?" Ulf strummed fiercely on his lute, hoping to drown her out, his voice too rose.

"Maybe, we could find you a wife." More strumming. She began to name some names of the young girls in the village. Finally, one name struck home and drew a deep blush.

"Ah, so it's Ethel. The blond." No answer, more strumming. Ethel was round and apple-cheeked, broad in the hips and a strong young girl who was a very good field hand. Her father was an older Visigoth but her mother a Cathar. "Maybe, we can help. A miller's son would be a good bargain."

"Zastra, enough." Chloe was tired of Zastra's taunting. Marriage and tempting of young men was not favored with the Cathars and Zastra, now purporting to want to be a Perfect, should know better and be more dignified. Ulf let out a sigh of relief and resumed his serenade. The horses continued their slow pace through the dappled path under the shade of the trees. It was a beautiful day and their mission now had a hope of fulfillment. Soon the path through the forest joined up with the Via Domitia with a number of other travelers going east and west on the old Roman paving. A few farmers had set up market stands along the way. They bought a huge bag of pumpkin and sunflower seeds and shared them, spitting the husks out along the way. At one point, a trumpet blared and mounted soldiers galloped down the middle of the road forcing everyone to the side and into the forest, but they passed and the travelers resumed their pace. It was late in the afternoon when the four peeled away from the road and on to Limoux. It was dark when they were able to dismount at their homes. But their journey had been fruitful. Time to wait for this unknown troubadour.

Raymond Visits

It had been a few days since their visit to Esclarmonde at Foix, but still Chloe and Zastra tingled in anticipation of some event, promised but undescribed, which would rid them of this odious Osric. About three o'clock in the afternoon, several particularly unkempt men shambled into the village and planted themselves in the town square. An old woman came up, as it happened, the town busybody, and asked if they wanted some water. This was a pretext to querying them as to whom they were and what they wanted in Limoux. One of the men complained of a series of ailments and asked for the town's apothecary. He then went into a long story as to why he didn't have any money to pay but would come back with some game he would shoot if he were healthy again. The woman went to Chloe's hut and told her of the man. Chloe came out to see the men.

"So, my good men, what is it that ails you?" she said with an airy professional manner.

They complained of a bad cough, a bad cold, and an earache. It seems they had been sleeping in a damp area. "Uh-huh," Chloe mused, calculating in her head what was needed. She and Zastra returned with some Echinacea, some eucalyptus and some garlic. She brewed the collection of herbs into a tea and threw in some valerian to let him sleep.

The men sipped the tea, and spoke of being wandering troubadours and offered to sing for the village. After a few minutes, they seemed to yawn and soon dozed off where they sat in the town square and snored loudly. By suppertime they rose and stretched and asked to speak to the apothecary again. They knocked furtively at her doorpost and Zastra came to meet them.

"We wish to thank Madame Chloe for her herbs. May we see her?"

"Of course," Zastra turned to get Chloe from the back yard where she was drying out some specimens recently collected from the woods. As the two returned, they saw the tall handsome gentlemen in red cloaks with a white dove on the shoulder. Before they could speak, and indeed they were speechless, one of the men said, "Madame, I am Roger Raimond sent by Esclarmonde. You have proven to be an excellent host. How may we serve you?" Once again, the women could not even catch their breath but hugged each other with tears running from their cheeks. After a few gasps, it was Zastra who related once again the indignities they had suffered at the hands of Osric, stepson of Lord Alphonso, as they travelled to local fairs to purvey their herbs. The men nodded thoughtfully.

Roger Raymond said, "Madame, it would be a pleasure to serve you. We see you both study to be a Perfect. We will put an end to this nonsense."

The men stayed for supper – a large pot of lentils and other stewed vegetables and fish. Halfway through dinner, Raymond said, "Ladies, we must follow you on your next trip to Carcassonne in the caravan. We will be in disguise, but we will assure you we will not be far off. When Osric appears again, we will be ready." The women looked at each other and nodded. They cleared the bowls from supper and arranged for the men to bed down in an empty hut nearby. As it would happen, the fair for Carcassonne was to be this weekend. So they prepared their cart on Thursday and were ready to join the first caravan to Carcassonne on the way north. The men had fed and watered their horses and gotten back into their unkempt disguises. At dawn, they all rode out to the caravan.

As before, the trip to Carcassonne was uneventful with the travelers in a long line plodding in and out of the dappling sunshine along the road through the trees. At Carcassonne, they put in for the night with the woman they usually stayed with. And so the market day started early Saturday as lines formed at the apothecary booth where Chloe and Zastra prescribed herbal cures.

And then, at about noon, Osric and his two retainers appeared. Once again, he taunted and teased Zastra who did her best to ignore him as she served her customers. Finally, he butted to the front of the line as he pulled away from the two retainers who tried to dissuade him.

"Little sparrow from Limoux I hear. You might be a Cathar. Are you not?" A very dangerous accusation. Even now the Cathars were being persecuted by wandering clergy, but still enjoyed the support of the Court of Toulouse. Osric's stepfather, Lord Alphonso, had no power in Languedoc, but the power of nobility of any sort was not to be trifled with.

"Sir, I am a good Christian woman." It was the truth, but did not answer his question. Cathars were a sort of Christian as well.

"Let me hear you recite the Apostle's Creed?" He meant the Nicaean Creed acknowledging the divinity of Jesus and the oneness of the trinity.

"Sir, I do not know such things. I am an unlettered maid." A plausible lie. Many peasants had little formal religious training.

"Perhaps, I should have some of the wandering priests interrogate you." By now, a crowd had gathered.

"Oh, good sir, why do you taunt me so? I only come to market to sell cures. As you can see, we do our job well." With this, there were a few voices in the crowd shouting to leave her alone. Masculine voices at first, then the crowd joined in. They were in heavily Cathar territory in Carcassonne, and Osric had no legal authority. As a teenager and the mere son of a local lord from a neighboring region, he was not on firm ground if some disturbance should arise. The shouting had drawn a few of the local constables who asked, "What is going on here?"

Osric was persuaded to back down and move on since his father had no power in Carcassonne. The crowd soon dispersed. Chloe and Zastra closed the booth for a midday meal and left their porter to guard it.

"Zastra, that was too close. I hope those men can do something," as they sat at a local inn and ate some of their fresh vegetables. Soon, a filthy beggar limped by and threw a few small coins on their table. Yes, the men were there.

They returned to the booth and were met with the usual long line of people complaining about one thing or another. Some asked to step to the rear of the booth to whisper their maladies in private. And at the end of the day a full cash box sat at the rear of the booth as they started to pack up their wares. The porter brought his wagon and escorted them back to the lady's house where they boarded overnight. They took supper with her rather than some public place where they might be at the mercy of Osric once again. The next day the porter brought the cart around and filled in the bundles of herbs. Chloe carefully hid the cash box on the cart and they wheeled out to join the caravan as dawn broke slowly to the east. Still there was no sign of Osric or Raimond.

After a few piercing whistles, the caravan slowly started on the road south. After a few hours, there he was. Osric, lurching drunkenly on his horse, followed by his two retainers. Drunk – at what, ten or eleven o'clock. The day before he had been dressed as a proper noble – tights with one green leg, one red, a hammered leather doublet, and a shirt with red and green sleeves. Hammered into the doublet was his father's seal in green and red. Today, he was covered with pieces of straw and smelled of… what was it… yes, vomit. He must have been drinking and vomited on himself somewhere. He had found Chloe's and Zastra's cart now and was making lewd gestures with his hands. The guards of the caravan usually rode up and down the sides of the caravan to protect it from bandits. They saw this slovenly person lurching near the caravan, and not taking him for a noble, and further remembering that he had not paid to join the caravan, they shooed him off. The retainers nodded as some form of apology shrugging their shoulders. The caravan moved on and Osric was left behind bellowing some curse or threat.

When the caravan was well out of sight of Chloe, three riders in ragged cloaks with hoods pulled off to the side and cantered back along the route. They found Osric sitting on a fallen tree head in hands while one of the retainers brought him water from a nearby stream. As the men approached, the retainer swirled around only to see three men in cloaks with broadswords drawn.

"On your knees if you wish to see tomorrow," one barked. The retainer did not need to be told twice and Osric was in no condition to resist. The other retainer came on the scene, sensed what was happening. He dropped to his knees as well. One of the cloaks collected the weapons and the horses.

"Now strip."

"What? Strip you say?"

"Yes. Strip and be quick about it." Osric and the two retainers looked at each other. What was about to happen? They stripped and left their clothes in a pile. The three naked men were told to kneel at the base of a tree, facing the tree. Their hands were bound securely around the tree. One of the cloaks got out a jar of honey and a brush and liberally painted the thighs and nether regions of Osric and the other two. Flies, spiders and hornets were already being drawn as the men squirmed.

Gathering up the clothes and weapons, hitching the horses to their own, the three cloaks trotted off to the next small town. There they found a boy, gave him the clothes and a few coins and told the boy to go to Carcassonne and report that three men could be found in the woods near the stream on the road to Carcassonne. The three cloaks trotted off into the distance.

The boy accompanied by his father on the family mule went on to Carcassonne and told them of the three naked men tied to a tree.

Without, of course, knowing who these three bound men were, the guardsmen took their time but eventually found the men as described near the stream on the road to Carcassonne. One of the men was in fact a teenage boy who was sobbing. All the men were wracked by mosquito bites, bee stings and were in great discomfort. Small streams of blood trickled down their thighs. Their bonds were cut and they shakily came to their feet.

"Who are you and what are you doing here?"

One of the retainers spoke up, "We were attacked by bandits. They stole our horses and our clothes." He was trying to appear dignified as he stood at attention but was red from his waist to his knees with bug bites which he occasionally reached down to scratch.

"Who are you?"

"We are the retainers of Sir Osric here, (pointing). He is

the son of Lord Alphonso." Osric was still sobbing quietly and scratching his buttocks and the backs of his legs. The men debated holding them for ransom or turning them over freely for a reward. They decided it would be better to let the Count of Carcassonne decide. With some diffidence, the guards permitted the naked men to climb on behind them on horseback and they cantered back to town. The arrival of three naked men walking into the castle at the heart of Carcassonne drew quite a crowd, most of whom jeered as the men continued to scratch their buttocks and nether regions.

The guards went to the throne room and asked to see the Count. It was late in the afternoon and the formalities of the court were over, so the Count was delaying in dressing and preparing himself for a court appearance. As he mounted the dais to his throne, he looked at the three naked men covering their privates and began to chortle. "My guards, what have you brought me?"

The chief guard explained that they had been asked to free these three men who were on their knees facing the trunks of trees. They claimed they were beset by bandits. They brought them into town because they were unsure to hold them for ransom or sell them as slaves. One claimed to be the son of Lord Alphonso, so we brought them here for you to dispose of."

"Mm. Very good. Yes, thank you, men. Yes, a wise move. These men will make an interesting bargain with Lord Alphonso. Yes, Quite valuable." With that, he dispatched a rider to Lord Alphonso to advise of his son and his retainers whereabouts. "Also, see these guards are rewarded for their wisdom. Put these three in the dungeon for now and get them some clothes." He rose from the throne still chortling over the good luck the day had brought.

Return of Osric

The retrieval of Osric and the retainers was to be delicately negotiated. It could not be called a ransom since Carcassonne and Gascony were not at war, nor were they considered to be unfriendly. Yet, there was some value in having rescued a noble heir from the hands of bandits, as the Count of Carcassonne claimed, in a slight but acceptable prevarication in the process of negotiation. So the sum to be paid would be less than a ransom, and an enlargement on a mere gratuity. Once the price was agreed upon, Osric and his companions were mounted on horses, but with their hands securely bound, and taken to a place outside Toulouse where the exchange could occur. Osric and the others were then bound to a tree and, while still dressed in their borrowed tunics, awaited the arrival of Alphonso. It was midafternoon when a contingent from Auch in Gascony arrived. Alphonso was not among them. Osric was not his own son, but that of his wife by a prior marriage. Nonetheless, a sack of coins was dumped at the feet of the contingent from Carcassonne. Wisely, the head of the contingent counted the coins and found them to be short. Without another word, he directed his contingent to draw their swords and tie Osric up and place him on a horse. It seems the Gascon had helped himself to a few of the coins and hoped it would pass unnoticed.

It did not, and the Gascon leader would suffer humiliation if he returned without Osric, much less the bag of coins. So he quickly capitulated and offered the balance which the leader from Carcassonne graciously accepted. For him to return with Osric might also not reflect well on him, but a completed mission was worthy of the Count's gratitude. And so the two troops departed on their way back to their respective realms.

This exchange had been fraught with problems. The Gascons were a difficult people. The area had been Basque country for centuries, and even now resisted inclusion in the now French life. Those from Carcassonne were descended often from the Visigoths but now included many Cathars. The two regions were entirely different ethnically and had little communication between them. The exchange of Osric had been a delicate matter and an embarrassment to the Gascons.

When Osric was delivered to Alphonso's court in Auch, he was not welcomed warmly, but he and his retainers stood at attention in the throne room.

Soon, a sedan chair burst through the double doors to the throne room, as six men carried the chair to the dais front of the room. As it swung around, the chair revealed a very pale and sickly Alphonso seated. As he stared at the three men kneeling before him, his color reddened and he grew more agitated.

"So, Osric. Explain yourself."

"Lord Alphonso, we were beset by bandits on our way back from the market at Carcassonne."

"Did you know these men?"

"No, Sire."

"Had you been drinking?" Alphonso was well aware of Osric's proclivities.

"No, Sire, it was morning."

"What did these men do?"

"Sire, they took our weapons, our horses and our clothes, and tied us to trees."

"Your clothes? Why your clothes?"

"I don't know."

"It seems they wished to embarrass you and to teach you a lesson. Had you offended someone at the market?"

"No, Sire."

"Had you given offense to the caravan?"

"No, Sire."

"Why your clothes then?" He turned to the two retainers. "How is it you did not protect Osric? What happened here?"

The two retainers looked at one another and shrugged. "Sire, there were quite a few men and they ambushed us."

"If they ambushed you, they must have known you were coming. This sounds like a story. If I find out otherwise, I will see you both hanged. Someone has insulted my demesne and I must avenge this wrong. Now, I must know what happened. Did Osric give offense to anyone at the market or the caravan?"

With some hesitation, the older one of the retainers spoke up. "Sire, Osric had been drinking and he was flirting with one of the maids at the market."

"Flirting…? Maids at the fair…? Explain yourself!"

"Well, sir, he was suggestive with her… When she rebuffed him as she had the previous market…"

"The previous market. He had done this before?"

"Yes, Sire."

"Well, Sire, a crowd gathered, and Osric became angry and asked if she was a Christian and where she lived."

"She said she was a Christian, but by then the guards at the fair arrived to keep the peace and bade us move along."

"Was that it?"

The retainer cast a wary glance at Osric, shrugged his shoulders, and went on. "We went drinking that night and slept in the forest. When we awoke, Osric had a headache and began to drink again. He got sick and vomited. Then, he ordered us to accompany him to the caravan which we could hear in the distance."

"So did you?"

"Yes, Sire, on Osric's order and against our advice. But yes, we went to the caravan, and Osric again found the maid and began to say lewd things to her. But then the caravan guards came by and shooed us away.

"Osric was sick again so we found a stream in the glade near the road and sat down. At that point, several men on horse drew up with swords drawn. I was sitting with Osric, and Elderic was coming back with some water. We had no chance to get our weapons. The men told us to strip and tied us up kneeling and facing a tree. They then put honey on our private parts. This attracts many bugs and flies. They left. After a few hours, some people from a small town came to free us. They were led by a young boy to us. The boy said our captors told the boy to bring the villagers to free us."

"And so, the villagers took you to Carcassonne."

"Yes, Sire."

"Your clothes. Did they have my shield on them?"

"Yes, Sire."

"And Osric's sword, was it the fine one from Spain with my seal on it?"

"Yes, Sire." Alphonso had been growing angrier as the story spilled out. He abruptly motioned to some of the others in his entourage to confer with him. As they talked, he was already using a string of unintelligible words from the Basque dialect. In a half hour, he returned with the entourage.

"Osric, I have been burdened with your care by your mother and now you shame me, our realm and our people. I will now see to your further education. You will stay in the army barracks and be trained as a common soldier until I receive word that you are properly trained. You will further receive religious training at the monastery at Armagnac. You will not receive any inheritance from me."

Now, turning to the retainers. "You two, I had hoped you could keep better watch on him. I see that you have not. But I acknowledge he is difficult and you had little power. Yet you have been truthful and I respect that. Accordingly, I will not punish you for this. You shall be returned to the rank of the army from which you came. Now, it is so ordered." Alphonso was borne on his litter from the room followed by his entourage and guards approached Osric to take him to the military camp. He was starting to whimper. He still was wearing the same dirty tunic they had given him in Carcassonne and his rump and thighs and elsewhere stung and itched from a thousand bites.

Alphonso then was borne by his entourage into the large dining hall and where he made them sit. "Gentlemen, we have been humiliated by this young maid's people. While they may well have had provocation from that ass, my step-son, it is an insult I cannot let go unanswered. I want all of you to find out who this maid is and where she comes from. Start at the market at Carcassonne and be quick about it before word of this incident spreads."

The entourage nodded. It would be done.

One of Alphonso's nobles quietly left the room. Knowledge of this meeting was worth something to someone. This sounded like a word to the Cathars would be well rewarded and the Cathars had money. He saddled quickly and rode to Foix and Esclarmonde. He returned to Armagnac with a nice purse in two days.

Alphonso's Men Meet Caravan

It was not hard for one of Alphonso's retainers to find and identify
Chloe and Zastra on the next market at Carcassonne, but the
Gascons were out of their territory and could ill afford an event
under the nose of the Count of Toulouse. So it had to be done
with great speed and delicacy before anyone could guess what
had happened.

They chose the caravan south from Carcassonne. It was
smaller and the woods were thicker. Alphonso had planned
well. Twenty mounted men led by his best knight stalked the
caravan at a discrete distance as the women's cart waited on
the road outside town for the one south. For this brief time
they were alone. They pulled the cart under the shade of the
tree when the contingent of mounted men road up in a flash to
surround them. The women could barely scream before they
were bound and gagged and secured to the bottom of their cart.
They could note that the men spoke the Basque dialect. Soon
they were trotting off back to Auch in Gascony and Alphonso's
court. It had happened like that! They were outside town and
far from curious eyes. All those eyes except Roger Trencavel
and his two men who had been assigned to protect the women.

As the Gascons and the cart pulled away, Roger pulled onto
the trail and stared up the road. He did not have enough men
and he had little knowledge of Gascon ways. Would the women
be harmed? He must report unhappily to Esclarmonde.

The women had been bound with their arms to their sides and around the ankles. A gag was securely tied at the back of their heads. Then they were lain on their backs on top of the sacks of herbs. They could see the sky, but not move or cry out. The cart then followed the clatter of horses' hooves and the women could hear the familiar sounds of the cart wheels rolling on the Via Domitia west. At some point, there was a perceptible turn north and west, on a worn earthen path among trees. The shadows and sun beams drifted past as Chloe and Zastra lay immobile. It was not long before they began to climb hills and wound through different turnings. It was already dark when the troop came to a halt, and rough hands lifted the women, unbound their ankles and rustled them towards a large wooden enclave of buildings. They were thrust through a set of double doors to the middle of what looked like a large dining hall. There, they were told to kneel. Their knees became painful and they relaxed back to sit on their heels. Anxiously they looked at each other and signaled fear with their wide-eyed looks.

Not much later, several men bore a sedan chair through the double doors and carried it up to a raised level in the dining hall, and a sickly man, not old but in his 30's, hunched out of the sedan and lurched for the throne-like wooden chair at the center of the raised level. Men slit the gags binding the women's mouths.

"Women, who are you and where are you from?"

"I am Chloe of Limoux and this is my daughter." The man was consumed by a fit of heavy coughing and sat back in the chair for a while and rested.

"What have you done to my son?"

"Sire, I know nothing of your son. " He gestured impatiently and wiped his mouth with a cloth.

"Osric… Osric… don't tell me you don't know Osric. I'll have you flogged." He breathed heavily, gasping the words out.

"Oh, Osric, that rude drunken boy from the market at Carcassonne.

Yes. We know of him."

"Admit what you did to him."

"Nothing, Sire, nothing. He was rude to us at the market and again on the road with the caravan. Both times the guards bade him move on."

"So you had nothing to do with his attack?" Again, the man became agitated, red in the face, and began to cough.

"No, Sire. What attack? We know nothing of this."

"Do you deny capturing him and tying him up in the woods?"

"Yes, Sire. We know nothing of this. He was quite drunk when he left us alone, but he had two men with him. What happened to him?"

"The three were found naked in the wood, tied to trees with their nether areas slathered in honey to induce bug bites." Chloe could not help looking at Zastra and breaking a smile.

Timidly, she asked, "Was he bitten, Sire?"

"Yes, quite severely from knee to navel." Chloe and Zastra could not restrain themselves further and laughed out loud.

"Did you do this?" his voice raising.

"No, Sire. How was he found?"

"A young boy came into a nearby town and said men had given him a few coins and told to say where Osric and the others could be found.

The Count of Carcassonne recovered them and sent them back to us."

"Were they robbed?"

"Yes, their clothes, their weapons, their purses and their horses. And… uh."

"And their privates covered with honey."

"Yes, quite so." Again, the women barely concealed their smiles.

"So they were bandits then."

"I doubt it. They would have held them for ransom or sold them into slavery."

"But they told you where to find him?"

"Yes."

"So it seems someone wanted to teach Osric a lesson."

"Perhaps, but it is an insult to my house."

"Sire, Osric himself is an insult to your house. He is a lazy drunken lout who has no manners. He insults decent women earning their living. He certainly speaks poorly of the upbringing you have given him. If he is to be the next ruler, your house is doomed."

"No. He is my stepson. He came with my wife who was much my senior. She has spoiled him."

"Then he needs much discipline anyway. He will provoke others, and you will find yourself at war over him."

The man was quite taken aback by Chloe's boldness. After all, she was his prisoner, kneeling at his feet, awaiting his judgement. Justice could be swift and brutal for her and her daughter.

"Why do you speak so boldly to me? It is I who have you captive."

"Yes, Sire, you do. But my body is but a temporary shell, and my soul belongs to God. Before His eyes, we are equal."

"You anger me, woman."

"Chloe… My name is Chloe. And while I'm angering you, with little more to lose, I see you are a sick man. My daughter and I are healers. We dispense herbs and medicines to cure many ills."

"Alas, it is true. I am sick of something my physicians know not what. Since the Jews were chased into Aragon, there are no good physicians left."

"If I may be so bold, may my daughter and I examine you? We may be able to help." The guards surrounding the women stepped menacingly forward and roused their weapons. Alphonso waved them back.

"Healers, you say."

"Yes, Sire. That is what we were doing at Carcassonne, purveying herbs and cures when Osric chose to harass us."

Alphonso sat in thought for a moment. His recent illness had left him vulnerable. He was not an old man but suffered from fatigue and pains that his own physician was incapable of alleviating. What harm could come from having these women at least examine him? Of course, they probably were the cause of Osric's humiliation, but quite obviously they had not done it by themselves. From all accounts, a band of armed men had done this, and the women did not even seem to know what had been done. The apparent punishment inflicted on Osric and the two was actually quite minor, but undoubtedly embarrassing and very public. It could have been much worse. Osric's recovery had been inexpensive and his bug bites would heal, and might even teach him a lesson. Alphonso was not happy in this marriage in the first place. He had been matched by his parents at age 14 with a woman 10 years his senior with two children from a prior marriage. Of course, she came from a noble family to the west and secured the western border, and protected a trade route through the Pyrenees which was very valuable to the Gascon region. But still, she was a plain insipid woman who constantly complained about her living conditions. She was haughty to those who spoke the Basque dialect and did little to warm Alphonso's bed. And now, her son Osric was an embarrassment. At least, this latest episode had given him the opportunity to banish him from court and make him grow up. He had endured his wife's complaints about her desire for revenge, but now he enjoyed separating him from his mother. It also gave him the reason to ban him from ever nourishing a hope of succeeding him as Count of Gascony. If these two women were able to cure his disease, he would keep them as members of his court and a constant irritant to his wife. They would have the status as prisoners or hostages for those who had attacked Osric, but, in reality, this Chloe was an interesting woman. She spoke up even when possibly facing severe punishment, and she had made a few provocative comments, something about her body being a vessel and meaningless, while her soul belonged to God. Interesting. So yes, he would let them examine him and try to cure his illness.

"Approach then, what do you see?"

Chloe and Zastra rose painfully from their knees and arched their backs. Their hands were unbound and they slowly approached this noble in his sedan chair.

In the manner they followed with ordinary peasants at the Carcassonne fair, they examined him. They checked his pulse, felt his forehead, probed his neck. He was at this range quite a handsome man with long straight black hair and piercing black eyes although now dulled by a rheumy glaze. His beard and mustache were neatly trimmed, but he had a foul odor to his breath. They checked his neck and armpits for lumps. Meanwhile, Chloe and Zastra mumbled back and forth their observations and possible diagnoses.

At about this moment, the Countess of Gascony, Alphonso's wife came into the room with several ladies in attendance. "Good Sire, what is the meaning of this?"

"Fulgencia, these women are healers from Carcassonne. They are trying to cure my illness."

"They look like ragamuffins to me." Chloe and Zastra had been lying on their backs in the cart for many hours and had straw and dirt over their shifts and in their hair. "Why must they touch you?" Chloe and Zastra had stopped and now faced Fulgencia.

Chloe spoke. "Madam, it is necessary to determine the cause of his discomfiture. We believe we have some cures for his condition." Then,

turning to Alphonso, "May we proceed, my Lord?"

"By all means," Alphonso directed his stare at Fulgencia.

"My Lady, please leave these women to their profession."

"Are these the women who attacked my Osric?"

"No, my Lady. They did not attack Osric, some men did."

"Did they see Osric?"

"Yes, they were rudely insulted by an inebriated Osric in front of their customers at the fair and again on the road to Carcassonne."

"And for this, you have sent him into military service?"

"He needs discipline and maturity. If he is to become a noble of this demesne he must have both. This episode must not happen again."

"But Alphonso…"

"Enough, Fulgencia, leave these women to their work and leave me in peace." This public insult was more than Fulgencia could bear, and she turned on her heel, followed by her feminine entourage and left. Alphonso, red in the face, and now coughing heavily turned to Chloe, "You say you have some cures?"

"Yes, my Lord. We are not sure, but believe you have a number of ailments. We will need some herbs from our cart. And we must send for some others. May we go to our cart for now?"

"Yes, yes, by all means. What is my illness?"

"We will have to explore a few possibilities, but will start on a few items first. Some will relieve this cold and cough you have brought on by your weakness. Some will relieve what we believe is high blood pressure and high sugar. Some will make you sleep better. Then we will try the most serious matter. For that, we will need to brew an ancient Greek remedy which requires a mixture of herbs, some rare."

"What is that disease?"

"Possibly a weak heart condition. Possibly fatal."

"How is it my physician does not know this?"

"They learn their medicine from the Romans and the Visigoths. We have studied Greek and Hebrew papers. The Romans, and then the Visigoths destroyed much of this. Our people brought it with them centuries ago. But, Sire, we have not eaten since yesterday. We would like to know where we will stay, and we need someone to help us bring our herbs to a place indoors where we may prepare them for you."

Ah… Quite so." He motioned to his chamberlain, "Get these women something to eat and see to their needs."

The chamberlain bowed and gestured for the women to follow him. They were seated in a small room and a large bowl of stew was brought out. It was apparently what was to be served for the midday meal to the rest of Alphonso's court later. Chloe and Zastra looked at each other with some dismay. Their Cathar beliefs had a number of dietary restrictions including any animal's meat. However, this potage smelled of fish and a thick vegetable soup. They sampled it warily, shrugged and ladled out full bowls. It was fish, but not the sort they were familiar with. This catch must have come from the Atlantic rather than the Mediterranean. But it was hearty and had considerable garlic in it. Garlic was a constant staple in their diet. Yes, it was quite good. When they finished, a serving girl asked them to follow her. They were conducted to a large room with a large bed, and on the floor in a corner were piles of their sacks from the cart. They both sat on the bed to test its softness and fell into a deep sleep. It was near dusk when they woke up and stretched. Cautiously, they opened the door to their room and found two armed guards. Apparently they were just as much prisoners as healers to Alphonso.

They were told that Alphonso expected some remedies before the evening supper. Chloe asked if they could have a table and a bucket of clean water. One of the guards left and soon came back with several servants carrying a small wooden table and a bucket.

Chloe assembled a work space on the table and began to sort the herbs. Each concoction for Alphonso they wrapped in a leaf and set aside for later. As they worked, they hummed a few Cathar hymns and settled into a pleasant routine. The leaves contained fenugreek to relieve high blood pressure, Echinacea for the cough and cold, eucalyptus for the cough and some primrose and valerian to aid in sleep. These herbs were common in the area and easy to harvest locally. A list was made of the rarer. The most significant would be theriac – an ancient Greek concoction with many rare herbs. Chloe made a list of some of the herbs, but still did not have a recipe for assembling the combination. This was contained in some old manuscripts presently in the custody of the ruler of Foix, now Esclarmonde. This elixir would be absolutely necessary for Alphonso and because it was expensive and rare, was not often made available to ordinary folk. For Alphonso, it must be obtained.

Now with a small sack, the women descended toward the dining hall with their armed guard, but were directed to a small room off to the side. Alphonso came in aided by several men and a cane and dropped heavily into a chair.

"My Lord, we have assembled a few minor remedies which must be brewed into a tea each morning. This leaf contains fenugreek for your high blood pressure which puts a strain on your heart and makes you dizzy. This leaf contains a mixture of eucalyptus and Echinacea for your cough and cold. At night you must put this into a tea to aid you to sleep better. It contains primrose, valerian and chamomile. This is a start for now. It will clear up some of your discomfort, but it is not the most important we seek. Try this for now and we will speak to you about the rest tomorrow."

Serving girls were summoned to brew the mixture into a tea. The women were escorted out and to a table by the corner of the dining hall and seated. The chamberlain came in followed by a few servants. Chloe waved to get his attention.

"Sir, we are apparently to be here for some time. Our beliefs restrict our diets to only certain things. Is it possible that they could be accommodated?" As the chamberlain frowned, Zastra was able to speak. "Good sir, the fish stew yesterday was excellent. Is that your recipe?" This brought a smile to the chamberlain. He knew he was being charmed by these women, but could not resist a spark of pride go through him.

"Yes, it is from my mother. She is Basque."

"What fish was that? We have not had it before."

"That was an orange roughy."

"Very tasty."

"Thank you. Now what will you ladies require?"

"Good sir, we do not eat the flesh of animals, but we do eat fish."

"Simple enough. No meat."

"We prefer vegetables, fruits and nuts. We eat all kinds of bread and found yours of last night wonderful." Again, a slight blush of pride from the chamberlain.

"Also, good sir, we have given mixtures of herbs to be given Lord

Alphonso in the form of tea."

"Yes, I have already instructed the kitchen on this."

"Then, thank you very much and may Alphonso benefit from tea." "My wishes, too, ladies." He turned and left.

The supper that night was a mackerel. Also tasty. The women were beginning to relax in this captivity.

That night, there was a timid knock on the door of the women's bedroom. As Zastra opened the door, there was a small pale serving girl about age 11. "I was told to give you this and wait for an answer." She handed Zastra a leaf. On the underside it said, "Are you safe?" Zastra showed it to Chloe who wrote underneath, "Yes. Well fed." She handed it back to the girl who curtsied and ran off.

Cures

For the next several days, the women continued to brew teas and grind herbs for Alphonso. It became necessary to replenish their store of herbs, so they asked to be permitted to gather herbs in the neighboring forests. He was feeling much better and was able to walk about with just a cane. Something good was definitely happening. He readily agreed and dispatched two guards to take them into the forest.

It was pleasant for the two to seek about in the Gascon woods for herbs, mushrooms, nuts and berries. They would wrap each find in a leaf and put it into a large basket. Although just a short distance from Limoux to the east, this location had new species – perhaps they were higher up in the foothills, maybe it was the wind and rain from the Atlantic. After a brief midday meal and rest, the women scavenged the brush until late in the afternoon. By now, the baskets were full and the guards lifted them onto the cart and drove the women back to Auch.

Word of their prowess had spread around the castle, and soon nobles, knights, courtiers, and even servants requested time to present their maladies. Chloe and Zastra explained to Alphonso that they charged customers for these services and did not dispense them for free. So on Tuesdays, they were permitted to set up a booth and dispense their cures as they did in Carcassonne. Of course, the two guards were again ordered to keep an eye on their activities.

By now, Lord Alphonso had improved markedly. His cough

was gone, he was well rested, but still he complained of fatigue and pains in his chest and joints. As the women had suspected all along, he had high blood pressure, and heart trouble. They knew they needed two remedies: Hawthorn and theriac.

Hawthorn came from a low bush and had red berries which could be ground into a jelly or paste. It was essential to restore health in the heart and reduce this high blood pressure. Yet it was not a local plant. Chloe had heard of it and acquired some from traders from the north of France and also from Britain. Someone must go to a seaport to acquire a supply.

More important was theriac. An ancient Greek remedy, maybe even from Persia, it had reached Palestine and was widely regarded as almost a panacea; but certainly it would cure Alphonso's illnesses.

It was an exotic combination of herbs and spices, and even animal parts, but the formulation was not known in these times. It had appeared in Greek medical formularies on parchment or other scrolls which had unfortunately been destroyed by the marauding Roman armies, and, if not by them, the plundering barbarians of all sorts. Yet, Chloe and her people knew that many of these documents were preserved by the Cathars over the years. It was rumored that these documents had come over from Africa with Mary Magdalene and passed down in the sect she had founded as she preached in the Languedoc area centuries ago. These documents, it was said, were all in Aramaic – the form of Hebrew in use in Jesus' times and had to be translated. Chloe had heard that the formula for theriac was kept by Esclarmonde in her castle in Foix by other Cathar healers, but would need to be translated if in Aramaic to at least some form of Latin or Greek. Only Jews it seems possessed this knowledge. But theriac was proving to be a necessity for the final cure of Alphonso. So an elaborate plan for its discovery must be laid before asking Alphonso for his permission.

Female God

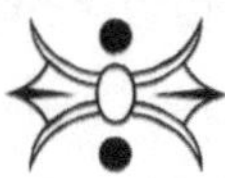

Chloe and Zastra came into Alphonso's chambers accompanied as usual by two guards to administer their cures. Alphonso had improved markedly. Many changes had been made to his diet, and the combination of teas and soups laden with herbs and now minerals was a constant in his therapy. It seemed odd that there were still guards present since the women could easily poison their ward at any time and never have it detected. But the guards remained.

As the women checked his eyes, his armpits, his throat and other places for signs of inflammation, Alphonso was impelled to ask, "What kind of women are you? You read. You have little regard for your superiors. You now have many coins from those you treat, yet you indulge in no finery."

Chloe with a cautious look at Zastra said, "Sire, we are educated. We read the scriptures, and we know several languages. We…"

"You read the scriptures. But… but that is forbidden. Only the priests may read them. Some places it is a capital crime for lay people to do such. Especially women."

"And no wonder. These priests you say are not well schooled and make gross errors. They have only minimal schooling.

"What else do we read? Of course we read medical texts from the Arabs and the Greeks. They are of great help to us in our cures." "I fear you are not like women I know."

"And that is good. Your male priests teach that women are a source of evil. In your worship and the preachings, you speak only of two women. Mary, the Mother of Jesus and Mary Magdalene. One is a perpetual virgin, a passive drudge who obeys her husband, and one is a whore – submissive to the desires of men. The Hebrew bible has many wonderful women whom you ignore: Ruth, Deborah, Moses' wife, Zipporah, many. Yet you Catholics hold us women in low regard and your priests never speak of the Hebrew women."

"I feel I am hearing a heresy."

"No… What we say is in the holy writ."

"But St. Paul tells us to avoid women and avoid sex. Women are not to speak in church and must only learn from their husbands at home. He admonishes us to avoid sex and only for reproduction may we indulge."

"Does that sound like a normal man, Sire, do you avoid sex and women? Do you fear such as we?"

"Well… no."

"Do you not enjoy other women?"

Alphonso looked anxiously at his guards now. He ordered them to leave.

"I hesitate to ask this but you women sound very strange to me. What are you? You have been very good to me, and you may trust that I am very grateful for my improvement, but you are not like the Christian women I know. Are you Jews?" Are you Arabs?"

Chloe again furtively glanced at Zastra. "Sire, you must know that we are Cathars."

"But our priests say that you are dangerous, blasphemous?"

"Sire, do you feel danger?"

"No. I feel I am lucky to have found you. You and your hand do not seem at all warlike."

"Nor are we, my Lord. You worship a form of God who is only masculine. You train for war, you constantly fight battles, you hunt and kill animals for sport, and you abuse your bodies with heavy drink and the meat of slain animals. We abhor killing – anyone, or any animal.

We worship the female side of God – the holy feminine – we nurture, we cure, we practice love as Jesus and Mary Magdalene preached. You believe that faith is all that is necessary for salvation. We believe good works are more important."

"My head is spinning. This is too much. I must think on this."

"Sire, we have observed that you are a man capable of clear thought. Yet you have been raised by Catholic priests. We are telling you what we have learned from both."

"It is all too much."

"Sire, are we now in danger?"

"No. No."

"You see we believe our bodies are but a shell which contains our soul. If we die, our soul lives."

"Enough, enough. Let me think on this. It is too much for today."

"One more thing, Sire, we must ask."

"Ask."

"There are two more medicines we need to cure you. Your heart is not healthy. There are two cures we need. One is Hawthorn. This is a red berry which grows on a bush much further north than we are now. We have looked around in your forests, even at higher altitudes and could not find it. We have found it before from traders in the ports with ships from Britain or caravans from northern France in Toulouse. Zastra has seen it and knows how to test to see if it is real.

"The second is theriac. We have read about it in texts from the Greek which come from Persia. It describes a very complex mixture with many ingredients. I have seen such texts but did not know how to read them. Some Arab doctors we met told us about this and they say it is a miracle."

"Where are these texts?"

"We believe Esclarmonde de Foix has a collection of old documents which contain these Greek texts. The Romans and then the Visigoths have burned many valuable old texts, but the Jews and the Arabs have saved some. I need to send Zastra to Esclarmonde to get a translation of the text on theriac. I will stay here while she goes. I will remain as a hostage."

Alphonso was no fool when it came to the craft of managing a feudal demesne. Letting Zastra go could easily mean she might never return. Besides, a young woman traveling alone even the short distance to Foix was risky. Yes, Chloe would remain. She has been a great benefit to him. But she was a Cathar. Now he knew. Might Zastra tell Esclamonde, a known Cathar, to mount an offensive against him to reclaim Chloe. Not likely – a whole army to rescue one low born woman. And would Esclarmonde release the knowledge contained in such a valuable cure? If she was a Cathar, as Chloe had said, she was interested in good works and healing. That is what Cathars do. Besides it might be a good thing to make good dealings with Foix and Esclarmonde. Yes. He would send Zastra, with a valuable present, and secure her good will. So he granted Chloe's wish and assigned two guards to Zastra on her trip south to Foix. He also dispatched courtiers to Bayonne to seek out Hawthorn. That port traded regularly with vessels from Britain.

That evening after supper, there was again a timid rap on the door of the women's room and again the little serving girl stood with a leaf in her hand. The leaf again had a note, "Are you safe?" Chloe jotted on the leaf, "Yes, Z to Foix soon." She gave the girl a small coin, she curtsied and left.

As they readied for bed, Chloe and Zastra debated the wisdom of their revelations to Alphonso. Zastra would soon be gone, and Alphonso seemed very interested in getting these cures that Chloe had asked for. He certainly would not want to harm Chloe. But what of the future? There were few Cathars in Gascony, but the church was even now spreading sermons of the evils of Cathar worship.

To Foix for Theriac

The trip to Foix was short and without incident. Zastra's and the two guards' horses plodded up the slope of the foothills past a few outlying huts, and past the more populous area to the gate. The guards were ordered to halt and surrender their swords and pass through the narrow gate as it shut behind them and then a second gate opened to let the three through. They were asked their business at Foix and Zastra explained that she and her mother from Limoux were seeking to read an old medical treatise on theriac. A boy was dispatched to the castle with this message. Zastra knew that, if Esclarmonde or her people did not remember their names, they would recognize the village of Limoux. After some time the boy returned and told the guards to let them pass and he ran before them to the open courtyard before the castle. He directed them to a small building to one side of the steps leading up to the castle, and told them to sit. He took their horses to be fed and watered.

Soon, Esclarmonde and two men came in. Esclarmonde was dressed in a simple white tunic and a black cloak with a high collar. The men wore white shifts. "So, my child, Chloe needs theriac. Why?"

"My lady, she is helping to cure Lord Alphonso in Auch. He suffers from a disease of the heart. We have heard of theriac and its powers but never used it. We're told you have old documents that describe its compounding and uses."

"So, Zastra, how is it that you are in Auch in the court of

Alphonso?”

"Do you remember when we sought your help about Osric, the stepson of Alphonso? Well, Osric was taken by a band of men, along with his retainers. We are told they were stripped of their clothes and tied naked to trees along the Via Domitia and had their privates covered with honey. These drew many insects to them…”

As she continued her story, Esclarmonde and the two men began to laugh heartily and tears streamed down their cheeks as she went on.

"And he was discovered by a boy who had been given some coins. They were taken to Carcassonne and later returned to Auch. We believe Alphonso's men discovered us at the fair in Carcassonne and kidnapped us. We were taken to Auch.”

"What has Alphonso done to you? Were you safe?”

"Yes. Chloe looked at him. He was quite sick and weak, so we started to cure him. He has done quite well. But now Chloe needs some theriac and Hawthorn to heal his heart. I was sent by Alphonso to ask you to allow me to see the theriac treatise if you have it.”

"So he released you and kept Chloe.”

"Yes. And he sent you this present.” There was a large box of wine bottles. It contained the famous brandy of Armagnac. "He says he wants to meet you and make a friendship.”

"Ah hah!” Esclarmonde looked at her two men. "Zastra, the treatise on theriac is written in Aramaic, an ancient form of Hebrew spoken about the time of Jesus. You will need one of our learned Jews to translate it. This and other documents, some say, came to our area with Mary Magdalene when she and Jesus escaped from the Romans.

Can you wait until we get a Jew to do the translation?”

"We will wait, if you will permit us.”

"Of course, my dear. Please follow these men to some quarters and join us for the midday meal." The men motioned her to follow them and they were given rooms in the town near the castle.

Esclarmonde turned to her adviser. "Do you think Alphonso wants peace and friendship? Does he know anything of the Cathars?"

"My Lady, it cannot do harm to discuss this with him and discover his true intentions. He has been suffering from some maladies it is said. Perhaps the goodwill Chloe has shown him has done some good."

"I do not have any alliances with these Basques, but they are neither French nor English. They are very independent and have resisted the English from Aquitaine for centuries. Let us send him this theriac as a peace offering."

It took several days for Esclarmonde's translator to decipher the old Aramaic. It was a language that had not been in use since the Romans destroyed Jerusalem, although there were said to be a few groups who kept the old scrolls and codexes and used Aramaic daily. But the elderly rabbi Esclarmonde had been sworn to secrecy and worked in complete isolation in a room where the other documents were kept. He was finally able to parse out a presentable translation and gave it to Esclarmonde. Zastra and her two guards were summoned to the throne room and given a small scroll as well as a sack of dried berries.

"Zastra, I have given you some dried Hawthorn berries as well. I enclosed a note to Alphonso wishing him a fast recovery, and a hope for peace in the future. You may leave tomorrow when you like." Zastra had very much enjoyed her stay at Foix as the guest of the Countess, but missed her mother as well. At dawn, the next day, they departed the castle on the smooth dirt road down the Pyrenees foothills.

However, at a glade off to the side of the road, several armed men with iron helmets crossed the road. "Halt and identify yourselves."

One of the guards stammered, "We are from Gascony and return this day."

"And who is this girl?"

Zastra spoke. "I am Zastra of Limoux returning on an errand for Lord Alphonso of Gascony."

"What is that in the sack?"

"Some medical remedies only, sir." One of the armed men looked into the sack.

"Zastra of Limoux, come with us. Guards, you may deliver this sack to Alphonso. Now be gone." The guards trotted off and Zastra's cart was now directed east to the Via Domitia.

"Sirs, what are you going to do with me?"

"Hush, girl, and say no more. It will go better for you." The men and Zastra continued at a leisurely pace. One of the men pulled out a lute and began to play and sing. It was a love song that Zastra had heard. If these men were troubadours they might be Cathars. She decided to sit quietly on the cart as it was pulled ahead.

Theriac in Auch

The guards without their prisoner continued on to Auch and miserably discussed what punishment awaited them. The distance to Auch was not long and they could feel doom about to descend when Alphonso discovered their loss. Slowly fearing the worst, the two guardsmen meandered through the forest road to Auch. Upon arriving, the gate sentries who had been alerted for their arrival, shouted, "Halloo," and ran to meet them. Their horses were then trotted into the castle courtyard and they were marched with their sacks to the large dining hall where Alphonso now sat at court.

"What news then, men?" his chamberlain shouted.

One of the guards, head bowed, said, "Sire, we have returned with a scroll of translation and a bag of dried berries, but along the way, the young woman was taken from us by armed men."

"I see," said Alphonso. "Armed men. What did they look like? How many?"

"They were covered by their hoods. They were about five. They sprang from a glade on the way north from Foix."

"Hmm. Did they take anything else?"

"No, Sire. They left a message from the Countess and a gift for you from her."

"So, they only took Zastra?"

"Yes, Sire. They let us keep our horses and weapons."

"I must see Chloe, bring her here at once."

In short order, Chloe was brought in and told the guards'

story. She could not contain a smile, and then, "I'm sorry, my Lord. It must have been some of my countrymen."

"Can you still work your cures?" She looked at the scroll and perused it quickly and examined the dried berries.

"It seems we have the translation I sought and the Hawthorn. It seems Esclarmonde has sent a message of peace. Yes, I now have the cures I wanted."

"Can you do this without Zastra?"

"I may need a servant girl to help me."

"Done." He motioned to the chamberlain, who motioned to another servant and the young girl who had been delivering messages was brought up from the kitchen. Her apron was still wet and dirty.

She curtsied and stared at the ground.

"What is your name, child?"

"Celine, Sire."

"Fine. Celine, you will work with Chloe now, now wash up and follow her." Alphonso turned to Chloe, "When can you have these cures ready?"

"My Lord, the Hawthorn, I can mix for tonight. The other, I must collect a few more ingredients. I must go to the forest tomorrow."

"Fine. Take Celine with you and train her in your arts. I will assign new guards for you." Turning to Zastra's guards, "You two need more training. You will report to the barracks and tell the centurion you need more training."

The two guards, happy to have received so light a punishment, bowed their heads, said, "Yes, Sire," and exited the room as fast as they could.

"And Chloe," Alphonso said. "I must see you in my quarters after supper."

"Yes, my Lord.

Alphonso waved everyone off and continued with his meal.

Chloe's Cure

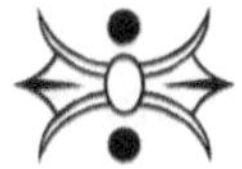

Chloe came into Alphonso's chambers to examine him. It was now several weeks after her cures had been administered. Most of the external signs of illness were gone. He was walking, he no longer had a cough, his face had coloring and he appeared cheerful.

"Chloe, do I have any illness now I could give to someone else?"

"No, I don't think so. The problem is with your heart which seems better with the Hawthorn."

"You know, Chloe, I have never met a woman like you. You are well read, and interesting. You…" Chloe began to think as she had long expected that Alphonso was strongly attracted to her. Was it something new? In her marriage she had been young and inexperienced. The man picked for her to marry was older, and while pleasant, not very strong or experienced in amorous matters himself. She had borne two children, but then his interest seemed to wane. Their household was then a convenience for them. The Cathars however placed little importance on sex. It was a function of the body which was but a temporary shell for the soul. Affairs of the body were meaningless and unimportant. When Chloe said she wished to end the marriage and begin a life which would lead to her becoming a Perfect, her husband had no objection. So they separated amicably and she became celibate. Zastra was a close companion and she was content in her life. But Alphonso was a strong and vigorous man even in his illnesses. He commanded his underlings and kept a close watch on his estate. She could feel the attention he gave her as she tended his medical matters. As she felt his armpits and under his jawline, he would gaze on her face. When she took his arm to feel his pulse, he rested his hand on her side. Of course, he was married under the Roman Catholic rite, and to a noble woman who was a relative of a nearby lord. This meant strong political ties and the marriage vows were to be taken seriously. But the Cathars ignored and had actual disdain for Catholic sacraments. They had no respect for the corrupt clergy, or the ignorant priests who kept their parishes in fear of not attaining a place in heaven, while accepting money from the rich for absolution. They had little regard for the stories of Jesus' crucifixion and resurrection since their own closely guarded tradition held that Mary Magdalene landed in Languedoc over a millennium ago bringing the frail Jesus with her. Those thoughts swirled through Chloe's head as she grasped Alphonso's left arm to feel his pulse and the gland in his armpit. This brought her face close to his, and his hand rested on her hip. As he was finishing something that sounded like the beginning of a declaration of love, he pulled her to him and kissed her full on the lips. She did not resist. She felt stirrings throughout her body. Was she some helpless young girl feeling things for first time? She had not felt this before. She was now a mother of a teenage girl and an initiate in the Cathar rite of becoming a Perfect. Yet she felt stirrings. She lingered on his lips and fell awkwardly to his lap. As she fell, she felt his manhood growing in his lap. When their lips parted, he was flustered and embarrassed.

"I'm sorry, I shouldn't have…" She did not know what to do, so she just smiled.

"Alphonso, it was an act of love. God does not despise them."

He again kissed her lightly on the lips. "Chloe, we must keep this a secret… my wife…"

"Yes, I know. This is a political marriage. You owe loyalties. I would not harm you."

"But you are a Perfect, like a nun."

"We Cathars do not respect these prohibitions, or abstinences."

"So… um… sex is not forbidden."

"It is an act of the body. What matters is the soul."

"You are indeed a strange woman. St. Paul forbids sex except for procreation, but you…"

"If it is not an act of love, it is meaningless."

"Can you… er… examine my blood pressure after supper tonight?" She said looking at the extension of the codpiece in his lap, "I fear it may be elevated."

"Oh, sorry then," he murmured.

"Oh, Lord Alphonso. I am not some silly young girl. I will… um… examine you this evening."

As she left, she could not forget that Lord Alphonso was a powerful ruler and was married to the female relative of an important Spanish ally he could ill afford to antagonize. Yet the thrill in her stomach and the lightheadedness were there as she pulled herself up standing and marched out of the room. She had not had these feelings before. She had married, or such as the Cathars call it, as a young teenage girl to a very nice older man. Cathars do not accept traditional Catholic sacraments because they shun rites administered with a priesthood whom they deem corrupt. Yet her pairing with this man had been amicable, but passionless. Her delight was in her daughter Zastra. But when time had run its course and Chloe wished to become a Perfect, he was not averse to separating. But now these feelings, in her thirties! What was God doing to her? The body as she and the Cathars saw it was simply a shell to house the soul. It could be a source of evil, materialistic evil, as such to be avoided. Was her body, or God, tempting her? Or was this attraction a God-given benefit, a joy to be pursued? Certainly, her attraction to Alphonso could not be made public. Nor could she freely express her feelings to him. If he tired of her, he could cast her off or relegate her to the kitchen. She must remain aloof and hide her feelings. Not only was she in reality a prisoner of his but a Cathar – a sect much at odds with the Holy Roman Empire which was regularly sending out priests to stamp out this heresy.

So she retired to her room, quietly sorting out her herbs, and mixing the complicated concoction of theriac as she read from the translated formula. She had acquired most of the important ingredients from nearby fields and forests, and sent the Lord's men for others in local fairs and markets. And yet, she could not resist humming quietly to herself, it was a troubadour's song about love, but an unrequited love. The little serving girl by her side could only look up at her with a puzzled look.

Supper with Alphonso

The regular supper for the Gascony count was a formal event.

The minor members filed in and took their places at the wooden table and benches. Chloe took her usual spot at the corner of the room, and the little serving girl now followed her wherever she went. Soon, the upper level dais would be laid out with servants putting the better crockery and forks in the places reserved for the nobility with Alphonso and Fulgencia in the middle. Since Osric had been banished away to military service, he ate with the men in the barracks.

A smile came to Chloe's lips which she could not suppress as she saw Fulgencia parade in with a kind of strut she had interpreted as befitting her noble position. By now, she had grown plump and soft, but her hair was arrayed up in a series of ribbons, and her gown was imported from Toulouse. She was a comical figure putting on airs as she refused to recognize the minions gathered below her. Part of Chloe's smile was also because she had had the serving girl add some Yohimbe powder to the bowl of lentil soup, reserved for Alphonso.

Like most holding positions of power in this age the possibility of poisoning was high. Alphonso's meal was prepared separately and tested by those responsible before it was served to him. If they did not die or get sick, neither would Lord Alphonso. Chloe's serving girl had come from the kitchen and because of her stature was for the most part ignored. The kitchen staff was now familiar with Chloe's concoctions added to Alphonso's meal and paid little attention as the serving girl added Yohimbe to the lentil soup destined for Alphonso by his own personal waiter.

Since Chloe expected a liaison with Alphonso that night, she wished him to be ready. He had recovered from many of the illnesses which had plagued him before and seemed ready to engage in a proper secret liaison that night. But to be on the safe side, Chloe added the Yohimbe to increase his manly prowess that he would not be disappointed or discouraged. She had a passing thought that this new potency might direct him to Fulgencia, but the fatuous noblewoman now had little attractive powers. Although they sat side-by-side during the meal, they hardly spoke and he enjoyed the comradery of the men to his right.

For Chloe the meal proceeded slowly. Somehow the serving girls were dragging their heels and the courses of fish stew took forever to ladle out. Chloe turned to her now worshipful serving girl.

"Child, where are you from?"

"Madame, I was orphaned at a battle in Aquitaine when I was little. My name then was Amalafrida. Some of the men found me crying over my mother and brought me here. Now they call me Celine."

"Were you Basque?"

"No, they say I was Visigoth."

"Are you Christian?"

"I think so."

"Have you heard of the Cathars?"

"No, Madame."

"Do you like to mix herbs with me?"

"Oh, very much so."

"Where did you sleep before?"

"On the floor of the kitchen."

"Do you remember who gave you the notes you passed to me?"

"I think so. He is one of the cooks."

"So you came here, worked in the kitchen and never lived outside the kitchen since they brought you here?"

"Yes, Madame."

"Were the cooks nice to you?"

"They mostly ignored me or ordered me about."

"Would you like to learn about medicines with me?"

Her face brightened for the first time. "Oh, yes, Madame." With this new happiness, her pretty Visigothic features became more apparent. Her high cheekbones, and small almond eyes, and her lank blond hair. She could be a beauty one day. In the absence of Zastra, Celine could be her companion, she would see to her wellbeing.

Meanwhile, a wave of raucous laughter rolled through the room, as the nobles and military commanders drank and grew louder. Alphonso could not help bumping Fulgencia as he gestured with his left arm while telling a story that amused the men. Fulgencia accepted the slight and moved to her left. The female companion to her left had come with her from Aragon. She frowned at Alphonso and patted Fulgencia.

The meal drew to a merciful conclusion and people filed out as they were finished. Chloe and Celine now went back to their room.

Once there, Chloe took Celine by the shoulders.

"Celine, can you keep a secret?"

"For you, Madame, always."

"I have a meeting tonight and may return late. Can you keep this to yourself? It is very important."

"Yes, Madame, I understand." The squint of her eyes as she said this told of some intelligence in that head. Yes, she could keep a secret – and now she was loyal to Chloe.

Chloe could hear the guards marching down the hall and knew it was vespers. She walked carefully down the hall to Alphonso's chamber. Although a handsome man now that he had recovered his health, he like most Gascons bathed rarely and had a strong smell about him. Chloe had brewed a mixture of mostly sandalwood which she brought now in what most of the court knew was her medicine bag. She slipped quietly into his bedroom.

"Ah, Chloe, I've waited for this."

"For what? I have given you treatments for several weeks now."

"But you said… I said."

"Yes, yes and you are a count and married. I am a prisoner."

"No longer you…"

"I have a different treatment for you now. Please remove your shirt." She then began to massage him with the sandalwood.

"That smells great. What is it?"

"It is a rare spice from India." As she drew close, he pulled her to him and kissed her.

"Chloe, I've…"

Chloe let her lips fall on his again. He then held her in a strong embrace and began to caress her with his hands. He now smelled of sandalwood and his own musk. She did not resist. He pulled her to his bed, and began to raise her shift. He also pulled his own tights and wriggled out of them. His lovemaking was quick and abrupt, like the 14 year old boy he had been. It was nonetheless effective. Chloe lingered in his room as the session became even more passionate and heated. The church bell rang for lauds. She had been here from compline to lauds, and now must slip unnoticed back to her room. She walked barefoot swiftly down the wooden floor and closed her bedroom door quietly behind her.

"Is that you, Madame?" she heard from Celine.

"Yes, Celine, you must go back to sleep."

"Yes, Madame. I was worried about you. You might have been stabbed." Chloe grinned to herself, yes, she had been stabbed and more than once. What was this mirth? At a function of the body. Why had God given us this? Well, no matter for now. Now was the time for sleep. Celine was already breathing heavily by her side. A lingering scent of sandalwood brought a smile to her lips as she drifted off.

Afterglow

Alphonso and Chloe lay quietly side by side. It had been another pleasant night visit. He broke the silence.

"You know, Chloe, that I cannot offer you much."

"I don't want anything. I would like to see my daughter and my village again."

"Will you return?"

"Of course. But what about Fulgencia? She must know. There are few secrets here."

"Oh no, she is content. I have an older soldier, now a widower, who is her bodyguard. She seems to like him."

"What about Osric? Does he want to succeed you?"

"Never. Fulgencia had been married before, but her husband had died in battle before Osric was born. She was the niece of the King of Aragon and my father thought it a good idea to arrange this marriage.

I was 14 and she 24 with a child."

"Was she a good match?"

"Hardly. She was still mourning her husband, she was still nursing Osric, and she thought I was a crude peasant and she was the niece of a king. All true I guess. I mean I am a Gascon, and my family were Visigoths. We don't care about courtly refinements. So she didn't seem interested in a teenage boy. She was already too plump and she never was a beauty. No, it wasn't a good match. We have been polite and from time to time she endures my requests to visit my bed chamber.

When I was sick, she was heard plotting with a few nobles for my successor. I should have had her exiled or sent to a nunnery, but I need the good will of Aragon. So she stays. I put up with Osric. She has her bodyguard and she stays to herself. I am sure she is happy not to visit me at night now."

"That is sad."

"Not any more. I have been blessed with you. I have never met a woman with your brains. The ones in court are such ninnies."

"Alphonso, Cathar women are not taught to be subservient. We can read, and think. We often lead in our villages."

"I am not sure if that is dangerous. St. Paul says women should be quiet and learn from their husbands."

"Ah yes, St. Paul. Well, we believe in Mary Magdalene. She was an educated woman and was Jesus' closest companion. She is worshipped by the Cathars. Some believe she came to the shore of France with Jesus and founded our religion."

"Our priests say she was a prostitute and possessed by demons."

"I see. And how many women are the leadership of the Catholic
Church?"

"Um, none. None that I can think of."

"You see. Someone has made her a whore. What do the women in your church do?"

"They pray. They tend the fields. I think some care for orphans."

"But they do not lead."

"No. Never."

"We Cathars believe that God is part feminine. The holy feminine God, the Shekinah, teaches the opposite of the male

God. Men pursue war, oppression of the weak, hunting, drinking and lack mercy. We believe as did Jesus in love, compassion for the poor and healing. The two halves of God must be joined."

"That is nothing like what I was taught."

"Do you read the words of Jesus?"

"No. They are in Latin. Only the priests can do that. They tell us what he said. Sometimes they read them out in Latin."

"But no one speaks Latin anymore."

"True."

"Do they teach you about St. Paul?"

"Of course. That they quote in French."

"You see we are quite different."

"I would agree. But I am very fond of you."

"And I of you. Now I must go back to my room."

"Adieu. I understand." If these regular visits to Alphonso's bed chamber were to become more public, it might endanger Chloe. Around a ruler there are always many with fierce jealousies. Better not to tempt them to action.

Fulgencia

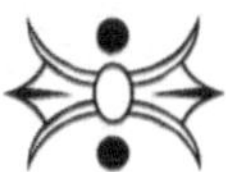

Chloe and Celine were sitting quietly at their corner of the large dining hall, dabbing at the fish stew with pieces of bread they had torn off the loaf. They sat with the kitchen women in a back row. So it was a startling event when Fulgencia had her entourage of ladies in waiting stop by her table on their way to the raised dais in the front of the room.

"Chloe, I would speak with you after the midday meal in my chambers." She asserted this as a command and used the lower form of "you" as one would address a servant.

"Yes, milady." She rose, curtsied and nodded. It would not do to avoid showing full respect for the Countess. She rustled as she walked by – a sound made of petticoats and silk by her and her ladies, all clicking fans.

What was this about? Alphonso said she was no longer interested in him. Could she have heard? Could he be jealous? Should she tell Alphonso? No. This was an announced public meeting. She would not dare cause her harm. Maybe a threat but she must go. Maybe she wanted some herbs or a cure of some kind. Chloe was already treating many in the court, from servants to nobles, and was well paid for it. Would the Countess announce so publicly a need for a cure? Not likely. The only way to find out was to go to her chambers. So after the meal she washed her face, daubed a bit of flower scent and took Celine with her to the chambers.

Fulgencia's Chambers

As she approached the door to the Countess' chambers, a large older man sat on a bench. He was dressed as a soldier with a hammered leather breast plate but was clearly past the age of military service. He rose.

"Who are you, miss?" Clearly Chloe was no longer to be addressed as an unmarried woman, and the surly tone with the lower "you" was an assertion of superiority and disdain.

"Sir, (he was clearly not a "sir") I have been sent for by Countess Fulgencia. I am Chloe. This is my assistant Celine."

"Wait here." He opened the door to the chambers and returned shortly. "Please enter." Ah! A "please" this time.

Fulgencia was seated on a large padded bench. Several women surrounded her in chairs. "Please leave us." She waived her hands dismissively and the women scurried out the door. "Who is this?" she said, gesturing at Celine.

"She is my assistant. She helps me to mix my cures."

"I see. She may leave, too." The same hand gesture. Celine, already nervous, was more than happy to leave.

"So, now, Chloe, you administered cures to my husband, Lord
Alphonso?"

"Yes, milady."

"And he is well now."

"Does he pursue things with vigor?" She was using an

uncomfortable tone now. She must know. Is she jealous?

"So I am told." Not a lie, not a denial.

"I see. Does he thrust himself into the affairs of state?"

"It seems so." Unmistakable. Yes, she knows.

"I might need some of your medicines." What was this, a new tack? "It would be my pleasure, milady."

"One of my um… ladies complains of her husband's flagging interest."

"Ah. I see."

"Can something be done?"

"Probably. It would be best if I could examine him."

"No, no, no. That wouldn't do. This must be discrete."

"So, one of your ladies. Hm. What does this man lack?"

"Um, vigor."

"So, he is not upright in his ardor?"

"His ardor is fine. He is not so upright."

"Ah, I see. Yes. There is something that can be done. Is he older or young?"

"I would say older."

"How, umm… regular was he upright?"

"Why, every night… I am told."

"Well, milady, I must counsel you on two things. As men get older, they are not able to fulfill their desires every night. It is common as men get older. I would say every other night or twice a week. How old is this man?"

"Maybe in his forties."

"Does he have any other ailments? Does he breathe well? Does he drink much before he attempts to be upright?"

"No, he is healthy as a horse and exercises with the soldiers. He breathes clearly. But he does drink to excess often."

"I see. Well, he must have a healthy heart, but he cannot drink so much before his other activity. It slows the blood."

"I have a good remedy for the condition. Celine will deliver a powder to you. His woman friend should mix a pinch of it in his stew or soup in the evening before any planned activity and he should limit his drink of strong spirits that meal."

"Will that work?"

"I have seen its beneficial effects before."

"May we keep this inquiry a secret?"

"Of course, milady."

"Not one word to Alphonso. Do you hear?"

"Of course, milady." (I will wait at least a half hour before telling him.) "Is there anything else?"

"Not for now, Chloe. And thank you." Chloe curtsied and left. As she passed the guard at the door, she paused and smiled at him. "A good day to you, sir. And a good night." He looked quizzically at her, but smiled. Ah, now a smile.

Post Fulgencia

Alphonso and Chloe again lay side by side. "So what did Fulgencia want? Is she angry at you?"

"I would say no. She seemed pleasant that you were healthy again and asked if you pursue things with vigor and if you 'thrust yourself into affairs of state.'"

"Ah, very sly. So she knows."

"Then she asked for some medicine for a 'friend' because of her friend's lover's flagging interest. It seems this friend is in his forties.

He is not so 'upright' in his ardor."

"Could you help her?"

"Of course. I gave her something to put in the man's stew and told her he should not drink so much before coitus."

"Did that help?"

"I don't know yet."

"Do I need anything like that?" Of course Chloe had given him his regular dose of Yohimbe, but a man's ego was not to be trifled with even in the Cathar world.

"No, Alphonso, you are doing very well on your own." He nodded quietly assured of his virility.

A few minutes passed. "Chloe, I have heard some disturbing news. It seems the Pope is worried about the so-called Cathar heresy and has sent a new order of monks called the Dominicans around Toulouse and Languedoc to preach and interrogate Cathars. Those are your people are they not?"

"Yes, Alphonso. So I have heard, too."

"We have very few Cathars in my demesne, but I am worried about the Pope and these Dominicans."

"Why so?"

"They cause unrest and disruption. My people have had peace for many years now. The Cathars bother nobody. But I fear the Pope has ulterior motives."

"Like what?"

"The king of France is a very nasty person. I think he could take advantage of the unrest in Languedoc and seize land to expand his kingdom."

"I can see that."

"So far the Dominicans have not done very much in Gascony, but a war in Languedoc could spill over into our land."

"So what can you do?"

"I don't think I can do much about a few monks who wander about preaching. I might send an envoy to the Pope to ask what he intends for Gascony and ask for his intercession with the Dominicans."

"How are your relations with the French king?"

"I have never met him."

"Maybe you could send him some of your Bordeaux wine and ask for a meeting."

"Yes, I could. But I think you should warn the Cathars in Gascony to be on guard."

"If you will permit me to do so."

"Of course you have been very good to me and I owe you much. Your people are not a problem, and I will protect them if I can. Just like the Count in Toulouse, but he is already suffering because of it."

"Thank you, Alphonso. But I must go now."

"I wish you could stay all night."

"Me too." She kissed him and scurried out the door back to her room, nodding to the guard as she went.

Fulgencia Again

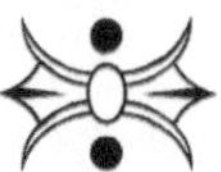

Once again, Fulgencia flounced into the dining hall followed by her entourage of ladies. She again stopped at the outer bench where Chloe and Celina sat. "Chloe, I would see you again in my chambers." What was this now?

"Yes milady. Would three bells be acceptable?"

"Yes." On, she flounced up to the upper dais where the royalty ate. Celina looked at Chloe grinning shyly. She knew what she had prepared for Countess Fulgencia. Chloe frowned at her for possibly revealing a secret.

That afternoon, Chloe was greeted by the Countess' bodyguard, this time, enthusiastically. "Please enter, Madame Chloe." (Now, she was addressed as Madame.) There on her large padded bench sat Fulgencia who bade Chloe sit beside her after she had curtsied and greeted her. (So now she could be seated.)

"Yes, milady. How can I be of service?"

"I must say that my friend reported that the powder you gave me did very nicely."

"So her man showed some encouragement."

Fulgencia grinned a bit lewdly. "Apparently, he showed some engorgement." She laughed and blushed.

"I am happy to see I have promoted the cause of love, milady." "We have a slight problem."

"May I help then?"

"Yes, it seems the man has an abrasion on his member. It seems he or she was a bit too vigorous. Do you have an unguent that can heal him?"

"Oh, yes, milady. That is an easy matter. May I also suggest that they use the unguent liberally before entry? It would help prevent future occasions."

"I am most indebted, Chloe."

"I will send Celine around with a mixture promptly."

"How is Count Alphonso these days?"

"Quite well, milady."

"I hope he will need the unguent as well." With that Chloe could not resist a heat rising to her neck and cheeks. Was she a teenager that she should blush so? Fulgencia enjoyed her little game, but she was also signaling her approval. Chloe had no dynastic aspirations and did not threaten Fulgencia's position. She insisted on no finery or preferment. It was now an unspoken state of peace. "By the way, Chloe, I hear that you may know of troubadours that sing songs of love. You come from that region, yes."

"Yes, I do, milady."

"Could you have some come to our court? (A dangerous turn for the conversation. Troubadours were often Cathars.) I fear Gascony does not enjoy the culture of Languedoc. Do you know of any such?" "I will make an effort to see if any can come to our court, milady." Was Fulgencia now telling Chloe she knew her to be a Cathar?

After all, it was known that most troubadours were Cathars. Their songs for the first time glorified love, love between a man and a woman. It was unheard of until now. Certainly most noble marriages were arranged and designed to fulfill political objectives even more binding than treaties. But at the lower levels, a man negotiated a dowry for his bride and thus acquired a bed companion and a servant for life. A most commercial arrangement. But now, these troubadours spoke of a love – often unrequited for a woman. But also unknown, this reference to a woman was also a secretly and intricately worded hymn to the sacred female aspect of God – a central Cathar concept. It was raising the status of women from Mary Magdalene, the whore, or Mary, mother of Jesus – a passive untouchable perpetual virgin to a flesh and blood woman who had divine powers. Was this what Fulgencia was referring to? It could not be. Fulgencia was an unlettered spoiled noblewoman. There is no possible way she could have absorbed any aspect of Catharism or culture. It was more probably she just wanted to hear love songs. Or could she be sending in her covert way a message to Chloe that she too was sympathetic to the Cathars? After all, she was not stupid and had a keen sense for intrigue and hidden meanings in her words.

It did not take long for Chloe to scribble a note for Celine to deliver to Raimond Roger de Trencavel. Trencavel had been keeping watch on Chloe's situation in Gascony. Celine had faithfully been the conduit to exchange messages through a worker in the kitchen between the two. When Fulgencia out of the blue asked Chloe to request a visit from the troubadours to sing love songs in their court, it was a complete surprise, but a welcome one. Of course, Chloe had to harbor doubts that this might be a trap set by Fulgencia for the troubadours and Cathars, but it was unlikely. She was from Aragon – over the Pyrenees – which had little to do with the king of France or the Pope. They were tolerant of the Cathars, what little they knew of them. Besides, Fulgencia seemed to be grateful for the aid Chloe had given her in her love life. She discounted any suspicion and welcomed the response from Raimond Roger that he and a fellow troubadour would appear for a courtly performance.

Benches were set round the courtyard and a raised platform was set against the wall of the castle. The courtyard was filled with onlookers arranged by rank and calling, soldiers here, kitchen maids there, with the nobles surrounding Alphonso and Fulgencia. At the signal, the two troubadours swept through the gates and strode up to the stage with their red cloaks swirling behind them. On the right shoulder of each cloak was a white dove – the mysterious and clandestine symbol of Languedoc troubadours, a covert homage to the sacred feminine and Mary Magdalene.

The performance was a mixture of many different forms. Most of the songs were about love – a knight for whom his beloved is forbidden, or love – carnal and gritty with many obscure references and puns, but some were about nature – beautiful spring, graceful deer, pure brooks. Known only to a few were songs to the divine Goddess, the sacred feminine. Many had tunes from familiar Latin hymns, some were original. The show ended with a ballad specifically written for Count Alphonso and the Gascons. Uproarious applause greeted each rendition and a thunderclap broke at the end of the ballad of Alphonso. At the love songs, Fulgencia stole glances at her bodyguard and many of the ladies peered over their fans at the lovers or those whom they wished to attract. All was followed by a sumptuous feast with roast pig and never an empty goblet of burgundy wine from just north of the Count's town of Auch. Revelry and songs spilled out in the night until people staggered off to the beds or simply snored where they lay. Of course, Fulgencia crept off quietly to her bed chamber on the arm of her lover.

Chloe and Celine did not drink and enjoyed watching the antics of the court. Secret alliances were revealed and open embraces betrayed hidden desires. She took leave with Celine dozing on her shoulder.

At about nine bells, there was an unmistakable gentle rap on Chloe's door. Alphonso never came to her room and she hoped not to have attracted an inebriated unwanted admirer with new found alcoholic courage and the inspiration of the love songs. She cautiously opened the door and saw Raimond Roger de Trencavel.

"Chloe, we must speak." She recognized the lead troubadour. "I am Raimond Roger de Trencavel sent by Esclarmonde."

"Of course, Sir Raimond, please come in." Celine snored gently in the bed. Chloe and Raymond sat at the small table at the corner of the room.

"First, are you safe, are you well kept?"

"Yes, Raimond. Alphonso has taken to me. I now dispense herbs to the entire court and do very well."

"Does Alphonso treat you well?" At this, even though a woman in her thirties, she could not repress a nodding of the head and a growing blush. Raimond – a man of great experience – could not help but chuckle at this teenage shyness.

"So he does, eh? Are you lovers?" He enjoyed his little moment at her discomfiture.

"Oh, Sir Raimond. Stop."

"This is very nice. A good Cathar perfect with a Count of Gascony.

Quite a story for the village of Limoux."

"Please Raimond, no. You must keep this between us."

"But how can I deny the village such wonderful gossip?"

"Please, Roger. I still seek to be a perfect and a serious woman."

"Oh, very well. So you are happy and safe."

"Well, I have much to tell you. Things are not going well for the Cathars. The Pope has been embarrassed by his crusaders and seeks money and lands. He is becoming more concerned about the Cathar heresy. Some local priests are forced to inquire as well into the beliefs of their townspeople. Some are questioned in open public forums, some in the confessional. It is becoming very dangerous. The Pope has demanded action from the Count of Toulouse, but so far he has remained quiet. Meanwhile, I suspect the French king who will profit handsomely if Toulouse should become divided in a religious war. Even now, some claim it will become a crusade and a duty of the French to rid the land of heretical Cathars. Of course, they have been promised the lands when the Cathars leave. Pleasant no?"

"So what shall I do?"

"For now you are safe in Gascony. Also, your village of Limoux is safe and so is your daughter. My advice is to go see her now if you can. Then, if things become dangerous in Gascony, escape over the Pyrenees to Aragon or Castile. If you can get to Esclarmonde in Foix, she will help you."

"Thank you, Raimond. I am most grateful. And I must say your concert tonight dazzled everyone. It seems you have ignited the lamp of love in more than one couple."

"I can see the fingers of dawn on the horizon, I must leave you now."

"Safe trip, Roger. And eternal thanks."

"Adieu."

Debates and an Assassination

Many matters controlled the thoughts of Pope Innocent III. The failure of the Crusades in which his loyal Christian knights chose to sack their brother Christian capital of Constantinople instead of Muslim-held Palestine. Richard the Lion Heart of England was returning from the Crusades, but had been captured along the way and was being held for ransom. His inept brother, John, had in his absence lost control of the kingdom and was forced to sign that evil paper, the Magna Carta, which gave his nobles power and ended his absolute rule. Yet John persisted in an unending war with the French king, Philip II Auguste, over the lands of northern and west France. A number of other wars perpetually broke out in Eastern Europe and even his own Italian peninsula had erupted from time to time in land disputes. Even Rome itself had violent confrontations by warring families. Innocent moved his offices to the neighboring area of Trastevere. Although deemed the supreme religious leader of the western world, Innocent III was still a feudal lord who had to expand papal territory and acquire more rich fiefdoms and serfs and the generous income they brought in.

Of course, he always had simony the so-called donations from the wealthy world could buy a remission of their sins and a cleared pathway to salvation at the promised Day of Judgement. There were also contributions from the many pilgrimage sites and their churches replete with specious relics of the holy family and the saints, their bones, their clothes, their shrouds said to be hidden away in crypts or on murky display. It was feared that some of these relics might turn out to be chicken bones. These brought seasonal crowds to the pilgrimage sites to worship and to ask for favors from these venerated objects just as had the pagans from their idols and statuary in the past. They brought with them large donations and enriched the towns en route.

Yes. The Holy Roman Empire was indeed wealthy, but was plagued with the worries of managing the many problems of controlling such a large temporal empire.

So Innocent III was a wealthy descendent of the Segni family, a powerful player in the banking business who profited substantially from their relative's high success and power, but now he sat head in hand on his throne. He wore the high peaked mitre in colors of white, red and gold, and was berobed in a red and gold wrap encrusted with pearls. As such, he represented the cause of the humble Jew, Jesus. His ministers stood before him to start the day's affairs. The Pope was trained in the business of acquiring wealth not in the holy devotion to piety and peace.

One of the ministers clad in black was the first to speak. "Your Holiness, we still have left undone a decision on the sack of Constantinople by the Crusade. Some 50,000 Christians were killed and the churches were looted. And what of the bastards fathered by the many rapes?"

Innocent III rumbled, "But I have excommunicated all who participated in this. As I have said, a noble rules only by grace of God, and the Church decides whether he is in a state of grace. These men are not. What more can be done?"

"Alas, Your Holiness, the Eastern Church wants to know what is to be done. Are these men to return to their lands not knowing their fates?"

"Perhaps, it was by the grace of God that this incident happened. It was meant to reunite the Holy Roman Empire east and west."

"And what of our crusaders? They return home only to find they have been excommunicated. How can they reclaim their lands without the church's blessing."

"They have given us much in the stolen gold, silver and art, I am told."

"Yes, Your Holiness."

"Well, then we must let it pass. It was a horrible mistake, but I cannot excommunicate so many of my most loyal nobles. They must reclaim their estates and continue to send us their tithes. I will lift the decree. Send an envoy to Constantinople and have him give me a report."

"Yes, Your Holiness."

Another bishop rose to address Innocent III. He had a distinct Frankish accent. "Your Holiness, we continue to have problems in the south of Francia. There is much heresy."

"Ah, the Cathars again."

"Yes, Your Holiness."

"Let me review the parties. Now, this Philip II, who calls himself the Auguste is the French king, yes."

"Quite so."

"Why does he not do something?"

"The Count of Toulouse controls the southern region and he is not willing to go after his own subjects."

"Is he a Cathar?"

"No."

"I see. Send for this Philip. I would talk to him. And send out some priests to convert some of these wayward people."

"Understood, Your Holiness." He bowed and left the chamber.

The business of the day continued on as each minister presented a troublesome situation and asked for guidance. The Pope was brought a tray of food so that he could continue on. Soon the vespers bell rung and the Pope adjourned for the day.

The next day, clerics were dispersed throughout Toulouse to preach against the Cathar heresy. They were in a quandary because they simply did not know what Cathars believed or how to preach against it. They followed the message of Paul as refined by the Nicaean Creed – Jesus as the son was co-equal to the Father and the Holy Spirit, and belief in this was the sole source of salvation and entry into the Kingdom of Heaven. Side issues were of course raised: The death of the Son ordained by the Father freed those who believed from the original sin of Adam and Eve. Good works or repentance was not necessary only faith; complete faith in the divinity and resurrection of Jesus. Lack of faith would lead to an eternity of damnation in Hell. These were time-honored preaching standards, but did not meet the questions raised by the parishioners who were confused by all this intricate theology. For the simple, the question was how could three things be one and why did it matter anyway what one believed. But Toulouse and the region around it was not a backward collection of farmers tilling soil and raising pigs. It had become a wealthy and prosperous area which had attracted educated men. It had become a center for the arts, philosophy, music and culture. Its people did not accept easily the old formulas of faith. Only recently, the Visigoths had been persuaded to discard the Arian philosophy which denied the equal standing of Jesus and the Father in the trinity and, on occasion, questioned the divinity of Jesus itself. The lay people saw the evils and corruption in the church. Rich people could buy their way into heaven by the practice of simony – paying for a remission of sins. The poor might be sent to the eternal fires of Hell. Questions innocently raised to these envoys of the Pope confounded the simple priests and the message came back to the Pope. Was this the faith Jesus had preached? Somehow, a public conference must take place to resolve these issues. After all, well-educated theologians certainly could best an unknown bunch of Cathars who had never attended the fine universities in Italy and France. And so, the debate was to be arranged in the public square of Toulouse. Again, word of this was diffidently relayed back to the Pope. Stronger measures were needed. The Pope proposed a meeting with King Philip II Auguste of France forthwith. He also sent out a brutal Cistercian legate to speak severely to the Count of Toulouse.

This situation must be resolved.

Friars in Toulouse

Count Raymond IV of Toulouse had been getting reports of missionaries pouring into his demesne, the Comte of Toulouse, and creating incidents in the rural villages. Raymond's feudal holdings including his own lands and those of his vassals were the vast majority of southern France. He had been both prosperous, and generous. In addition to rich farm lands, there were many trade routes in the area known as Languedoc. From Rome and northern Italy, to Spain and Aragon, and north to Paris and Lyon, merchants and caravans plodded along old Roman roads laden with cargo. Raymond and his predecessors had all been educated and fostered a golden age in Toulouse in the arts and sciences, philosophy, astrology and astronomy and poetry. His lands tolerated and welcomed a potpourri of faiths: Arabs left over from their previous occupation of the region, Jews, and Cathars. Raymond saw little reason to discourage their presence and enjoyed their contributions to his demesne. The Cathars especially had prospered and held many areas of rich farmland and paid substantial tribute to his coffers with little protest. They were a peaceful lot and kept to themselves. In Toulouse itself, their particular blend of Christianity met the Jewish sages, and formulated jointly many interesting concepts. The Kabbalah fit nicely with their beliefs in the holy feminine aspect of God, reincarnation, and the value of Mary Magdalene. The troubadours were born during these times and they sang for the first time of courtly love, the romantic quest for a woman's love, which in euphoric terms, also revealed an adoration of the feminine God, the Shekinah. People were happy and delighted in the financial and intellectual prosperity of the region. Churches were erected venerating Mary Magdalene and John the Baptist as well as Sarah, Jesus' daughter by Mary Magdalene.

But now! Now these emissaries from Pope Innocent III were creating unrest. They spoke of eternal damnation and warned the evil consequences of heresy. The parish priests emboldened by their flock now listened intently in the confessional for the infusion of heretical ideas. The parish priests and the traveling friars were now beginning to note who those espousing Catharism or having Cathar influences were. Reports came back of distress in many towns as the neighbors resisted this intrusion in their lives.

The Counts of Toulouse had for several centuries been loyal to the Roman Catholic Church. They, at the behest of the Popes, had answered the call to join the Crusades. They had provided money and soldiers, they had transported boatloads at their own expense to Africa and the Middle East through the treacherous Mediterranean. At one time, they held the port of Tripoli in North Africa as their own fiefdom. They helped found the Knights Templar and the Knights Hospitaller in Europe. Of all the areas causing unrest for the Roman Catholic Church, the Counts of Toulouse was among the least. And yet, the Pope was now fomenting discontent within Raymond's lands.

A messenger had recently come from the Pope, it was part request, part demand, that Raymond cooperate in ridding his demesne of the Cathar heresy which was infecting it. Word from the Pope was not to be ignored, but he had many loyal subjects who were Cathars. The area was at peace. He had always been a tolerant ruler and it had always served him well. Now, this disruption from the Pope. He told the messenger he would comply with the Pope's wishes.

Dominic at St. Peter's

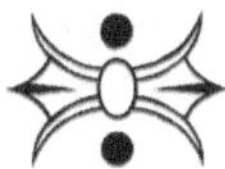

Dominic Guzman and his followers sat in the shade of the arches of St. Peter's as he awaited an audience with Pope Innocent III. While not from a noble family, he was nonetheless wealthy, well-educated and drilled in the theology of the Roman Catholic Church. He had left his cart and horses at the livery at the edge of Rome and walked barefoot with a staff. He had chosen for the audience a threadbare cloak, a grimy shift and dirty feet. Raised in Castilian Spain, he had already made some headway in the politics of the church hierarchy by accompanying his loyal bishop on a diplomatic mission for Alfonso, King of Castile. He burned with ambition and set up residence in Rome with his followers, but he chafed under the control of the Duke of Toulouse who would not let him persecute the heretics in his realm. So now he sought an audience with the Pope to form a new order, reporting directly only to the Pope and bypassing the local bishops and feudal lay rulers. He felt this was ordained because he told of a dream his mother had before he was born in which she gave birth to a dog with a torch in its mouth who set the world on fire. If the Pope could grant the rights to Guzman to form a separate order, it would be called the Dominicans, making a pun of the Latin term Domini Canis or Dog of God for the name of the order, Dominicanus, Latinization of Guzman's name. But for today, Dominic Guzman was still in search of the imprimatur for his order.

At last, a papal secretary came out to meet Dominic and his followers. The secretary was dressed in a brilliant scarlet cloak with brocade trimmings, and a lace shirt with a high lace collar. He wore a red and white satin cap. On his fingers were a number of rings signifying the seals of his noble family, the Papal authority itself, and several lands his own noble family controlled. A tall thin man with a long thin face and hands with long fingers with long finger nails. As he approached Dominic, he sniffed the air as if detecting odorous body scents and shuddered at the sensation. Dominic and his followers had freshly bathed that morning, so the secretary's pretense was ignored.

"Who are you and what do you seek?" intoned the secretary in a stilted form of church Latin and using the contemptuous form of "you" in addressing the group.

Dominic, not to be intimidated, replied in perfect church Latin, "We seek the Pope for an audience to combat heresies in the Toulouse area. Surely, he will wish to cure the world of these dangerous beliefs." With that he presented letters to the secretary from the King of Castile, the Bishop of Osma and several other high ranking clerics in the south of France, all sealed for the Pope's eyes only. Unsure whether to dismiss the men as presumptuous ruffians or recognize them as worthy nobles, he took the less dangerous course and lead them into the Pope's throne room.

Guzman had chosen the doctrine of asceticism or extreme denial of creature comforts as a way to secure the blessing of heaven. He believed that God wished extreme bodily discomfort as a sacrifice. While neither Jesus, nor any of the Hebrew notables or sages, nor the Muslim clerics had elected such a path to salvation, many of the Catholic monks now sought asceticism and even self-inflicted pain as an ideology. It was a mystery how self-inflected pain could absolve some else's sin. And so, Guzman sought this way to impress the Pope with his piety, rather than any actual good works. Ritual behavior was to triumph over good works.

As they were ushered into a large throne room, the Pope sat on a high marble throne amid carved wooden galleries. Several clerics sat facing the carpet on which the monks now made their way to the foot of the throne.

Pope Innocent III came from a long line of popes. His father was Count of Segni, and the Segni house produced nine popes. Thus, the Segni family was able to assert its power in both the religious and secular realms. As was the usual practice, the pope previously known as Lothar of Segni was not the first born in his father's family, and so was sent into the clergy to consolidate power. It was certainly a life of study and reverence, but as most popes did, he enjoyed all the emoluments of a noble life except official and overt marriage. Celibacy, while preached, was more often rarely practiced by the noble clergy. The lower level clergy were of course enjoined from pursuing the women in the nearby villages, but the nobles among the clergy not so. And Innocent III was a formidable character.

His recent embarrassment from the Fourth Crusades was a blot on his historical record he wished to be erased. Although the earlier crusades had some measure of success, the Fourth was a disaster. Although sent to re-conquer the lands of Palestine, recently lost, the western Christian forces in a bizarre turn of events, had succeeded, not in conquering the Muslims in Palestine but in sacking, looting and raping their way through Constantinople – an eastern Christian ally. Apparently, the Pope's trusted leaders of the Fourth Crusade had planned to raise 35,000 men, depart Venice for Egypt and attack Palestine from the south. However, they never raised enough money to compensate Venice for the cost of the enormous undertaking, and had agreed instead to attack an enemy of Venice, Zara instead on behalf of Venice. Flush from the sack of Zara, the forces got it into their heads that Constantinople would be a better prize. And so, they descended with an army on Constantinople, the capital of the eastern Holy Roman Empire and destroyed what a thousand years of barbarians had tried and failed to do. Pope Innocent suitably embarrassed by an attack on fellow Christians rather than the targeted Muslims, excommunicated the entire lot. But then on second thought reinstated them when they arrived in Rome and turned over a large portion of their loot to the Pope.

Innocent had continued to reap financial success in the practice of simony by the sale of indulgences. Rich people could actually buy a remission of their past sins even if unconfessed or unacknowledged and received their place in the Kingdom of Heaven which by some unexplained miracle had been granted to the Pope rather than God. He also unsuccessfully engaged in a number of territorial wars in Europe which expanded the feudal estate and wealth of the papacy. This sale of indulgences made not only the Pope, but all the local bishops quite wealthy as local burghers and nobles were persuaded not only not to commit sins and seek repentance, but to buy their souls as pardon from the clergy. It is not known how the clergy acquired this power for itself rather than having forgiveness come directly from God, yet the laity were convinced it was so and poured their wealth into the church coffers. Along with the tithes from his religionists, he received generous portions of the profits from the many monasteries the papal state controlled.

So, as Dominic knelt on the marble floor of the Pope's throne room, the Pope had many items of political and temporal conflict on his mind. The barefoot and threadbare Dominic and his followers were asking for the sanction of an order from the Pope himself bypassing the local bishops and feudal lords to seek out and rid the south of France of its heretics. Dominic's plea was based on theological grounds and not so incidently the power and control of many Cistercian monasteries. The Pope's consideration was based on political and financial grounds and the advancement of the papal state.

As Dominic spoke, his eyes opened wide and his pupils dilated. "The south of France, Toulouse, has accumulated vast numbers of heretics." He spoke in perfect church Latin. "First, there was the Arian heresy which denied that Jesus was one and the same as God the Father, and possibly denied his divine nature. That was resolved centuries ago. Now we have the Cathar heresy."

Moving his arms wildly, he went on, "These Cathars revive the gnostic heresies of years ago. They entertain dualism: that there are two forces good and evil at contest with each of us. They believe the body and the material corrupts the spirit, and that in the lifetime of an individual, the spirit is trapped and corrupted by the body." Innocent nodded thoughtfully. In his mind, he wondered how these Cathars were a threat and who he knew in Toulouse. What were the politics there? It was a fertile area for farming. Who were his people there? Should he send this angry monk back to the area with a papal blessing to root out the heresy? We need more on this. Dominic and his people were politely dismissed with a promise that their quest would be considered.

Popes Meet Philippe II Auguste

For several weeks, emissaries rode back and forth between Pope Innocent III and King Philippe II to arrange a meeting place. Of course, the prestige of each was at stake because one could not travel to the other without seeming to be the petitioner and the other the beneficent grantor. In reality, the Pope had so many enemies in his domain, the Papal Estates, and even the city of Rome that he could not risk having his whereabouts disclosed if he left the heavily guarded confines in his enclave on the Trastevere outside Rome proper. King Philippe II Auguste was beset by problems with the English who perpetually engaged in a war to acquire power over the north and west of the Frankish kingdom. These days, however, the Pope because of his power to enthrone or excommunicate rulers had superior clout. And so, the very prize Philippe sought had to be so great that he would risk a covert mission to meet the Pope and plot a joint course of conquest: the conquest and subjugation of southwest France – Languedoc and Toulouse.

Philippe and fifty armed knights mapped out a route south to the Alps and near the town of Avignon at the estate of a friend of the Pope. Philippe was able to arrange for some commercial barges to carry him east on the Seine, take a short portage and drift down the Rhone in style. His barge was fitted out with a dining hall and a floor for performances on the deck. The pope who frequently would go to the south of France in the summer, drew no curious onlookers as he followed the Roman roads to Avignon. The two men set up large tents in the fields and planned to meet.

It was to be an advantage for each as they each looked hungrily at the rich farmlands and wealthy holdings in southern France to their west. The question was who would lead the attack, who would benefit from it and how would the men be motivated to fight.

Philippe strode into the meeting with the vigor of a warrior. He was a large beefy man with a bald head and a round face. He was a jolly sort fond of eating, drinking and enjoying himself, but that exterior belied a shrewd and manipulating mind. He had heard that the Pope was a wily negotiator as well and welcomed the chance to consult this spiritual leader. He dressed as a king. He had a large royal blue cloak with gold fleur de lis, and a navy and gold tunic. By his side he carried a largely ceremonial epee, and on his head he wore the French crown.

Not to be outdone, Innocent III sat at the throne on a raised dais. At the back of the throne was an immense cross bejeweled throughout. He wore the full papal garb of one conducting a mass in white and red with gold trim, and a tall mitre in white with gold trim. His fingers had many rings encrusted with jewels.

As previously agreed, these men were about to determine the fate of the humble Cathars.

Kneeling before the Pope, Phillipe said, "It is such an honor to greet you, Your Holiness. I have heard about your many successes in the Italian peninsula, in the Crusades, and in Hungary. Your family must be extremely proud." (The Crusades had either been embarrassments or failures and the Italian peninsula was in a perpetual state of disarray.) The pope who took great pride in his international dealings was duly impressed that the French king would have heard of his trumpeted conquests which were in fact embarrassing disasters. Of course, both men were experienced in dealing with other rulers and knew it was not only good practice but a necessity to praise extravagantly the abilities and accomplishments of the other. But Phillipe went into further detail in describing the labyrinthian maneuvering Innocent III had utilized in expanding the power and influence of the church.

Not to be outdone, the Pope had obviously paid great attention to Philippe's battles in defending the north and west against the English – a war which had been going on in battles in Normandy, Burgundy and elsewhere for at least a generation. The battle had severely depleted the royal treasury and the taxes assessed to pay for war had impoverished his people. The male population had declined precipitously. Philippe had been parlaying alliances with different nobles to distract and delay the more powerful English kings. Yes. Philippe beamed. Yes he was known and respected by the Pope. Both men gloried in their supposed accomplishments and were happy to have their failures overlooked.

"And so, to business." The Pope anxious to draw this meeting to a successful conclusion. "I look to your realm and see a few demesnes who are not in vassalage to you. Especially the Count of Toulouse. A rich prize. And a noble who has not been willing to be strong against heretics who would defy the tenets of our faith."

"Ah, the Cathars."

"Just so. They refuse to convert or abandon their inane practices." Philippe was not slow to see where the Pope wished to go. He was dangling the rich farmlands and wealthy cities of the south of France before him and asking him to participate in a joint effort to result in their conquest and subjugation to the French crown. Philippe was now weary of war, however. These interminable confrontations and battles with the English, the constant negotiations with the northern nobles and their not so petty demands. But Toulouse, and Languedoc. Why it could be double the size of France! What did the pope have in mind?

"A crusade."

"A crusade? But they have been against the Arabs and even Constantinople. How do we conduct a crusade in our own continent?"

"I will again call on the crusader spirit. 'Deus Vult.' God wants it. You will promise men the lands they conquer and wrest from the Cathars and anyone else in their way. We will consider it the will of God to rid the earth of this heresy, which to this day, I don't fully understand."

"So, you will call on these men of faith who wish to receive lands in southern France, to champion God in a holy war from which they will become wealthy landowners. And, these landowners will be your feudal subjects, paying tribute and honoring defense obligations as true knights of the French realm."

"But my resources are depleted in my fights with the English. I don't think my armies are ready for more war, and I cannot afford it. The people are now overburdened with taxes to pay for my adventures."

"But you would be able to repay loans with the tributes you will receive."

"Who would lend me this kind of money?"

"Sir, you do not know me. I and my family are powerful bankers in the Italian peninsula. We could underwrite loans for these nobles of yours."

"But why are you interested in such a campaign, your

Holiness? That is, in addition to setting these heretics on the true path to the Kingdom of Heaven?"

"Do the monasteries pay tribute to you in northern France?"

"No. They are exempt from tribute and the requirement of military service."

"To whom do they pay tribute from the bounty of their rich farmlands?"

"Why, to you, Your Holiness."

"So they are like feudal enclaves loyal to me that are resident in the land of a secular king."

"Ah, so you will gain a fresh portfolio of feudal estates in my realm which it would be my duty to defend. As well as more benefits from pilgrimages and indulgences."

"Ah, you have it. And at the same time they would preach the gospels to your subjects and make them worthy of heaven. And yet, these monks would have no heirs since they would be celibate and the monasteries would remain from generation to generation under the control of the Holy Roman Church."

"But, your Holiness, I have many entanglements with these lords in the south. Marriages, military alliances, treaties. If I were to lead such a crusade, they would contend that I had broken vows of friendship and mutual alliance. I even have some of these connections with lords believed to be Cathar, or at least Cathar sympathizers."

"And so, do not lead it. Encourage others quietly to do so. Lend them our money, give them your tacit blessing, and stay discretely in your Paris, behind the magnificent wall you have built."

"Oh, you've heard of my wall."

"How could I not? So are we of the same mind?"

"May I discuss this for this night with my court?"

"Of course, of course." With that, Philippe bowed and left.

The Pope motioned to some unseen figures behind the curtains and gestured that they should follow the king. Only a ripple was seen along the tent wall as they left.

Debate

Three scholars of the Roman Catholic Church nodded peacefully as their horses ambled along the Via Domitia from Rome. They would take the road north to Toulouse. They were accompanied by 10 Swiss guards dressed in their vibrant multicolored uniforms. Make no mistake though, these men were armed and ready to defend the scholars from any and all attacks as they made their way through what might be a thicket of bandits, enemies of Innocent III, or other feudal lords who sought territory and power. This trip had been planned for months. Innocent III had been warned repeatedly of the socalled Cathar heresy. He had been irritated by Dominic Guzman who, at a requested papal audience, had asked permission to interrogate and persecute these people who claimed to be Christians but espoused what these scholars and others condemned as heresy. But they were a peaceful lot, living in a quiet corner of southern France and posed no military threat to the papacy or the king of France. They had no leader, no priests, no cathedrals and seemed to live a life of good deeds and healing others. But they paid no tithes to the church, bought no indulgences from their sins, and did not attend mass, take communion or make confession.

They quietly rejected the mystery of the trinity, and the Nicaean Creed – the ultimate test of faith for the Roman Catholic Church. They held the church sacraments and the venial priests in contempt. They were an embarrassment to the Church. More embarrassing, the Count of Toulouse enjoyed their support and often sought to protect them. This disobedience by a Christian feudal lord irked the Pope. After all, did not these noblemen accede to their stations in life by the grace of God as determined by the Pope of the Holy Roman Empire?

To calm Dominic Guzman's frequent requests for a more aggressive approach to this heresy, Pope Innocent III settled on the more peaceful and diplomatic method. He would send the finest of his scholars to confront and debate the Cathars in their own capital city, Toulouse, and thus, convert the lot to the true faith. The finest scholars of Rome were to join the most learned scholars of Paris in Toulouse for a debate hosted by the Count of Toulouse. Dominic Guzman was permitted to join the entourage, but not participate in the debate.

This would be no contest. The Cathars had no scholastic training and were probably country bumpkins living in small villages on the fringes of civilization. It was rumored that they had a variety of backgrounds. Some held them to be from Bulgaria and espousing all gnostic myths long since discredited. Others contended they were remnants of a faith founded by Mary Magdalene who landed on the southern coast of France and began to preach a doctrine with her frail husband Jesus by her side. This myth had survived nearly 1,200 years, but still the child of Mary Magdalene, Sarah, was worshipped extensively in the area, and Black Madonnas, purported to be Mary Magdalene herself, adorned many churches of southern France. The Pope's men cared little for these myths and approached the day of the debate calmly and confidently. They hoped to baptize many souls as they were born again in the true faith. When they reached the Castle of Toulouse, they were greeted by the Count's chamberlain and directed to a palatial suite of rooms near the Count's castle. They were wined and dined on all the local delicacies. It was the Count's time to curry favor with the Pope and the extension of hospitality would be elaborately described to the Pope on their return.

The city of Toulouse also awaited anxiously the confrontation. But Toulouse was not an ordinary city serving as a mere market place for the exchange of local produce and the housing of a feudal lord. Because of its location as a trade center, and a stop on a pilgrimage route, it had grown to be a widely recognized center of knowledge and culture. The liberal laws set forth by the Count permitted Jews, Arabs and other cultures to settle without threat of persecution or ruinous taxation. The arts, medicine, the sciences, philosophy, poetry were celebrated around the city and much supported by Count Raymond. Old Greek and Arabic texts were collected and studied in the large library. An affluent class of merchants arose to support this learning as well. It was not as the Pope had suspected a region controlled by the Visigothic barbarians as many of the cities were.

The Cathars also came to Toulouse for this high moment in the history of their religion. They were housed by their co-religionists in their homes around the city. The debate was to consist of five people from each side presenting issues to be answered immediately thereafter by the opposing scholars. Unknown to the papal group, however, two of the five Cathars on the dais would be women.

Soon the day of the event approached, and the crowd began to assemble in the village square. The people stood in clumps; some monks, some Jews, some Cathars, some merely curious staked out their places. It was also to be a festive day; vendors of many sorts of delicacies set up tables at the periphery, others hawked religious medals or implements. To keep the peace, 100 armed guards of Count Raymond's were stationed throughout and paced menacingly among the assemblage.

Count Raymond climbed the steps to the dais, and gave a speech of welcome to the Pope's men and their Cathar opponents, to the assembled multitude. He offered a simple prayer to God which asked that His wisdom might be on display this day. He introduced each of the speakers who mounted the dais and bowed to the crowd. A murmur rose up as the Cathar women were introduced. It was possibly an evil omen that women would be allowed to speak in public on religious matters. Had not St. Paul forbade it?

The Pope's men were dressed in the garb of celebrating mass on important holidays. They wore brilliant red robes with white and gold lapels over a white lace alb. Some of the men were cardinals and wore their red galeros – wide brimmed hats with long red tassels. Some were not cardinals and wore the white and gold archbishop's mitre or a brilliant red biretta. They took the right side of the platform. As they mounted the dais and were given their introductions, murmurs of awe rose from the crowd at the presence of such elevated members of the church. The Cathars too were introduced but had no titles and were designated by their first names and the village they resided in. They were each dressed in a bright white tunic belted with a braided rope.

At the front of the dais, facing the crowd, were two lecterns with a chair behind each. The first two to address the crowd, one cardinal and one lay Cathar woman, approached their respective lecterns. The Cardinal went first. It was a common sermon of the church and began with the sin of Adam and Eve.

The sin of Adam and Eve was direct disobedience to God and was therefore the Original Sin – a sin which all mankind must bear. Jesus who was the begotten son of God was made to suffer for that sin and to wash it away by the pain of the crucifixion.

Therefore, if we believe in Jesus' divinity and his resurrection after death, that is if we are born again, we are absolved of this original sin and may therefore enter the Kingdom of Heaven. The Cardinal was considered an eminent scholar and he was not about to disappoint. His points were carefully crafted with references to past Christian scholars – Origen, St. Thomas Aquinas. The Cathar woman sat politely in her chair and knitted. As the Cardinal drew to a close, he bowed to polite applause, as Catherine of Aude came to her lectern.

"I speak of love as Jesus did. Love does not fight wars or harm the weak. Love cures the sick as did Jesus." And then in a timid voice, she recited in the French, for the first time heard about in Toulouse, the Sermon on the Mount. The people had heard this before in Latin as explained by the priests but never in their own tongue. When she finished, there was a smattering of claps then as people stood with tears in their eyes then there was a crescendo of applause. She sat and picked up her knitting.

The rest of the debate went on. The Cathars were accused of being from Bulgaria, or being sodomists, of many things. But the locals knew them from being in their midst. The Catholic speakers made fine arguments, laced with threats of condemnation of the soul and threats of hell. The Cathars pointed out the vain sporting of material wealth in the priests' outfits, the corruption in the act of simony which permitted rich people to pay to the church for the remission of their sins. They contrasted this with Jesus' words themselves from the gospels and Jesus' own simple ways. They reminded the people that Jesus and all of his apostles were Jewish and believed in peace. Jesus threw over the tables of the money lenders and condemned the "den of thieves" his church had become. While simple and direct, the Cathars' speeches betrayed a deep familiarity with Christianity by the apt quotations from the

Hebrew bible and the gospels. A common theme of corruption on the church was hinted at as Jesus' words were quoted. However, there were occasional odd differences between the words of Jesus from the gospels and the words the Cathars used in their quotations. They suggested their gospels came from a different source.

The Catholic clergy could not conceal their discomfiture at being bested by these unknown locals in a major city before a large crowd. As the session drew to a close, the Cathars came to shake hands with their opponents who, while dumbfounded that these peasants should presume to shake hands as equals with such as they, they nonetheless accepted the proffered hands.

As the city square slowly emptied, the Cardinal – obviously the leader of his faction – turned to one of the male Cathars, and with barely concealed anger, asked, "Where do you people learn your scripture?"

"Good Father, (an address to a village priest not an eminent Cardinal) most of us here are literate. We educate our young."

"Even the women?"

"Aye, even them. Although Paul would have our women be silent in public and ask their husbands at home."

"Who are you to quote Paul?"

"We read him, too."

"Do you accept the divinity of Jesus and the mystery of the trinity?" This now was an out and out threat which might mean torture or death if the acceptance were not wholehearted.

"Good Father, we believe in Jesus as you have heard today. Some of us say he came to our shores with Mary Magdalene and began to preach here. Some say our faith is derived from him. But that is a discussion for another day." He bowed politely and turned to help other Cathars pack their items and descend from the dais. The Cardinal was not sure what he had heard. Was it an admission or a denial? Jesus in Languedoc? Preposterous! He must see Innocent III as soon as possible.

Friars to the Towns

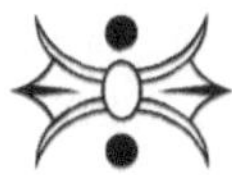

By now, the word of the fiasco of the debate in Toulouse had reached Pope Innocent III. Several of the church's chosen advocate now appeared before him. Cardinal Scialfa, the only cardinal, stood in the center. A tall thin man, wearing a red silk galero, a wide brimmed hat with tasselated strings hanging past his ears, and a red satin robe with gold and white embroidery around the collar stood before him. Their heads were bowed and the Pope paced furiously back and forth. "How did this happen Vincente?" He was addressing the cardinal by his first name.

"Your Holiness, we preached the Nicaean Creed, the divinity of Jesus and his resurrection. That faith in Him would provide salvation while heresy would lead to eternal darnation. Of course, we each took an aspect of the gospels and explained them. I thought your surrogates were quite eloquent and convincing. They were well prepared."

"What do the Cathars say?"

"First they preached that the church was corrupt. They said Jesus did the same thing when he condemned the money changers. They recited the Sermon on the Mount in French. They preached of love and good deeds over the sacraments and self-torture.

"They said poor people were not held to the same standard as the rich, since the rich could buy their salvation by payment to the church. Jesus had contempt for the rich. His parables on the subject were recited in French for the first time."

"Not in Latin?"

"No, sire."

"Heresy! What else?"

"And they said good works were more important than faith. They quoted St. Paul Then they read from the gospels in French. Someone had translated it from Latin. The people were amazed to hear His words for the first time in their dialect. Then…"

"Enough… enough." He paced more, then sat and stared off into space. The clergymen fidgeted. "Alright now. I want 200 friars to go among the towns. Not Toulouse. There are too many Cathars and Jews there. The small towns. I want the friars wearing their robes, I want them tonsured and wearing sandals or barefoot. They will speak local French. They will preach the gospels. They will assure that true believers may enter the Kingdom of Heaven. I want sample sermons prepared for our review. They will preach in the local parishes. Do you get my point?"

"Yes, Your Holiness."

"Now, you are dismissed until you have produced sermons for the people."

"Yes, Your Holiness." The clergy turned and went out of the room. There, they had a prolonged discussion. They considered themselves lucky not to have suffered some punishment. Now, they must craft a form of preaching which the local townspeople could accept. Then there was a messenger sent from Innocent III who asked them to return. Again, the cardinal and his underlings followed the messenger in.

"Vincente, I also want each of these friars or their assistants to prepare rolls of all the Cathars where they go. I want the names of the leaders and the towns where they reside. Do you hear? I want the names of those who do not make confession or take communion."

"Yes, Your Holiness."

"Now, go and do God's work."

"Yes, Your Holiness." They filed out once again.

Dominican Order

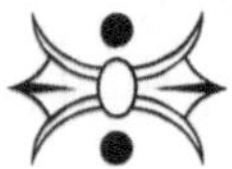

Following the disastrous debate with the Cathar representatives, especially the women, the Pope knew he would have to resort to other measures. He could not rely on that weak Raymond IV, Count of Toulouse to rid the world of this heresy. It was becoming clear that he needed people loyal to him. That meant knowing the wishes of that Dominic Guzman and several others to form orders blessed by and loyal directly to the Pope. Above all, they would owe little to the local rulers or to the local priests. They would take what measures were necessary to convert these blasphemous Cathars. Then he could rely on the King of France to force Raymond to require only the Orthodox Church doctrine in southern France or Philippe would take his land from him. King Philippe II Auguste had seemed willing to aid him in this matter when last they met. So, Innocent summoned this Dominic Guzman who had been staying in Rome for several years hoping to be granted the right to form an order to rid the world of the Cathar heresy. The Pope had not liked Guzman before; he had an air about him that was somewhat like a fanatic.

Innocent III had not been at all happy to entertain Guzman's request for a separate order. He, it must be said, did not like his looks. Although Guzman had what might be considered to be handsome features, a fine nose, and thin lips, and piercing eyes, there was a strangeness to them. Perhaps they were a bit pinched, or betrayed a heart of fanaticism. This fellow could be dangerous and difficult to control. Innocent had heard he conducted himself as an aristocrat back in his region of Aragon, but lately had begun to dress in meager and ragged monk's robes and to go barefoot. He also had the hair on his head cut into a tonsure. This sudden conversion was worrisome; was it a recent affectation, an effort to curry favor with the Pope or a true belief? It was clear that the debate of Toulouse showed the common people were not overwhelmed by the rich dress of the senior church officials. They might well be affected by the simplicity of the Jesus of the New Testament. Dominic must have divined that the people of Toulouse sought humility from the clergy. But this Guzman had a Spanish accent, he was from Aragon. What could he do in the land of Languedoc – the language was distinctive. Innocent mulled these thoughts.

But then, the thought of an order loyal directly to the Pope had favorable aspects. Now, missionaries would be sent out loyal to Rome, not local priests loyal to maybe the local bishops, the local rulers, but inaccessible to Rome. The idea of monasteries sitting on rich farmlands, paying rich tribute to Rome, and transmitting strict Roman doctrine to the peasants; this was an opportunity not to be missed. All it would cost would be a signature on a decree. After all, how much harm could this Guzman inflict? So the Papal authority was granted and Dominic Guzman left Rome with what he sought: The power to create his own order of friars and monks, to accept land and funds from Paris nobles for his monasteries, and to grant indulgences for past sins. If he were successful, he would soon rule over a rich series of monasteries scattered over southern France.

It was to some small degree that Guzman referred to his order as the Dominicans – the dogs of God in Latin. It fulfilled his mother's vision of a dog carrying a torch which would set the world on fire.

Guzman left Rome with a blaze in his eyes and a fire in his belly.

Confusion and Turmoil

The countryside in Toulouse was astir in mass confusion. It was not long ago that the genial local priests were welcomed as part of the larger family. They officiated weddings, funerals, baptisms and heard heartfelt confessions. They were neither rich, nor presumptuous, and were pillars of the villages. An example had been set for generations by the Counts of Toulouse, and continued by the present Count Raymond VI of toleration of the Jews, the Cathars and the few remaining Moors.

Then, at first appeared, intense Catholic scholars, theologians and lawyers who attempted to explain intricate and profound doctrines of Orthodox Catholic faith. These men of the prestigious Cistercian Order were commissioned directly by Rome and held the local priests in contempt. After all, they had been educated in the fine universities and were answerable only to the Pope. They wore rich formal priestly garb and spoke in educated French. The local peasants stared at them in dismay as they threatened eternal damnation or excommunication, but, above all, they condemned the Cathars and the Jews. They paid no taxes to the Count of Toulouse or other local lords. They insisted that Raymond VI join in their mission and impose sanctions and taxes on these heretics within his borders.

The villagers would speak behind their hands and say, "That bee is buzzing around again." They were told of the Cathars who they saw and knew in everyday life, that they worshipped the devil in the form of a black cat and kissed the devil's anus.

As time passed, their vitriolic messages became more strident. They pressed Raymond VI for more support in their efforts.

But Raymond VI had many ties within his demesne, he had many vassals among the Cathars and his people had intermarried with them. He owed loyalties sworn under time honored vows of mutual defense, peace and commerce. He tried to ignore these demands and keep the peace.

Meanwhile, Dominic Guzman trod a different path, he and his now called Dominicans. They dressed as the ragged poor, in tattered monk's robes and walked barefoot from town to town, surviving on handouts from the faithful. He preached also an angry message against these Cathars who had threatened the true faith. His intensity and that of his order frightened the populace, but made little headway.

One more theologian joined the ranks of missionaries sweeping through Languedoc. Pierre de Castelnau, a fiercely ambitious priest who had already survived a battle in the papal courts in Rome to acquire his position as an archdeacon in Miquelon. This village was actually an island, wholly owned by the papacy, and an enclave in the Comte of Toulouse controlled by the Pope, but not the Count. Castelnau was now a recognized jurist and joined the other papal clerics fanning out in Toulouse, and seeking an end to the Cathar heresy. But Raymond VI in Toulouse and his vassals throughout Languedoc were passive, reluctant now to disturb the peace and cause trouble for their Cathar subjects. Castelnau frustrated by the lack of support from the lay nobility, began to preach more virulently and seek an armed intervention against this heresy. As a papal legate, he assumed the power to excommunicate Raymond VI. He was also able to convince the archbishops to undertake a purge of the clergy who did not support him. The

Archbishop of Narbonne and the Bishops of Viviers, Agde and Toulouse all were deposed. These tactics still met with failure. The Cathars heresy persisted and these foreign delegates of the Pope were ignored.

In the meantime, Dominic and his Dominicans began to imitate the Cathar methods. Traveling in pairs, they roamed the country in absolute poverty. They preached love and simplified their sermons. But Castelnau and the Cistercians – the rival Roman-French order – refused to adopt these methods. The Pope, well aware the hostility these Cistercians fomented, himself tried to persuade Castelnau and the others to adapt to the more humble methods. The Dominicans and Cistercians vied for power and control and there were frequent confrontations.

By now Castelnau had acquired many enemies. The lay nobility were disturbed by the constant calls he made for their support, the local townspeople dreaded the incursions into their peaceful town life. Raymond VI was embarrassed by his excommunication. The townspeople were under constant fear of the inquisition that the two orders visited on their families and neighbors.

A more ominous force loomed to the north. King Philippe II Auguste; although in accord with the Pope's desire to rid southern France of the Cathar heresy, remained overtly unmoved. His vassals and knights from the north of France who well knew the turmoil brewing in Languedoc and were hungry for land to conquer and rule, had been told they would be permitted to attack and secure the Cathar's lands if a war broke out. They watched and waited for news of the discomfiture of the Comte of Toulouse. The fertile lands and rolling hills of the south of France filled their every thought and beckoned.

And then, Pierre de Castelnau was murdered. As he attempted

to cross the Rhone River on his way north, he and his companion were found fatally stabbed at the crossing ferry. Although he had many enemies and rivals, a squire from the court of Raymond VI was blamed. The Pope moved swiftly. Raymond VI was held responsible for the death of a papal legate and excommunicated. Pierre de Castelnau was promptly beatified – declared a saint within a year of his death. Promptly many miracles were attributed to him to satisfy the requirements of sainthood. Raymond VI quickly assessed the situation arising out of the death of Castelnau. Although Castelnau had many enemies and rivals it was no surprise that Raymond was held at fault for this murder, nor that the Pope excommunicated him and beatified Castelnau. Raymond VI rode swiftly to Rome, and humbled himself before Innocent III and begged to have the anathema lifted. He knew immediately that the papal clerics wandering his countryside preaching against the Cathars would be emboldened to rail against him and seek further and harsher penalties against the heretics. Dominic Guzman wasted little time demanding the forceful interrogation of every one of the Count's subjects and subjecting them to torture and confiscation if their Cathar learnings were not confessed and renounced. Now with the clear backing of the Pope himself, these humbly dressed monks terrified the townspeople and demanded obedience and not only threatened with eternal damnation but immediate corporal punishment as well as death by fire – a public burning at the stake known as the Auto de Fe.

With the death of Castelnau and the Pope's excommunication of Raymond, it also did not take long for the hordes of nobles and knights massed on the border of Toulouse and Languedoc to plunge into battle with the subjects of the Count of Toulouse. As with the Crusades against the Muslims, the Pope's encouragement was contained in a single phrase. "Deus Vult" – God wills it. And so with the same ardor which inspired the Crusades to the Middle East, the men sought lands, plunder, rape and glory all in the name of religious purity with the full blessing of the Pope. It was a new crusade, this time against a nearby and vulnerable foe with rich farmlands. Men of all levels of society, nobles, knowns, thugs and peasants sought the promise of heavenly salvation for their particular past sins as well as lands and booty. Philippe II Auguste, the King of France, now espoused the cause while at the same time by promising them that they could now acquire for themselves the lands now free of the Cathar heresy. After many losses to the Saracens in the Holy Land, the French fighting men saw an easy foe to conquer.

Yet Philippe II, the self-styled Auguste, remained above the fray despite urging from the Pope but sat in his walled city of Paris as his minions carried out his designs.

Even so, there was confusion. The Cathars for several generations had intermingled and intermarried with the inhabitants – including former Romans, Visigoths, Lombards, and a polyglot of other races and ethnic groups. It was difficult to tell who was a true Cathar and who was not. And what was a Cathar? In this, the papal orders were not only helpful, but the accusatory arm of the Crusade. They identified those Cathars they had interrogated previously, and compelled answers from those they had not yet questioned. But, on points of abstruse theological points, it was difficult to get a definitive answer. Some peasants learned the right answers, some confessed the error of their ways, but the confessional and the mass in which people must profess their beliefs was a supreme test. And yet, it was still confusing. Backed by armed men from the north, Dominic and his Dominicans spread from town to town conducting inquisitions into who were true believers. Those unable to give proper answers were tortured or burned at the stake in increasing numbers.

The military effort was coordinated at first by Arnaud Amaury, a close associate of the deceased Castelnau. Those towns that had offered little resistance were subjected to public inquisitions and public punishments of unimaginable barbarity. On one occasion, there was a frail elderly woman who was about to receive the Cathar rite – the consolamentum – on her deathbed. When Dominic Guzman heard of this woman, he went to see her. Since she was not in good health, she believed that Guzman was a Cathar elder administering the consolamentum rite. Since she readily and earnestly confessed her Cathar beliefs, Guzman had her carried into the center of the village where her heresy was exposed. She was then burned alive for all to see the error of her ways.

Soon, the Cathars began to arm themselves and offer resistance to the onslaught led by Amaury. The reputed but closely guarded secret identity of the Cathar leader was Raimond Roger de Trencavel.

It fell to Arnaud Amaury to lead this new crusade. He had been a close associate of Pierre de Castelnau, both of the Cistercian Order. With the pronouncement of "Deus Vult," by the Pope, the military effort consisting of greedy nobles, thugs and adventurers was labeled the Albigensian Crusade, after the meek town of Albi which was home to many Cathar religionists. In the beginning the Cathars were not prepared for armed conflict. These ravenous bands of armed men lead by those holding papal orders could simply march into a town, assemble the inhabitants and conduct public inquisitions as to each person's personal faith. Of course, for a considerable reward, informants would come forward to condemn a neighbor, particularly if there had been a history of bad blood with that neighbor.

Eventually, Cathar opposition began to form under the leadership of Raimond Roger de Trencavel and towns began to resist the onslaught of these would be crusaders lead by the Amaury Amalric – the Cistercian monk and his followers, or by Dominic Guzman and his. But with resistance, it was now difficult to separate the Cathar inhabitants from their Orthodox neighbors. There could be no public inquisition to root out the heretics from the faithful.

Raimond Roger Trencavel, viscount of Beziers, with a small entourage, met Amalric at Montpelier in an effort to save his Cathar followers. He was rejected. The lure of lands and booty was too strong and the heresy of the Cathars too divisive. Raymond Roger sped back ahead of the advancing crusaders to prepare his defenses at Carcassonne. He brought with him a following of Cathars and Jews.

Amalric pressed on. The bishop of Beziers came out of the city to again try to dissuade the papal legate or sue for peace. He was sent back to the city and told it would be spared if they surrendered their Cathars. He drew up a list of prominent Cathars, some 222, to sacrifice themselves for the city, but he was met with strong resistance by the citizenry.

Meanwhile, a small group of the townspeople fearing the onslaught in the making, attempted to escape to the south, but were met with a small force of crusaders. In the ensuring skirmish, the ragtag crusaders were defeated. As they retreated and told the other crusaders, a hue and cry went up and the common soldiers joined the defeated crusaders and burst into the town. Seeing the success of the common soldiers and not wanting to be left out of the robbery, the knights, the rest of the mélange of soldiery fearing they would lose out on the booty, joined in what was now becoming a rout.

The abbot of Beziers now was dismayed at the outbreak of fighting while he was still attempting to negotiate the release of his Catholics. From the hill where they stood the Bishop, Amalric and their retinues could see the disorderly outbreak of fighting.

"But, Legate Amalric, if this should become a defeat, how can we save our Catholics?"

The legate smiled benignly and quoted Timothy 2:19 in church Latin and then in the vulgate. "Caedite eos. Novit enim Dominus qui sunt evis." "Kill them all, for the Lord knoweth them that are his." By now, the northern barons and knights seeing the common soldiers had begun to kill vast members of the townspeople, and were taking plunder, rushed to the scene of battle and began to slash wide swaths through the defenders.

Soon, a large number began to seek refuge in the cathedrals which were jammed by now with asylum seekers. The Cathedral of St. Nazaire held a mélange of Catholics and a few Cathars. The raiders quickly set fire to it and, as the roof collapsed and spread its burning timbers throughout, as many as 5,000 died as the structure collapsed on them.

For days afterward, the forces of the papal legate fought among themselves over the meager possessions of the now deceased as Amalric and the Bishop watched from their hilltop vantage point.

Buoyed by this success, Simon de Montfort now saw his opportunity to claim lands and titles if he took charge of this papal crusade. Onward to Carcassonne, the loosely organized band of marauders swept.

Soon Carcassonne was in view. It was originally an old Roman fort and was surrounded by high walls and defended naturally by the Aude River. As the dust and shouts of the advancing crusaders were heard approaching, Raymond Roger Trencavel, the Count of Carcassonne, under a flag of truce with a few retainers trotted slowly up to the massed horde. Papal Legate Amalric and now Simon de Montfort came through the ranks of men before them to face Raymond Roger.

As the military engagements increased in size and large towns were encountered, Simon de Montfort took full command of the ragtag northern Frenchmen. Simon had fought with distinction in the previous crusade and was summoned by Philippe II to take over the forces aligned against the Count of Toulouse and the Cathars. He displayed the same brutality for which he had acquired a reputation before. Dominic Guzman was a loyal participant and source of inspiration in Simon's frequent forays.

"Come back to my tent," the legate beckoned. Sensing possibly a way to save his city and its inhabitants from the disaster at Beziers, they followed. Once out of sight of the city, Montfort signaled to his men who promptly unseated Raymond Roger from his horse and held him captive. He was never seen alive again and was found strangled in a jail cell in Carcassonne three months later.

The papal legate now drew near the battlements and demanded, "I will spare your lives. You must leave this city with nothing more than the clothes on your backs. You will be searched. You must leave by the third bell." Slowly the people began to trundle out of the gates. When they attempted to bring food baskets, they were relieved of even that and sent on their way. The people now bewildered and without a place of shelter, wandered into the forest to the west.

Simon de Montfort rode in and took possession of the city as his men searched the abandoned homes. Within months, the lands of Carcassonne and its surrounding fields were awarded to Simon and he became Count of Carcassonne. The crusaders spent the next few weeks carousing, drinking the rich wine for which Carcassonne was famous, and gambling over the plunder they had been able to amass.

Move South

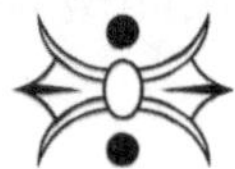

The Dominican purge of the Cathars started slowly at the northern edge of Languedoc. This peaceful region supplied the rest of Europa with a vast array of farm produce. Most of it was ruled by the Count of Toulouse for many years and he had been tolerant of his Cathar subjects. He had prospered and so had they. Toulouse became a center for learning and culture. The university attracted scholars from all over – Byzantium, North Africa, Greece, and included Muslims and Jews. But the Pope and King Philippe looked hungrily at this rich expanse of farms. The urging of Dominic Guzman and then the murder of the Cistercian monk, Pierre de Castelnau, gave them the excuse they needed for what they called a crusade, not against the Muslims this time, but against their own people, the Cathars.

Now, the Dominican friars – a loosely educated bunch – intent on torturing their fellow countrymen – spread out first among the more vulnerable small towns. They demanded of the local Roman Catholic priest the names of those who did not attend his masses, and thus were not in "a state of grace" because they had neither confessed, nor received communion weekly. The church, of course, taxed them anyway but largely ignored them otherwise. The passive parish priests were overwhelmed by visits from the Dominicans who bore the imprimatur directly from the Pope to inquire of his parishioners, their beliefs in order to root out heresy. And so it went. The friars dressed in a much soiled white robe and tonsured as monks barefoot often, with their vow of poverty descended on the towns and looked to a few mounted knights from the northern lords for protection.

Routine matters of doctrine were the subject of this interrogation. The unlettered peasants of Languedoc were often poorly educated in the fine points of the theology of their faith and stumbled over the questions. The trinity was a total mystery to them. They were unable to read the bible in an ancient form of Latin, and the barely educated local priests told them bible stories in their weekly sermons. The Cathars were more educated and understood the rudimentary fine points of their difference from the Roman Catholics. The local priests were compelled to expose some of the local villagers they passed and nodded to on the roads each day.

This day, a band of friars and men-at-arms walked slowly into the town of Tauriac, just north of Toulouse. The men-at-arms were loose ruffians assembled from the northern areas. There was a selfproclaimed knight on a horse. He was the younger son of a landed noble, but not by law entitled to any inheritance. These men were drawn by the promise of lands and preferment to join in the crusade against the Cathars in hopes of becoming landed nobility or gentry by extracting their share of the crops from their peasants who worked the soil. They were convinced of holiness of their quest by the words "Deus Vult" – a battle cry of earlier crusades from an exhortation of Pope Urban against the Saracens but now applied to the Cathars in the midst. The friars wore what were once white robes now mud stained and tattered. With some rudimentary religious training, they now sought the protection of the church. But they also were drawn by the promise of a life of ease in a southern monastery to be carved from the Cathar lands.

As they trundled into the small hamlet, word spread of their arrival in the late afternoon and the townspeople came out of their huts to view the new visitors. Of course, they had heard of the spread of these Dominican friars but now they had come to Tauriac.

The elder of the friars barked out, "Bring out all your people, the Pope demands it." To these meek villagers, the reference to the Pope was an undeniable threat. The Cathar adamantly opposed a church hierarchy of any sort, and held well founded suspicions of the corruption of the clergy. But with no defense, a few of the young boys were sent to bring out the rest of the villagers. Soon, nearly all were assembled before the friars and the men-at-arms.

"Now, who among you is a Cathar?" A sullen silence. "Come now, we have come to spread the true faith. It will do you no good to remain silent." The word Cathar was one used by the Roman Catholics as an insult, because by the "ar" syllable, they implied they were Arians – a belief which questioned the divinity of Jesus or the concept of the trinity. These men meant to convert or kill all those who opposed the church orthodoxy.

The elder friar motioned to the largest of the men-at-arms to fetch one from the group, one of the meeker men to stand before him.

"Kneel," he ordered. He knelt.

"Are you a Cathar?"

"I don't think so, your grace." His reply which elevated this ragged friar well above his station.

"Do you believe in the holy trinity?"

The man now held a debate in his head to deny publicly his true faith and save himself or to confront this friar and suffer extreme torture or death by fire.

"Yes…" he said timidly. He was not a strong man and had a

wife and children.

"Recite the Hail Mary."

Alas, the church Latin for this prayer was one recited by rote among the many Catholics, but never heard in Cathar circles. The man tried bravely to remember what he had overheard in the past, but could do little more than the first phrase.

By now the men-at-arms had already drawn their weapons, mostly clubs and axes, and had begun to encircle the group. One of the men stopped behind a young girl who started to tremble. He came up behind her and began to fondle her breasts. She was a plump girl in her early teens who had even now large breasts. She was plain and standing in a soiled shift from her recent work preparing food. She started to cry. She knew a rape was now imminent and it might mean her prospects of a decent marriage would be lost. Thus, the violent spin of the wheel of fortune could spell doom or death for the unfortunate in seconds. As the man drew her back towards him and began to drag her to the now empty huts in the village, something intervened. She shuddered and her bladder let go a stream of urine which soiled her shift and now ran down her legs. She cried miserably in front of all those assembled, but the man threw her to the ground disgusted. "Ach, the cow had peed herself." She lay on the ground sobbing.

Yet the scene was not lost on the townspeople. These holy men would permit whatever indecencies or sins on them, so long as they rooted out the heresy. And so the men began to assemble a crude form of torture devices – a rack for pulling the individual limb from limb. As the men-at-arms assembled the device, the elder friar set up a rude table and some writing implements. One by one the townspeople were lined up and asked a series of questions. Of course, the Catholic terms used regularly in the Sunday mass were foreign to them. Some immediately offered to convert, some held steadfast to Cathar tenets. The latter were lead off to the rack. There they screamed as their hand and feet were bound and they were stretched on the device until their shoulders or hips dislocated.

At the same time, other men-at-arms were digging post holes in the ground and rolling off tree trunks from their wagon to fit into the holes. Soon three posts were in place and securely upright. The men then scavenged from the village kindling and firewood into a large pile near the posts.

Those who most adamantly defied the friar were led to the posts and tied hand and foot to the post. The men-at-arms now laid copious amounts of kindling and firewood at the feet of the men on the posts. A liberal splash of turpentine was now administered to the firewood and the man. A pot of glowing embers was then spread at the base of each of the three posts. In no time, flames were rising around the men on the posts as they screamed. It was like a wild animal scream – almost unearthly, high-pitched and trembling. Soon the smell of burning meat filled the air.

The townspeople stood aghast. People they knew every day were turned into grim fires and something inhuman.

They all vowed to convert. But the friars were not so quick to accept these easy conversions. They first examined their huts for stored coins or valuable objects, and then asked about the fields where they grew their crops. If they owned in free assign their fields, they deeded it to one of the men-at-arms and agreed to be their serf – paying over three quarters of the crops to them. When the people owned nothing, the women were raped or killed, the men simply killed even with the offer of conversion.

Now, left and shattered, the people who remained after the friars and their men went down the road to the next town quietly singing a Cathar hymn and decided to flee across the Pyrenees. Surely, nothing of this sort could occur in Iberia.

Back to Limoux

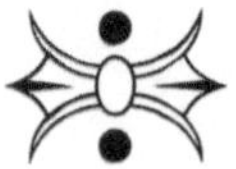

The lovemaking between Chloe and Alphonso grew less frenetic and more affectionate. Her nightly clandestine trips to Alphonso's quarters were still a closely guarded secret, but his endearment of her was becoming obvious. He would call her into private conferences during the day and have long discussions with her on what was still not known. But changes were happening in the kingdom. Scholars were imported to start up schools in the larger towns: Auch, Bordeaux, Pau and Bayonne. At first they came from nearby Toulouse, but then they were brought in from Byzantium, Egypt and Paris. They taught mathematics, philosophy, poetry and rhetorics. Teaching religion, of course, was not permitted, nor was history. These topics were deemed too dangerous. In addition, there were frequent concerts – especially troubadours. The count was observed enjoying them.

At the same time Dominicans were drifting into Gascony from the neighboring kingdom of Toulouse. As they went, they were accompanied by Frankish soldiers, not directly subservient to Philippe Auguste himself, but to his nobles. After conferring with the local priests who were intimidated by the friars, the friars were advised who were "in the state of grace" and those who were not. To be in such a state, one had to receive communion regularly, and make regular confessions. The rest were put on a list to be examined as to their faith. Since most peasants were not literate, and most masses were in ancient church Latin understood only by ordained priests, few understood the fine points of church doctrine, and were easily confused. Those who openly confessed to be of the Cathar faith, were subjected to torture of the most hideous kind until they converted, died in the process, or were burned at the stake. Those who were confused by the doctrine of the trinity might be similarly tortured. Often, angry or jealous neighbors might inform of a local out of spite. The Dominicans showed little grace in excusing marginal cases. Their body guards were not slow to confiscate the property or lands of those believed to be heretics.

The Dominicans now drifted across the ill-defined border of Gascony. Reports of their incursions came every day to Alphonso, and were discussed at length with Chloe. It became apparent that her village of Limoux might become involved in this inquisition if it were not already. Chloe asked Alphonso for leave to visit her daughter and her old village. Although loathe to lose her company, Alphonso gave her permission and two bodyguards to travel to Limoux. So she was waved off by a very tearful Celine, and an Alphonso who concealed manfully his loss. Even Fulgencia waved sadly farewell with ample supplies of Yohimbe and sandalwood at her feet.

The journey was neither long nor difficult; the old Roman roads from Auch to Toulouse and thence to Carcassonne were well traveled and in good repair. As they came to Toulouse, they stayed at a fine inn; the bodyguards had been well supplied with coin to make Chloe's journey comfortable. They rose early for Carcassonne and made good time so they could arrive at Limoux by nightfall.

As the two mounted and well-armed bodyguards rode into the small main street of Limoux, they were met with much fear and consternation until the townspeople could detect

Chloe driving a small cart and mule behind them. Then the buzz started. "Chloe has returned."

As they drew up to her old house, Zastra came to the door and, on seeing her mother, dashed and stumbled toward the cart, mumbling inaudible things. As the two women met, they embraced and wept in the roadway as the townspeople surrounded them grinning. The bodyguards dismounted and lead their horses to a nearby rain trough and waited.

Villagers gathered around the front of Chloe's house and welcomed her back. Eventually the crowd dispersed; Chloe and Zastra returned to the house to make dinner. The bodyguards followed and sat at the small table in the rear yard. Soon, a large bowl of lentil soup followed and a platter of grilled eggplant covered with a sharp melted cheese and a tomato sauce with ample garlic appeared at the table. Chloe brought out a bottle of the fine Bordeaux wine Alphonso had seen fit to load her carriage with. The bodyguards and the women ate heartily. The bodyguards made quick work of their wine and soon spread out their tarpaulins in the rear yard to bed down for the night. It was not long before they were snoring loudly but peacefully.

Chloe and Zastra sat on a small bench in front of the house and chatted about their time apart.

"So was Alphonso cruel to you?" Chloe tried to suppress a blush and giggled softly.

"Quite the opposite."

"Mother, what have you done?" Zastra raised her hands and smiled with wide eyes. "You haven't…?"

"I'm afraid I have, Zastra. I've fallen in love with Alphonso and see him in his chambers. He's really a changed man. He has regained his health."

"I'm sure," said Zastra, not losing the opportunity to have fun at her mother's expense. "But you are a Cathar. Bodily pleasures are bad trifles and interfere with our spiritual being's quest for perfection." She recited standard Cathar doctrine with great pomposity.

"Ah, Zastra. Sometimes, the body directs the heart and the soul to finer things. Our attention is of a deep and heartfelt kind. He loves and respects me. He is bringing culture to Gascony. The troubadours come often. But most amazing, he understands our view of Shekinah – the female aspect of God. He has begun to see that warfare and conquest is meaningless without the sacred female."

By now, Zastra had resumed her serious face – from teenage girl to Perfect aspirant. But then, Chloe had launched into her tale of Fulgencia and the "healing process" with her lover. Again, Zastra broke into squeals of laughter from the powers of Yohimbe and sandalwood.

However, a group of villagers lead by Sarah, the current village elder, walked down the roadway to Chloe's house.

"Chloe, we must talk. Can we meet in the morning?" The very serious expression on Sarah and the other elders betrayed a heavy concern that could not be denied.

"Of course, Sarah. I will be at the temple at six bells. Would that suit?"

"Very much so. We have much to discuss." With that, they turned and left. The mood had been broken. Chloe must now return to the very serious business of the Dominicans in Gascony. Zastra had similar tales of the surrounding villages. It was evident that this was what weighed most heavily on the minds of the elders. As the small fire at the feet of the two women burned low, they put it out and retired for the night only to hear the snores of the bodyguards mixed with the thrum of the cicadas.

Meeting at Limoux

The next morning, Chloe and Zastra were up at dawn. They knew the meeting would be important. They ate quietly at the small table in front of the house and let the bodyguards snore peacefully in the back yard. They left a pot of tea boiling on the table in the rear along with some fruit and bread. As a few of the villagers came down the street to the meeting area, Chloe and Zastra joined them. Anyone could attend these meetings. Cathars recognized no official leader or hierarchy and disdained any official clergy, but Sarah had been designated for this year to mediate the discussion. She was an older woman and had spent many years reading old texts after her children had reached maturity. As mediator, she was expected not to express an opinion but to call on those standing and asking to speak.

As enough people had trundled through the streets of the town to the meeting area, Sarah rose and began the meeting with a few of the traditional prayers – some of which were chanted. Mostly they sought guidance and wisdom. A few referred to Mary Magdalene as their founder, and to ask for the intercession of the divine feminine – the Shekinah. Since Mary Magdalene's presence in their history was controversial, a few elected to remain silent as her name and her wisdom was referred to. Many of the people had brought their own benches or chairs to the meeting place and surrounded Sarah in a rough semi-circle. When Sarah felt enough people were in attendance, she began the meeting by calling on Peter. He was a merchant who had been in the military of the Count of Toulouse and was respected for his worldliness.

"My friends, I am afraid the times are becoming laden with much difficulty and we must make changes to our lives. The Pope has sought to declare the Cathar religion heretical. He seems to have given a franchise to Dominic Guzman, a man not of our region but from Spain, to inquire of these residents of Toulouse who are followers of the Roman Catholic Church and those who are not. Others including the Cistercians are also doing so. At first they simply preached what they considered to be the true version of Christianity. Now, they intimidate the local priests and hold a court to compel those of us who are not in a state of grace to confess our Cathar faith. They have now begun to torture those who refuse to convert, and even subject them to death by fire in the public squares. This attack on our friends has led French nobles loyal to King Philippe Auguste to seize our goods and confiscate our lands. It seems the Pope has arranged this. To put it simply, our people are under attack. Even now, Simon de Montfort has been authorized to conduct a crusade against us. He has burned Cathars in the village of Minerve. In Bronn, he had villagers' eyes gouged out, and their ears, noses and lips cut off." The latter points of Peter's warning were met with gasps and tears.

Chloe arose to speak. "I have been in Gascony for some time now, and have heard the same thing. We must seek help and take action."

The village had been peaceful for several generations and had little trouble from the outside world. They paid taxes, of course, but the Count of Toulouse had left them in peace. After Chloe had confirmed Peter's warning, a silence fell.

Gerard arose He was by now one of the oldest in the village.

"I must admit I have little taste for war. I have never been more violent than to attack my weeds with a hoe. But we must take arms. We must volunteer to some Cathar leader who can oppose these Catholics: the greedy Simon de Montfort and the wicked Dominic Guzman. But how? We have no army."

Chloe arose. "The only man I can think of to appeal to is Raimond Roger de Trencavel. We must send a delegation to him and ask his counsel. But I must also add that we must hide our valuable possessions somewhere. We will need to make them available to one who would raise an army against these French. It will cost us much, but we have little choice."

Again, a silence fell over the meeting. At last, Sarah arose. "Chloe and Peter, I must ask you both to lead a delegation to this man, Trencavel, and ask what we must do. I will ask for others to accompany you."

A few of the elders raised their hands. Sarah said, "We thank you for your support. Can you please leave at your earliest opportunity?"

Peter asked those who wished to join the delegation to join him after the meeting. Soon the people dispersed and left Peter, Chloe and two others – a man, Charles, and a woman, Berthe. They went to sit in a circle. They had known each other from birth in the village, but only as those following peaceful occupations. Now they were a council of war.

Peter began. "I know nothing of war. I don't know what even to ask this Trencavel."

Chloe spoke. "I know him. He is a man of great capability. Let us simply go to him and ask what must be done."

"Can we leave tomorrow?"

"Yes, we must at dawn. We will go to Toulouse and ask for him. Hopefully, he will hear of our plight and come to see us."

"Good. Then it is settled. We leave at dawn tomorrow."

After the Meeting

Chloe and Zastra walked slowly back to their house in a state of deep depression. It was not the first time that Chloe had heard this warning, but she had been safe in Gascony and the danger had seemed far away and she had the protection of Alphonso. Now, it threatened her village, her friends of many years and their way of life. She could not have imagined that her peaceful religion which eschewed war and violence and sought the perfection of the soul could in any way be offensive to anyone. Now, two powerful enemies, the Pope and King Philippe of France, could unleash Dominic Guzman and others like him to eradicate an entire people and their ethos. She voiced these thoughts as she and Zastra walked, and often repeated, "Why?" There was no answer. They looked toward God. What would he do? Would he intervene? People had already been tortured or put to death. Was this God's will?

When they reached their house, the two bodyguards were sitting at the table in front, and leaning back, basking in the sun, "Henri, Gerard, have you slept well?"

"Yes milady." They addressed her as royalty. She was not, but somehow their king's obvious affection for her gave her a standing in court. She bore herself as an educated woman and had a serious demeanor. So, she had become 'milady.'

"My good men, you have been kind of enough to accompany me here to Limoux. Now, unfortunately, I and several others must leave. I don't expect you to come on this trip, I am grateful to you and Alphonso for your help thus far."

"Milady, may we ask where you are going? Maybe we could accompany you part of the way."

"We are going to Toulouse."

"Ah, that is dangerous these days. Bands of Dominicans and Cistercians are active on all the roadways and waylay people who they believe might be heretics. With respect, Madame, we know well whom you and your people are. It is unjust what you must suffer. But you should not put yourself in harm's way."

"Henri, your thoughts are kind, but we seek help for our people in Toulouse."

"Yes, milady, but you may be discovered. King Alphonso was most clear that we should protect you."

"Do you have any other way to get our message to Toulouse?"

"Milady, the Count of Toulouse is beset on all sides. He is obliged to allow the Dominicans free rein in their pursuit of, you will forgive me, heretics. The Pope has excommunicated him because of the murder of this Castelnau, another friar who was set against the Cathars. Lords from the north are looking eagerly at his lands as he suffers from the lack of affection from the Pope. He cannot help you. He has enough troubles of his own."

"Where should we go?"

"Perhaps Esclarmonde de Foix can help. She has always been independent. Some say she is a Cathar herself."

"Yes, she has been helpful to me in the past, and knows the Cathars." Chloe knew it was best not to even speak of Roger Raimond de Trencavel. While these men might be sincere in their desire to help, some information was best withheld. Besides, they probably knew of him already.

"I thank you for this warning. I will discuss it with my people." With little time to hesitate, Chloe and Zastra went back to assemble those chosen for the trip.

It was not long before a number of people from the meeting could be assembled. Chloe was quick to speak of the dangers her bodyguards had told her. A discussion ensued while the other Cathars questioned the loyalty and the knowledge of these bodyguards. Could they be spies? Were they interfering in the mission they must undertake? Chloe was forced to reveal her relationship with their count and the benevolent attitude Gascons held toward the Cathars. She carried the day. They would go to Esclarmonde. The route was much safer and Esclarmonde was known to be a good friend, and she certainly would know whom to contact on behalf of these petitioners from Limoux. So the following morning, they would go to Foix and accept the protection of the bodyguards. The route to Foix was an easy one over the old Roman road.

So the next morning at dawn, the Cathars, Henri and Gerard assembled on the road from Carcassonne. Once there, they would take some smaller roads to Foix. The bodyguards sat astride the large warhorses – bred for size and stamina. The women road in a small donkey cart with Chloe and the two Cathar men rode donkeys.

The way was short, but the cart was packed with provisions. Chloe brought a trunk filled with herbal medicinals. The road used from there was familiar to all and passed quickly. After the turn off the route to Toulouse to the north, the road became earthen with occasional clearings. The day was pleasant as the sunshine dappled the travelers and the road. The familiar cicadas sang and going was pleasant.

However, a noise of a company of riders coming the other way could soon be heard. The beat of horses' hoofs clopping on the occasional rocks grew louder. Soon a group of horsemen began to appear. There were several warriors with a white covering bearing a red cross came into view first. Then, some white clad friars seated in a larger horsedrawn wagon. As the travelers going in each direction came together, the warriors with the white surplice spread across the trail and refused to move. The friars' wagon halted in the middle of the road.

Henri road up to the white clad warriors and asked, "May we pass, good sir?"

The apparent leader grumbled, "You have some questions to answer, sir." He addressed Henri in the impolite "you." "May I ask who you are and what these questions might be?" "We are knights attached to the followers of Dominic Guzman.

We protect the faith. Are you Christian?"

"Yes, we are."

"Good, then, you must dismount and my friars will question you on the catechism."

Henri turned to the Cathars with a bewildered expression. One of the male Cathars rose in the stirrups, "Good sir, I do not know this word. We are peaceful travelers and mean no harm. Please let us pass."

"Sir, you are not versed in the true faith. The catechism is a series of questions you must answer to show you believe in the one true faith."

The Cathar man was familiar with the past efforts by orthodox Catholics and the priests to examine the Cathars. He used the usual play. "Good sir, we are simple peasants. We are unlettered and do not have an education."

"We shall see about that." The friars began to descend from their wagon and set up benches and a table in the clearing. "Sir, dismount and approach the table. Remove your hats and kneel."

This was not a good sign. Chloe, seeing the hesitation among her companions descended and approached the table. She made a sign to the bodyguards, who remained mounted. Three white clad warriors dismounted and stood behind Chloe, and one remained mounted.

"What would you ask of me, father?" she said addressing the one in the middle. On closer view, these friars were peasants themselves. They were missing teeth and had tonsures shaved in their heads, but their hair was filthy and bits of dirt clung to it. Their white robes were also dirty and hung on them.

"Do you believe in Jesus Christ?"

Fair enough for a Cathar. "Yes, father." Of course she believed. He and Mary Magdalene landed not far from here on the coast of the Mediterranean nearly 1,200 years ago.

Do you believe he was the Son of God?"

"Yes, father." As all men are the sons of God, except women.

"You are a woman. Are you educated in the one true religion?"

"Father, St. Paul tells us not to educate women, but to be silent in church and speak only to our husbands." She said this with innocent wide eyes. Surely, these buffoon friars were not educated enough to debate her.

"Aye, my dear," he said, shaking his head and looking around the gathering to see if there was an improper response to this gibe.

"Do you believe we should convert the heretics who every day commit blasphemy – a sin against God?"

"I do not know anything of this, father, but did not Jesus bless the Samaritan woman and the centurion? Were they Roman Catholics?" Again, a wide-eyed innocent expression. Of course, there were no Catholics in Jesus' time.

"Be careful, madam, you may burn in hell. Can you recite the Nicaean Creed?" (A key component of the Catholic doctrine.)

"Is that like the Noahide laws? I do not know such things." The church was confounded about those human beings not in existence by Jesus' time. Without knowing of him, they could not believe in the church doctrine concerning him. So how could they be saved? An intense debate as to whether those unable to be aware of Jesus but who followed the Noahide laws were capable of heaven. The friars could not comprehend this, but Chloe, well read in matters of the sort, was confounding them. They were unsure whether her answers betrayed her heresy or not. These friars were country bumpkins and had little learning other than rote dogma. They began to feel exposed in their ignorance.

"Enough woman. Bring us one of the men." As one of the white clad warriors began to pull up Chloe to a standing position, Henri and Girard sprang into action. It was required. If these friars had their way, all these Cathars would be hauled into the nearest town where an inquisition was in full swing. This would result in death by fire in the public square or a torture that would make life unbearable.

Henri and Girard had already planned their attack. They pulled out their broadswords. Henri sprang at one of the other mounted warriors. He was unprepared for the attack and had been staring at the dialog between Chloe and the friar Henri's first blow came heavily down on his right shoulder leaving his arm dangling loosely and unable to hold his weapon. The second blow struck at the shoulder and bounced along until it burrowed deeply in his neck. The man fell heavily to the ground spouting large gouts of blood.

Girard swung directly at the top of the other knight's head and came down into his skull by several digits. He fell to the ground dragging the broadsword with him.

By now, Henri had spurred his horse at the warriors standing behind Chloe. He slashed at the closest one, and ripped a large gash in his chest. Only a gurgle came out of his mouth as he fell face first to the ground.

Girard now without a broadsword, pulled a short sword from his saddle and dismounted. He lunged at the warrior holding Chloe and drove his sword to meet his belly and out the back. Only a look of surprise crossed his face as he fell to his knees and dropped to the ground.

There was now only one warrior left and he fled behind the table where the three friars now stood shouting and crying in dismay. Henri and Girard approached waving their weapons overhead for a lethal strike.

"Wait, wait!" Chloe cried. Henri and Girard in full blood lust now were about to strike as Chloe dashed in front of them. "Wait! We are not killers. These men may be useful. Tie them up and load them in their wagon." Henri and Girard stared at her in disbelief. They were panting and could sense a complete kill, friars and all. Slowly, they let their weapons descend and moved over to the warrior and friars.

"Very well. On the ground, on your belly. All of you!" These men were not slow to comply.

The Cathar men and woman stared aghast at the sudden burst of violence. It had been totally unexpected. As they slowly started to realize what had happened and saw the massive amounts of blood spurting and draining into the soil, they became ill. They stumbled down from their cart and lurched among the trees to vomit with their hands on their knees.

Henri and Girard slowly wiped their weapons on the clothes of the deceased and came to Chloe's aid. She too was shaken by the suddenness of the attack, but she had ordered it by her signal. She had seen military combat in Gascony as the men trained, but the sheer brutality of actual combat was beyond her grasp. She stared at the men on the ground who no longer existed. Cathars believed the body was a temporary shell to contain the soul and death a natural event to release the spirit. But this… this was not something she had experienced. Elderly people, sick people died, but peacefully and their passing was a moment for prayer, but not necessarily for grief.

These dead men had threatened the Cathar's existence. Chloe was well aware that her questioning could only lead to torture and death when they failed to answer the questions. There was only a brief time to act and Henri and Girard, two hulking Gascons, had answered her with acts of violence. As her protectors were asking her quietly if she was alright, her shock began to dispel. Yes, this was something that had to be done and done quickly, with no hesitation. Things now had to be done and Chloe must help do them. She called to her Cathar people to help.

Henri and Girard took the reins from the warriors' horses and bound the hands of the remaining warrior and the friars behind their backs and around the ankles as they lay on their bellies. Chloe and the Cathars gathered up the weapons and threw them in the cart with visible distaste. They took the horses' bridles and fastened them to the rear of their cart. They averted their eyes as the bodyguards dragged the bodies of the slain warriors into the woods to be eaten by the birds and vermin in the next few weeks. With much reluctance the friars and the surviving warrior were hefted up into their own wagon. After the shock of the encounter had worn off, the friars began to swear at their captors in common oaths, their solemn religious demeanor now abandoned, they reverted to their peasant roots.

Once assembled the party now continued on to Foix. A blanket was thrown over the captives and gags placed in their mouths. Discovery by other Dominicans would mean certain death, while peering inquiries by common Catholics could lead to arrest. The bodyguards were in a state of high vigil and would again protect their charges.

As they moved along the dirt road to Foix, Chloe spoke to the bodyguards. "My good friends, we cannot thank you enough. You have saved our lives and kept our mission safe."

"Milady, you are the… er… beloved of King Alphonso. We cannot let anything happen to you." Apparently, her frequent liaisons with Alphonso were not as secret as she thought.

"But my good men, we must be careful when we are near Foix. Prying eyes may well discover our captives whom we must deliver to Esclarmonde."

"Yes, milady, we must camp at the edge of town, while you ride into meet her. In this area, we do not know friends from enemies." And so, they plodded on the forest road and were blessed to see no one else. In the distance, they began to see the magnificent towers of Foix rise up against the backdrop of the Pyrenees. Soon they could see the huts of the peasants just past the edge of the forest. It was time to stop and set up camp. Dusk was approaching and a camp fire was set. The women set the fire as the men collected wood. Soon a pot of stew was bubbling over the fire. The men started to set the prisoners in a sitting position in the wagon and freed one hand so they could eat.

Just then, three armed riders walked slowly into the camp. They wore the green cloaks with the emblem of Foix on the right shoulder. The bodyguards were not near their weapons and the Cathars walked calmly up to the riders.

"Who are you and what are you doing here?" one of the riders barked at the Cathars approaching.

"Sirs, we seek an audience with Countess Esclarmonde de Foix in a matter of importance. We plan to travel to the castle tomorrow." "Where are you from?"

"The village of Limoux."

"We see two of you are from Gascony and have weapons."

At this, Chloe stepped forward. "Yes, Lord Alphonso of Gascony has sent them to us for safe passage."

"Who are you?"

"I am Chloe of Limoux. I have had an audience with the Countess Esclarmonde before. She will remember me."

"And what is in the wagon?"

"Sirs, they are Dominicans who attacked us en route. We bring them to the Countess for disposition." The riders drew together and conferred.

One drew back and said, "You, Chloe, must come with us now. The rest… surrender your weapons and sit by the fire." The riders rode up to the wagon and saw the Dominicans and a warrior tied and lying in the wagon under a blanket."

"Yes, Chloe, you must come with us. Can you ride the horse tied to the wagon?"

"Yes, sirs, I can."

"Then, mount and follow me. My men will guard the rest of you."

Chloe and two of the men departed for the castle. At the city gate, one of the men told Chloe to wait with him while he sent one of the gatekeepers into the castle. He and Chloe dismounted and walked their horses to a water trough outside the gate. It was now dark. They had been waiting for some time. Chloe had not eaten.

Soon, three more riders came to the gate. Two large warriors and a tall thin man wrapped in a large cloak with a large hood. The riders told the first three men to return to the others and directed Chloe to go inside the hut just inside the gate usually occupied by the gatekeepers. Chloe went inside and sat on a bench in the corner.

The tall thin man entered the gatekeepers hut and pulled back the hood. As the cloak fell from his shoulders, it revealed not a man but Esclarmonde herself. She stood in a long dark green dress with a high white collar.

"My dear, what are you doing here and why have you come?"

Chloe was still in a deep curtsy and managed to stammer out, "My lady, I am overwhelmed. You do me much honor."

"Yes, my dear, why have you come? I heard you were last with Alphonso in Gascony."

"That is true. But he had heard the Dominicans and some of the lords of France were persecuting the Cathars in Toulouse. I wanted to return to my village to see my daughter. But the village held a council and also explained their fear of the Dominicans and the French lords. We were sent to you to ask for help and guidance."

"Mmm. I see. Help and guidance. My men tell me you have captured three Dominican friars and one of their guards. Only one guard?"

"No, my lady. The friars and their guards accosted us on the way here and began to interrogate us on our faith. We believed they meant to detain us and take us to a public inquisition, so my guards attacked and killed four of them. We took the last captive."

"Where are they now?"

"In our camp just outside your city in a clearing. Two of your men are guarding my people and our prisoners now."

"I see. Let me think about this." Esclarmonde began to pace in the small hut and sat on the bench opposite Chloe. "I hear you are a particular favorite of Alphonso."

Chloe could feel color rising up in her cheeks. "And you, Chloe, a good Cathar woman who deems intimate relations a transient material pleasure to be avoided." Chloe hung her head and was now consumed in a blush. Was the Countess taunting her?

"Never mind, Chloe. I too have been in love. It is a God-given thing as long as it is not abused." She patted Chloe on the shoulder.

"First, Chloe, I must decide what to do with this gift of prisoners. So far I am not troubled by the Dominicans and do not seek their enmity. I certainly can't ransom back their friars and risk drawing the attention of the French lords who lust after Cathar lands. I think what I will do is sell them to a band of brigands who will ransom them back. Do your prisoners know where you are and that you seek my help?"

"I don't know. They have been lying on their bellies in a wagon since we captured them. I don't think they even know we are Cathars, nor where we are now."

"Very well, I will contact some local brigands and let them ransom them back to the Dominicans." She called for one of her warriors and had a brief discussion with him at the door of the hut.

"Now, what to do with the Cathars of Limoux." She paced again. "First, the men must train to fight. I know you are a peaceful people, but you must defend yourselves. I will tell Raimond Roger de Trencavel. You know him. He will send men to your village and take them to a site for training. Some of the women will be needed as well. They must listen to Trencavel. It may become a fight for your very existence. There must be no delay."

Chloe was shocked to hear this: her village mobilized for war. Yes, she could see it must be.

"But, you, Chloe, I have some missions for you. You will wait at your camp while I devise a strategy. I do not want you to be seen at this encampment. Meanwhile return to the people you came with and tell them what I have said. My men will take your prisoners. I will alert Roger Raimond to help your people."

"Thank you, my lady. We knew you would know what to do."

"Now, come with me, dear." Esclarmonde drew her cloak and hood over her and swept out of the gatehouse. She mounted her horse like a soldier and waited while Chloe mounted as well.

Chloe with her guards returned to her camp.

"What happened, Chloe?" The horse soldiers from Foix rode on either side of her.

"My good friends. I have met with Esclarmonde. She says our people must learn to fight and defend ourselves. She will send soldiers to train you in this." There was a stunned silence. Then, a mumbling. "Yes, you must learn to fight. I know it is not our way, but the Dominicans and the French lords from the north would destroy us. There can be no other way. Cathar soldiers will come to you at Limoux." Now, I must go with these men in the morning. Tonight I stay with you." Esclarmonde's men went over to the wagon hiding the prisoners and began to drive it along the road in a northerly direction.

"What are they doing with our prisoners, Chloe?"

"I have given them to Esclarmonde. She can use them to her purposes. We have no use for them. Esclarmonde believes, and rightly so, that they may attract those seeking revenge. We do not need to be discovered in this." The group nodded in agreement and began to disperse around the campfire for the night. Chloe had a bowl of the stew and also went to her place for the night.

The following morning, the Cathars assembled their possessions and had a light breakfast. By then, the soldiers had returned the wagon which had carried the prisoners. After many hugs and farewells, the Cathars headed east through the forest back to Limoux with Esclarmonde's men providing protection. When they had left, Chloe along with her Gascon bodyguards were lead to the north by Esclarmonde's riders for a short distance and told to stay in a house on the outskirts of the city until later.

Soon, two women in pure white robes came to the house where Chloe and her guards were resting. "Please come with us, Madam Chloe." The guards, always protective of her, wanted to know where she was going and with whom.

"Good men, we come from Esclarmonde, Chloe must meet in private with her. Please stay and make yourselves comfortable." A large bowl of rabbit stew was brought in with several bottles of wine. "Please enjoy."

Chloe followed the two women down several streets until they entered a house, plain like the rest of those along the street, but once inside, it was a clear span with a high ceiling. The entire room was a bright white with a few doves painted along the walls. There were several rows of benches facing the rear wall. She was led to a door in the rear which led to the adjoining house.

"Please, Madam Chloe, prepare yourself and take a bath in the tub." A young girl was pouring hot water into a copper tub. Chloe removed her shift and slipped into the tub. When she was finished, the girl stood holding a sparkling white shift to wear. She was then directed to sit at a table where a tea setting had been neatly laid out. As the young girl poured out a cup of tea, the door opened. It was Esclarmonde also dressed in a white shift, and about her shoulders was a red cloak with a dove embroidered on the left shoulder. She joined Chloe at the table and poured herself a cup of tea. She waved the girl away and sat alone with Chloe, staring into her eyes.

"Chloe, I must ask you to do several things for me of great importance. By your character, I have begun to trust you. But, first, I must have you initiated into the Cathar faith as a Perfect. Then, you will be asked to devote yourself to our cause."

"Yes, Countess Esclarmonde, you do me a great honor. I will serve you and our cause, as you direct."

"Come into the chapter room, and receive the consolamentum."

Several men and women sat around the outside walls as Esclarmonde joined them. Chloe was directed to kneel in front of an older woman in the center of the room, also dressed in a white tunic. The familiar question and answers from the Cathar catechism were chanted back and forth between the woman and Chloe. These were the vows and beliefs of Catharism, eschewing material pleasures and seeking the spiritual, doing good works and avoiding evil, adoring the sacred feminine – the Shekinah. At the close of the chants, the room sang hymns and reaffirmed their own vows. Many of the hymns were directed to Mary Magdalene and Jesus, who were venerated as founders of their religion. At the close of the brief ceremony, Chloe rose and was embraced by the woman. Those on the benches also came up to congratulate Chloe and then slowly slipped out to resume their daily routines.

Esclarmonde stood aside until the last had departed and then beckoned Chloe back to the side room from which they had entered the ceremony previously. Once seated, another pot of tea was brought in and the serving girl departed quickly.

"Now that you are a Perfect and have received your consolamentum, I have many things to say to you." Esclarmonde started, "I now consider you as one of my family. You have distinguished yourself in your actions. I would announce this formally, but, as you can well appreciate, things must remain secret.

"I wish to form an alliance with Count Alphonso of Gascony and would give you in marriage to him to bind our domains, but I cannot do this openly, nor can you marry Alphonso openly or otherwise. So I send you as an envoy to conclude a treaty with him in these times of stress when we Cathars are threatened. We seek his protection and ask to have him join us in our mutual defense. But we cannot do this openly. We – he and I – should not draw down on ourselves the enmity of the French lords led by Simon de Montfort or the Pope. So all must be covert. I would have you return to Alphonso to conclude this détente. Do you think he might agree?"

"I believe he might. He understands our cause and has spoken favorably about it."

"I am sending your prisoners to him as a peace offering to do with as he wishes. He may choose to return them to the Dominicans as a peace offering, or hold them for ransom, as he sees fit. They will be imprisoned near Auch until he decides."

"What shall I tell him about how they were captured?"

"Between loving partners, I would suggest the truth. You were right in your actions, and have the right to ransom them back. How they came into Alphonso's possession is a tale for him to tell. This will depend on how he feels his relations with Simon de Montfort or Dominic Guzman rest.

"I remember your Alphonso as a boy growing up. Of course, as a Gascon, he was trained in combat and he was expected to be strong and brutal when confronting enemies. He was raised as a Catholic. But I remember he had a good mind and a kind heart. Something rare among our nobles. He received some education of the sort never offered to Gascons, or many of our French nobles. I think you have been fortunate to find such a man. My blessings."

"Thank you, my lady."

"From now on, my dear, you may call me Esclarmonde, but in private. Our bonds must be secret."

"I fully understand… um… Esclarmonde." The words did not flow from her lips, but a warm feeling rose in her as she felt a motherly connection to this woman.

"I will have Raimond Roger de Trencavel look into your well-being from time to time. And you may send messages to us through Jules, in the kitchen of the castle at Auch. You may rely on our help."

"Thank you again, Esclarmonde. I will not disappoint you in this."

"I am afraid I cannot provide you with the trappings of your station – fine dresses, jewelry, horses, servants. You are entitled to them."

"These mean nothing to me. Let Fulgencia have them in abundance."

"So you are friends with Fulgencia?"

"In a manner of speaking. Although claiming to ask advice on behalf of a friend, she wished to restore a man's vigor, so to speak. I gave her some Yohimbe which apparently was more than adequate. Shortly after, she asked me for some unguent to soothe the woman's private parts and those of her lover." Esclarmonde could not help emitting a girlish chuckle. "In any case, she seems to know about me and Alphonso and is pleased with the arrangement. Her lover also seems to be grateful to me as well."

"It is good that you are so well versed in the medicinal arts."

"I might add that I do very well dispensing to the rest of the court. I have many friends, and a nice purse. I would forfeit all that, if Alphonso claimed me officially."

"Now, that we have said all this, I must ask you for one more mission. But I must first explain. As you know by my name, I am descended from the Visigoths, but I have adopted the Cathars as my people. My name is Visigoth. Esclarmonde means crystal moon. But from what are now called Cathars, I have been told of the heritage of our group. We are told that Mary Magdalene and Jesus landed on our shores after the Romans would crucify him. Jesus was sickly and had not recovered from his wounds. So Mary began to preach and so did her daughter after her and so began the foundation of our beliefs. However, the Christians from Rome gained great power from the conversion of Constantine and his mother, Helene. So we practiced, but venerated Mary Magdalene secretly in many churches. Mary began to preach of the sacred feminine – the Shekinah. Over the many years since, our people have intermarried and some have adopted what they call Catharism.

"Now, I must give you a secret. When Jesus and Mary landed on our shores many years ago, they brought with them a chest of their sacred documents to found their religion. Many were old hymns, prayers and portions of the Torah, some are collections of the story of Jesus as he preached in his early life. All this we are told, but they are all written in their ancient language – a form of Hebrew in use at the time. We do not wish to have the Jews near here translate these for us, so they must be preserved until someone versed in this ancient tongue can tell us what they say. I fear for the future now of this chest of documents which has been entrusted to me. I know the Pope and the Dominicans fear the intrusion of Jesus' own papers into their orthodoxy. It would upset them greatly.

"So I fear an attack by Simon de Montfort to my domain would have these sacred writings disappear forever. I need someone I can trust to hide them and, if we survive these battles with the Dominicans, they may surface and bring in a world enlightened by the Shekinah. This task must fall to you. I need you, your Gascon bodyguards and several of my men to travel to a place between here and Mont Segur to place this chest. It will be on the road from here to Mont Segur in a place I will give you directions for. I will also hide some gold there so that I will have a source of funds if I need to escape. Can you do this for me?"

"It would be an honor be of service to you."

"I will have a wagon laden with these things. Only you will know its contents. You must pick one man to help you carry these things to their resting place."

"That will be Henri, my Gascon bodyguard. He is very loyal."

"Fine. When this is done, return to me and I will send you back to Alphonso with a wagonload of gifts to celebrate our treaty. When you have seen him and had a chance to discuss this, Alphonso and I will meet to confirm our mutual defense."

"Esclarmonde, I will carry these things out. I can see their importance."

With that, Esclarmonde rose and gave Chloe a long hug, turned and left. Chloe changed back to her usual shift and folded the white one carefully. Now, as a Perfect, she would have many duties to perform. She left and met with her two bodyguards and explained the trip to Mont Segur. Much had been done this day. Chloe retired to sit and think of her new status.

Toward Mont Segur

The ride out toward Mont Segur from Foix was short, along the winding foothills of the Pyrenees, the sun was shining brightly from the east. The Gascon guardsmen brought up the rear with Chloe's wagon in the middle and the Foix soldiers leading the way. The wagon bumped smoothly through the muddy trail ways and came in and out of the shade of trees. It was midmorning when the Foix horsemen stopped and pointed to the north along a small trail going up a hill that rose out of the trees. Chloe thanked the men and dismounted from her wagon. Her chosen Gascon and she slid the large wooden box off the rear of the wagon. They slid the poles through straps on the box and put the poles on their shoulders. Esclarmonde had given Chloe a narrative of instructions to proceed along the path. The going was rough for Chloe with both the weight of the box and the uncertain footing among the rock outcropping of the narrow uphill trail. Although they were well off the trail by now, the path was remarkably well trod. At a large evergreen, there was a slash mark on the trunk. Chloe directed her bodyguard to go to the right. A small splash of white on a rock directed them further right where there was a small clearing and a cave. The entrance to the cave required Chloe to stoop and enter a large cavern while her Gascon waited outside. Once in the cavern, there was a small beam of light from a crevice in the roof which barely illuminated the interior. A packed earthen floor made the interior a flat surface in the middle of which was a large stone. The stone had a number of symbols on it including the white dove in a field of red. There was a cross of wood bearing leaves and branches. The letters JMS appeared throughout, signifying Jesus, Mary and Sarah. The cross bearing leaves signaled that Jesus was alive. Chloe felt the presence of this clandestine worship site and the Cathars meeting and praying over the centuries. As she rested in the cool damp air of the cavern, she pulled out the second set of Esclarmonde's instructions. They directed her and the Gascon further into the forest towards a smaller cave. She exited the cave and pointed the way she and the Gascon must go with the chest. These directions were not over a trodden path as before but through an underbrush of ferns and small bushes for about 100 paces. There, a small fissure in the rock led to another cave. There, Chloe and the gascon managed to slip the chest inside. They placed several rocks into the fissure so that it was now nearly invisible. They were only about 20 feet from the top of the hill by now, so Chloe climbed the rest of the way to the top. A small flat area of rock was just out of the bushes and gave onto a sweeping view of the valley. To the east, the castle at Mont Segur was visible and to the south and west were the castle towers of Foix set up against the backdrop of the Pyrenees. She could see both from this vantage point. On the rock table were old ashes from what had been a fire in the distant past. It was now clear to Chloe that Esclarmonde wanted to educate her as to some of what were probably many covert sites scattered about the Foix domain. These would serve as sites for refuge in the times of trouble and now, once in Esclarmonde's confidence, Chloe could locate in the future.

She and the Gascon descended as they had come along the defile to where the rest of their entourage were sitting on a few fallen limbs chatting amiably. They soon mounted and returned as they had come, with the sun now warming their backs.

As the wagon bumped easily along the road, Chloe began to think about the chest she had just deposited in the cave. It was too heavy just to have contained documents or scrolls. There had been a sound of what might have been earthenware or silver plates or goblets rolling and striking the sides of the chest. What was this mysterious Esclarmonde concealing out here in the forest? What was this strange cavern of the Cathars? Why had Esclarmonde sent her? Soon she would leave Foix and return to Auch and Alphonso. But now she was a minion for this noble Cathar female. Times were now perilous and it was clear, Esclarmonde meant to involve her in the affairs of the Cathars.

Back to Auch

Chloe and her guards were back in Foix by the afternoon. Chloe rested at a house on the perimeter of the city while the Foix soldiers returned to the castle. As always the Gascon guards kept Chloe within their sight while they bedded down in the rear yard of the house after putting their horses in the local livery. By dinnertime, they all were summoned to the large banquet hall. Chloe was directed to the rear benches. She was not to sit at the dais with the rest of the Foix dignitaries, but was to remain a covert ally of Esclarmonde. The meal however was delicious. Something had been done with eggplant as the serving women dished out slices of the plant smothered in something with garlic and, what was it? Mustard and fennel. The wine was a hardy local variety. Midway through dinner, one of the kitchen staff passed a slip of a message to Chloe. "Godspeed. Regards to Alphonso. Crystal Moon." The signature was a translation for Esclarmonde's name in Visigoth and now to be her secret appellation.

Chloe returned back to her small cottage at the edge of the city. Her guards while normally inclined to enjoy the opportunity to imbibe the local Foix wine were careful to retain their senses and escort Chloe. They had now grown quite fond of their charge, service was no longer a task but a pleasant duty.

At dawn, the guards bustled about assembling things for the trip back to Auch as Chloe prepared a breakfast of fruit and yogurt, and packed meals for the road north. The guards had by now gotten used to the Cathar nearly vegetarian diet and had trimmed down. They were pleased to explain that they were now quite regular, and their facial acne had cleared up. Of course, they had regularly been treated to herbal teas and unguents that Chloe had prescribed. She too now fussed over her guards and scolded them for bad habits. She was a few years older, so she had not exactly been matronly about it, but more of an annoying older sister. She also could not help inculcating them in eating tenets, as they plodded from place to place since they had left Auch some time ago. But now they were to return. Soon they were ready and plodded through the muddy paths to the old Roman road north to Auch. They had debated the route which took them through Toulouse, but decided the danger of the Dominicans and the soldiers under command now of Simon de Montfort were to be avoided. So they took the small back roads which meandered in and out of the forests. It was not a long trip – about the same to the one north and then west from Toulouse. There were few travelers along this route, mostly local farmers with hay wagons. It was midday when they arrived at the outskirts of Auch. Since they were now in friendly territory, Chloe excused her guards. "No, Madame Chloe, you are our charge. We will see you to the castle." She could only smile at how she was being treated as a wayward lamb by two large sheepdogs. And soon she entered the castle grounds, gave her wagon to the large livery and went to her quarters. Celine was cleaning the room as Chloe entered, she turned and without a word ran to hug Chloe. Celine blubbered quietly in their embrace. "Celine, how have things been since I left?"

Celine then embarked on a long and scattered tale of the gossip and events of court. Apparently, Fulgencia had summoned her for more of the "medications." The men from the kitchen staff had kept her abreast of Chloe's travels. Alphonso was now practicing regularly with soldiers and had fully regained his strength. Of course, the romances and pregnancies of the women of the court were fully recounted. As she spoke, it seemed that Celine had matured in her absence. She now had breasts appearing as small bulges in her shift. Chloe noted that it was time to explain the intricacies of sex to her before she stumbled into a perpetual life as a kitchen maid. Women who became pregnant while young and without a husband were subject to the cruel realities of feudal life. If they had someone to protect them and arrange a decent marriage, they thrived and raised a large family. Now 13, Celine must absorb this knowledge before she became an unwed mother whose life was a constant one of servitude and despair. Besides, Celine had been learning the apothecary businesses quite nicely under Chloe's tutelage and was able to handle some of the minor ailments in her absence. Chloe took a long refreshing soak in their copper tub and wanted to present herself, in secret as before, to Alphonso. She could barely conceal her joy at seeing him again, but she would have to wait until late in the evening to steal down to his chambers, even though it was by now an open secret that they were lovers. Yet they would have to endure a few stolen glances from her back bench to his raised dais during the evening meal. So she applied her tincture of almonds and roses to her body and waited. She checked her store of herbs and her bottles of medications, noting what would be needed in a trip to the forests tomorrow. She wanted to nap from the exertions of her travels but she could not tamp down her anticipation of seeing Alphonso again and so she paced around her chambers and around the palace yard until dusk. This excitement and activity would require more almonds and roses. And then, it was time for the evening meal in the large hall. The afternoon hours dragged on, but Celine's happy chirping at Chloe's side by their chores was a pleasant distraction. Fulgencia flounced into their room, welcomed Chloe back and got a large dose of Yohimbe and unguent for her "friend." Finally the evening meal came and went. As anticipated, there were more than a few stolen glances between Chloe and Alphonso which drew polite snickers from those in the know – of whom there were many. Chloe and Celine retired to their room, with Chloe pacing the floor. This would need more almond and rose oil, and while she thought about it - more sandalwood for Alphonso.

With Alphonso

When the church bell struck nine, it was a time when most castle residents were in bed. Chloe whispered to Celine as she left their chambers and made her way to Alphonso and past the two men who guarded his door. She rapped softly on the door which flew open immediately. Without a word, Alphonso wrapped her in an embrace and flung the door shut in one move. They kissed a long deep moment. She could smell the sandalwood over the undercurrent of hearty male musk. They parted gasping for breath.

"I… I… I've missed you." Alphonso, Count of Gascony, was able to blurt out. "I, too." They stumbled over to the large raised canopy bed and made slow, tender, delicate love, wishing to prolong each sensation, each shiver, each delight. And then bathed in perspiration they fell on their backs and stared at the ceiling.

For her, this was a revelation. She had been taught as far back as she could remember that copulation was only an occasional act necessary to keep the Cathar population viable. This was an element of the material world, a possible evil, which, if avoided, was better. The spirit, the soul was the prime focus, the material a distraction at best, a sin at worst. But yet the troubadours had dared venture onto the theme of courtly love, unrequited love, love for a man and woman, divinely sent to sanctify the human condition.

Chloe's marriage had been a chaste religious necessity. Her husband, a pleasant, accommodating fellow had treated her with respect and approached her in bed with timidity. What had he felt? She never knew. They shared the marriage, both worked, both tended the kitchen and the children. They were equals, partners in a passionless cooperation. When the children grew self-sufficient, she asked for and was granted her release from marriage. They would always be friends – as they had been all those years.

But now, this, this passion. What was it a sin, an errant path for a Cathar Perfect. Was she being led from God's path? What would Mary Magdalene do or think? Ah, yes. She had adored Jesus. Had God given her the same sense of passion she now felt? Yes. She must have felt it. And then the agony of the arrest, Pilate's cruel mockery and trial, the scourging. But she had felt the passion. Yes, it had been a gift. She lay back contented. Yes, it must be God's way.

He was bewildered. For years, he had trained to be a warrior and a ruler. He lived among men. He was a true Visigoth. Tough, brutal and strong. His marriage to Fulgencia had been cruelly imposed on him at fourteen by his callous parents who wished to count their friends across the Pyrenees. They had joined him with a woman 10 years older who brought with her a brat, an overly indulged son from a dissipated court. Now, the lad must be thrown to the Visigothic world of manly combat. Yet he demanded and preserved his prerogatives, and the tutors and mentors along with the other boys backed off. He insisted on his entitlements and was indulged as his mother doted on him.

Meanwhile, bed with Fulgencia had become abhorrent. She was vain, selfish and plain. She insisted on fine dresses, but on her they were an embarrassment. As she flounced about with her flock of ladies in waiting, her figure swelled from the sweetmeats and pastries which perpetually followed her on the trays of servants. Soon, he abandoned her chamber. She kept up the pretense of a romance, but few in the castle were taken in.

He was after all a handsome young fellow with years of arduous military training in the court of Gascony. He had no lack of interested mistresses. Women are often raised to a fever pitch by a proximity to power and many vied for his attention. But these women were women of the court, the daughters of minor nobility sent to find noble husbands. They served, they sat and chatted, and occasionally had lessons in the religion by the local cleric who, though avowed to be celibate, managed to have his share of their affections. These women were too available, too shallow and offered him nothing. So he remained, as it were, a soldier and a ruler. Then, Chloe. She was educated, beyond his experience, she opened a new vision of worldly knowledge and a light into a world of the so-called divine feminine. Something beyond war and conquest, something about mercy and knowledge, curing and healing, growth, growth of the human spirit and the culture. He had already begun to import men from Toulouse to run academies in the towns and cities. Not of the dry religious debates, but in poetry, philosophy, astronomy, science. These men were not clerics, but Arabs and Jews, and a few Irish monks. They taught the wisdom of the Greeks, and Byzantium, and Alexandria. He was beginning to see the wisdom of his friend, the Count of Toulouse. It was an exciting new world. For a man raised to be a soldier engaging in conquest and brutal war, he could see a new truth. And all this he could attribute to Chloe, whom he loved, yes, loved. What was this new thing?

The silence reigned, each in their own thoughts. And then,

"Alphonso, I have a present for you."

"Me, what could you give me, I have you."

"Very nice, but I have four prisoners in a shed out of the city. Three Dominican monks and one bodyguard."

Flung back to reality, Alphonso sat up. "What... Three Dominicans. How did this happen?" The possibilities flashed through his mind. He was back being a ruler now.

"On the road to Foix, three monks and their five bodyguards stopped us and wanted to interrogate us on the true religion. We answered a few questions which seemed to baffle the dolts who were now friars and an arm of the Pope it would seem. They wanted to take us into some city they held and subject us to a public inquisition. As this became clear, my bodyguards sprang into action and slashed at two of the monks' bodyguards. They died where they were. They then killed the other two. The last backed off, so we tied the remaining four up and threw them on the floor of the wagon. The other four were stripped and dragged into the woods. When we made it to Foix, I offered them to Esclarmonde, but she didn't want them. Since she was obviously a Cathar ruler, she didn't wish to provoke a fight with Guzman or Simon de Montfort., she couldn't appear to take part in their capture. So she sent them to you."

"Me. What can I do with them? If Montfort or Guzman hears I have aligned with the Cathars, they will use it as an excuse to cause trouble."

"Supposed you just turn them over?"

"Who knows what these men will say to Guzman or identify their attackers? I can't risk the security of my domain."

"Yes, yes. I see that."

"I could sell them into slavery in North Africa. They would disappear without a trace."

"I can see that. While I don't believe in slavery, these men did threaten me with torture and death. They are now a danger to you. I can see that. Are they worth much?"

"It depends on their condition. But, usually, they will fetch a good bit of silver."

"Alright. They are my present to you. You must send my bodyguards out to fetch them."

"We will put them on a ship out of Bayonne for Tangiers."

"Maybe they will find converts there instead of among my innocent peasants. Thank you for the present."

Chloe debated then in her mind whether she should tell him of the chest of old documents and other things lodged in a cave between Foix and Carcassonne. On second thought, that was a matter for a different day. They lapsed back into contented silence until the church bell signaled it was time for Chloe to return to her own bed. She stole out and down the hall, and crept into her room to the sound of muffled girl snores from Celine. She was soon under the covers, but with a big grin on her face and a hearty giggle.

Report of Carcassonne

Chloe was kneeling in the mud of her herb garden by the edge of the forest. The sun shone brightly on her back and she was humming a troubadour tune as she tucked a row of seeds into the loosened earth.

From her back, she heard a shriek from Celine running up the hill behind her. She was followed by an older man with a stained apron.

"Madam, Madam, Carcassonne is lost." Chloe rose stiffly to face them.

"What is this, Celine?" She looked at the two. The man bowed as if she were nobility. He was the man from the kitchen who brought her messages from Roger Raimond Trencavel.

"Madame, I bring news of the Cathars. Roger Raymond has been taken prisoner by the Dominicans and Simon de Montfort. They have taken Carcassonne and expelled everyone from the city."

"Where have they all gone?"

"Scattered, Madame. I do not know where. They were forced to leave or face a mass slaughter, so they left with only the clothes on their backs. Montfort's soldiers have taken over the city and are sacking it."

"What of Trencavel?"

"He came under a white flag to sue for peace and was taken prisoner. We don't know what has happened to him."

"And these people. Where will they go? What will become of them?"

"I don't know. My messenger says that many are walking on the Via Domitia. Some may seek refuge in Foix. I don't know."

"But they cannot be far from Limoux. What will happen with my old village?"

"Madame, I don't know. They seem to be moving south."

Chloe stood transfixed. Celine had been crying as she ran up the hill and now wiped her eyes to see what Chloe would do. Chloe hugged herself and shivered. And then a calm overtook her.

"I must go to Alphonso. Thank you for your help," she said facing the man from the kitchen. "Celine, finish the garden. I'll go in to see Lord Alphonso," and she rushed off.

Alphonso was sitting in a small garden by the castle speaking to a few of his generals as Chloe came up. They all glanced up.

"Alphonso, I must speak to you."

Although she had not addressed him as "Lord Alphonso," the generals demurred to her. She was now the unacknowledged mistress of their leader and a recognized advisor.

"Yes, Chloe, what is it?"

"Sir, may we speak alone?"

"Of course," he dismissed the generals, but told them to wait outside. They had already heard of the awful massacre of the people of Beziers and were aware of the advances of the Dominicans and the Pope's crusaders. Alphonso had dispatched men to his borders to report on any efforts by these outsiders to threaten his domain. So far he had heard nothing. But Alphonso was well aware that Chloe had sources from the Cathars who reported to her. "Now, Chloe, what is it?"

"Alphonso, Simon de Montfort has taken Carcassonne and taken Raymond Roger prisoner. He seems to be marching south to Limoux. The people of Carcassonne have been expelled from their city with only the clothes they wore. They seem to have scattered."

Alphonso heard her and stared off into the middle distance. "So Chloe, we must rescue your people and save the people of Carcassonne." He paused. "But I must not expose my hand in doing this. I do not wish to be drawn into this absurdity."

"Yes, Alphonso. What can you do?"

"I will assemble 100 men, out of uniform, but mounted, and with wagons. Wagons of food and clothing, yes clothing and blankets." He was thinking out loud. "You will go with my men… You will take the people you find along the road to the town of… of Aulus-les-Bains. They can farm there."

"Then, you will get your people at Limoux and lead them out. I will try to hide them in Gascony or Foix. Dispense the food… Yes… go save your people."

"But, keep my help a secret. Otherwise they will came after me. I am sure they have their eyes on Foix. You must hide these people carefully in Foix. Aulus-les-Bains is a quiet valley. I hope they can be safe there." He called for his generals to return.

"Men, I wish you to dispatch 100 mounted men and five wagons with provisions. Listen to Chloe here. We will be rescuing some people from Carcassonne and Limoux. Do as she says. Above all, keep my involvement a secret. No one must know I have helped these Cathars.

Do you hear?"

"Yes, Lord Alphonso. It will be as you say."

"Now, go. We must not lose time in this." The generals saluted and left.

"I thank you, Alphonso."

"Chloe. It hurts me to you leave again, but I understand. He rose and hugged her. Reluctantly he held her at arm's length.

"Now go, you have important work to do."

Chloe left and briskly went to Celine. "Now, Celine, I must leave again. You must keep up the garden. What you have heard are important secrets."

Celine nodded. She had grown by now. She was approaching maturity. Chloe hugged her and left to go to the yard where wagons had already been drawn up to the kitchen yard.

She came down and saw her old bodyguards Henri and Girard standing by the generals. They all saluted. "Madame, we are at your service."

"I think you. I believe you are doing God's work."
The men assigned continued to load the wagons.

By dawn the next day, the generals had assembled the horsemen and the wagons. Chloe climbed into the lead wagon and the column started south to the Via Domitia.

Onto Limoux

The route had been discussed and agreed upon. The horsemen and the wagon train slowly lengthened out of the gates of Auch in a southerly direction. They would avoid Toulouse and cross over the spine of the wooded foothills and then turn east toward Carcassonne. There would be no confrontations with the Dominicans or the nobles led by Simon de Montfort.

Chloe was in the front wagon. She had begun to cut off slices of bread and pieces of fruit as the horsemen trotted up to her wagon. They had raced through breakfast in the dark, but were not given a healthy portion. As each foursome came up and were served, they pulled away and allowed another group to come up. The route was not long but there were people from Carcassonne, who were adrift in the back forest roads and must be brought to a place of safety where they could resettle. There would always be the Dominican threat to torture or kill those who espoused the Cathar faith.

And so it was not long before the first groups of people were seen through the trees. The horsemen and wagon train halted at a large clearing and several of the wagons were drawn up and unloaded. Ten of the horsemen stayed behind in the clearing with the first group. This would be the assembly point to collect all those traveling west to take them to Aulus-les-Bains which perched at the lower foothills of the Pyrenees. The valley was pleasant and cool and would serve well to adopt the immigrant Cathars.

Chloe, the rest of the wagons and horsemen trotted briskly on toward Carcassonne. As more Cathars appeared, some of the horsemen would escort them back to the clearing where the first group now rested.

But then, a dust cloud could be seen arising on the road ahead and a clopping of horses' hoofs. At once the horsemen drew their swords and daggers. General Tomric stood up in his stirrups and waved one group to the left and another to the right. They each stole quietly through the trees several hundred feet off the roadway.

Soon, the main body came upon a group of horsemen and foot soldiers walking alongside a wagon holding three Dominican friars also going east. At a signal from General Tomric his horsemen spurred their horses and galloped to surround this new group. As they drew around the friars and their accompaniment, the general again rose in his stirrups and barked, "Halt." With some 100 men on horse now surrounding a body of 10, they obeyed instantly.

The chief friar, an elderly fellow with white hair shaved into a tonsure and clad in a tattered and dirty white shift, rose in the wagon. In the Frankish tongue of bastardized Latin, he demanded, "Who are you and why have you stopped us? You have no livery."

"I will ask the questions here. Who are you and where are you going?"

"As you can plainly see, we are Dominicans, invested with the authority of the Pope to root out heresy."

"I see. And where are you going?"

"Why, to Limoux." By now the wagons had caught up to the horsemen and Chloe in the front wagon, plainly heard the word "Limoux" on the tongue of the friar.

"Were you in Beziers?"

"Of course."

"Did you kill all the residents, as we heard?"

"No, a few escaped. Most died when the church where they sought asylum collapsed on them."

"Were they all Cathars?"

"We don't know. Many were."

"Then you are murderers."

"No sir, we answer to the Pope and Dominic Guzman."

"Then tell your men to drop their swords and knives at once and dismount."

"But, sir, who are you to tell us this? You speak like a Gascon but you have no insignia. Whom do you fight for?"

"Alas, sir. You have now said something unfortunate." Tomric signaled his men to collect the weapons and lash the men to their wagon."

Tomric trotted back to Chloe's wagon, motioned his lieutenants to join him.

"Lord Alphonso was most clear to avoid being identified. We have come upon these men and they say I speak like a Gascon. We cannot let them return to Montfort or Guzman with this information. We cannot simply tie them to trees and let them be found later. It will involve Alphonso in this war. Shall we kill them?"

"They may be found later, General."

"Quite so, the animals will dig them up and expose them." Another lieutenant spoke. "General, Madame Chloe came to us with some friars and a soldier. They were sold into slavery on boats to North Africa."

Chloe heard this and stared thoughtfully. "No, we cannot kill friars who are under orders from the Pope."

"Then to North Africa, my lady?" All looked to her as if she were Alphonso's queen.

"Yes… Yes… I don't like this violence, but it must be so."

Tomric ordered the men to strip some of his prisoners down to their loin clothes and throw them in the wagon. The rest he lashed to the back of the wagon. He dispatched them to Bayonne with five mounted guards and directed them to sell captives as slaves on a ship to Tangiers. When the friars heard the orders, they began to wail. "But… We are under orders of the Pope." At that, their guards beat them with the flat of their swords. Soon their wagon was headed westward to Pau to get on the old Roman road to Bayonne.

When they were out of sight, Tomric directed his caravan on the way east to Limoux. As they went, Chloe recognized the familiar landmarks and roads. They were not far now.

Soon the entourage halted just outside Limoux at Tomric's orders. "Madame, we must first see if the town is safe for us or whether we may have to fight our way in."

"Yes… Yes, I see, General. Do what is wise." Tomric sent the men into town to investigate and report back. For Chloe the minutes dragged on. But soon, they could see a cloud of dust as the riders drew near.

"It is safe, General. Montfort's men have not come here yet."

"Then we must hurry. On into town!"

As the large contingent came down the main street, Chloe's wagon lead the train. People peered out of their huts and then came out to greet her. Soon the whole town thronged around her. Zastra came running teary-eyed and jumped onto Chloe's wagon. They hugged, sobbing. But Chloe had to lead these people. She pulled away from Zastra.

"My people, we must leave at once." Pointing at two teenage boys, "Carl and Simon, go at once. Look into every hut and tell everyone to come out. We must leave now. Those with horses and carts, ready them now and take a few belongings. Those without bring some things out to the roadway now. We will put you on someone's cart."

These people were Cathars. They knew well the dangers that faced them and were used to acting together. Soon they were bustling about. They must assemble all they could take in a half hour and leave old keepsakes and memories behind. For months now, they had hidden their gold and a few pieces of jewelry. They had somehow pictured this moment. Although with a heavy heart, they knew what must be done.

Soon a new train of wagons, some donkeys, a few carts had assembled on the main road of the village. Those who did not own a horse or a donkey were put on other's wagons. A few climbed into the provision wagons where Chloe sat. With a cry of sadness, the train pulled out to the west, toward Foix and Aulus-les-Bains.

Chloe's bodyguards from her previous trip asserted their right to travel beside her wagon. The provisions she had been carrying had diminished and were stacked to the side while some of the elders and children from Limoux were now seated in the space vacated. Zastra sat by Chloe's side.

The train of armed horsemen and wagons lumbered along the road to Foix.

General Tomric had dispatched riders to ride several hundred yards to the north of the train to spot any of Simon de Montfort's troops coming down from Carcassonne. Tomric rode up front in the van guard. He wanted no surprises.

As the wagons were heavily encumbered now, it was not possible to travel with a minimum of noise. So restrictions on conversation or even the singing of hymns were lifted. The children were permitted to chatter, but Tomric and his men still maintained a tense vigil.

Then one of the advance riders came at a gallop back to Tomric.

"General, a group of armed men comes from the west."

"The west? What are they doing there?"

"They are armed and bear the emblems of some of the northern lords and a few friars in white."

"How many?"

"There were about 20 horses and as many foot soldiers."

"And friars?"

"About five."

"And from the west, you say?"

"Yes, General."

"Maybe they have been sent out as outliers to catch the stragglers from Carcassonne or maybe they intend to surround Limoux. The general sat in his saddle, musing to his lieutenants.

"General, these men all carry heavy loads. They have no weapons, but seem to be carrying booty in large sacks strapped to their backs."

"Over their broadswords?"

"Yes, General."

"So they must take off their packs to get to their swords. Interesting." "And they have been drinking. They sing and lurch as they go. I don't think they expect any opposition until they reach Limoux."

"Hmm. We must lay an ambush. They cannot find our people now that we are Gascons. That is clear. We must utterly destroy them. All right then. Remove all wagons into the woods and off the trail. We must not waste time doing this. Then we must ride ahead to set a trap. Move those wagons now."

Fortunately, a small side road led to a farm to the north, so the wagons drew up that road some 100 yards. The soldiers told everyone there must be silence now. The enemy was coming.

They must not know our location. The conversations ceased and the people in the carts looked grimly about as their wagons bumped up the small road and drew to a stop. Chloe as the lead wagon took up the last position and her two body guards and eight more men were assigned to guard the wagons.

The rest of Tomric's men were split to the north and south along the sides of the road. The horses picked their way carefully through the brush. Another contingent stayed some 200 yards back in the main road. The men dismounted and drew their bows from their saddles.

Tomric had instructed the men to await the sound of a horn to be blown. They would then rise up and shoot a volley of arrows, no more than three each. At the sound of the second horn, they would converge on the road on foot if the bush was too thick, on horse if not. They were to fall upon the enemy as quickly as possible, leaving no one alive.

Soon, the jostling of about 20 men and horses came down the road. At this point the road had narrowed somewhat so they walked leisurely no more than two or three abreast. It was true. They each had a large sack tied to their backs and moved quite slowly with the horses plodding along heads down in a slow walk.

For several quiet minutes, nothing happened as the horses and men plodded slowly along the road. Then a horn sounded with a loud blare. From three sides, arrows rained down on the enemy hitting men and horses in a deadly hail. The arrows were nearly silent as they flew to their targets and the men and horses fell quietly to the ground. The remaining few were bewildered as they struggled to shrug off their packs. The cries of those wounded by the arrows but not dead filled the air along with the thunder of horses' hoofs from the front and sides.

Before they could arm themselves, swarms of horses bore

down on them as the riders drove spears deep into the chests and necks of those afoot, some slashed at the horsemen with swords, gashing deep into their chests and severing arms. Those afoot now reached the enemy and had little to do. A few of the enemy were staggering onto their feet, but were met with shattering blows to the head and shoulders. Maces and large hammers came down on the pates of the men and drove deeply down into the brain pans. By now, the field of battle was awash in blood and slippery. A third horn sounded and the men pulled back. An eerie silence first engulfed the road, then a few gasps and cries of the wounded and dying came out. The warm blood on the ground had thrown up a mist. A few of the horses wandered about confused and riderless.

"Bring me a few of the wounded. We need to interrogate them. The rest, I want stripped and dragged in the woods. The animals will take care of them." As he said this, he pointed at some of the men dispatching them in various directions.

Soon his men were carrying the dead deep into the forest and returning for more. The wounded were now propped against trees by the roadside. Only one friar remained alive.

As Tomric strode up to each wounded man, he bent over him and demanded, "Who are you and where are you from? Where did you camp last night?"

It seemed these men all came from a small town in the north of France and had assembled to fight just north of Toulouse. Their lord had brought them down, but he was one of the horsemen killed in the early barrage of arrows. They had recently looted Carcassonne and were carrying their booty on a march south to root out and kill Cathars. The friar was near death with several arrows in his chest and a heavy sword wound to his side. He was not able to speak and motioned that he wanted his throat slit to avoid the pain he was in. The survivors numbered only four by now. The friar's wish was granted and he and the remaining men were all given a final slash to the throat and carried into the bush to join their comrades.

There were five horses which had survived the onslaught. Their wounds were dressed and they were fed and tethered in place. Dirt was thrown on the large puddles of blood in the roadway. Tomric was careful to leave no trace of the battle. No Gascons had been killed or wounded. Piles of sacks of booty were gathered to the roadside. They would be sold in Foix and divided among the men. The soldiers now sat against the trees by the roadside as a few riders went back up the road to retrieve the wagons of their charges. Soon Chloe and her entourage pulled back onto the road and came to the scene of battle.

The wagon train could see where the brush on the side of the road had been trampled and little else, but there was an unmistakable smell. A heavy earthy smell. The smell of blood. Although the bodies had been pulled deep into the surrounding forest, and the earth along the roadway had been raked evenly, there was still that smell.

At Chloe's direction, many of the Cathars in the village had begun some elementary training for combat, they had never seen or heard a battle. As they passed through the battle scene, they shuddered. Of course, they had seen animals killed but never men. What was this new force in their countryside? With many fearful backward looks, the wagon trains lurched forward. They could get to Foix soon enough. To calm their fears, a few began to hum the troubadour songs. The dappled sunshine, the thrum of the cicadas and the peace of the forest once again returned as the train rumbled on. But there was still the ominous pile of captured weapons and military gear piled in one of the wagons.

Onto Aulus-les-Bains

After the skirmish, the train of horsemen and wagons again bumped along the road. Outriders on either side of the road had been sent deep into the surrounding woods to keep an eye out for other possible enemies. None developed and so the short remaining trip to Aulus-les-Bains drew to a close. As the horsemen entered the small clearing at the edge of the town, the Cathars and other townspeople came out to greet the caravan. As Cathars recognized and saw the rescue of their fellow Cathars, they rushed out and embraced one another. Tears flowed. The horsemen circled with their horses shifting about impatiently. Soon, an immense stew was set boiling in the town square as the townspeople collected their share of ingredients. Large swathes of pita bread were flattened on griddles and then stacked. The Cathars spread tents and blankets on the ground and brought over bowls of the stew and piles of the finished pita. They ate and sat and talked for hours in the late sun. The old villagers not used to this large influx stared at the new arrivals, but envoys from Esclarmonde had already told them of their new townspeople. These people, it was explained, brought with them knowledge of herbs and healing practices. The town had for years been a local center for a spa as the warm sulfuric waters of "les bains" drew local Gascons. As envisioned by Esclarmonde, the admixture of Cathars with their herbs and ointments would go well with the healing waters of the baths. And so, the residents were induced to welcome these new people into their midst. A new area had been swept from the brush and scrub of the wood side for the Cathars to build huts and living amenities. The Cathars were led by the townspeople to the new quarters where the Cathars now staked out their homesteads and laid out their tents and put down the furniture and house goods they had managed to stow on the wagons from Limoux. Being ripped from the town these people had occupied for generations was indeed a cruel disruption, but the threat now well recognized of the advancing Dominican inquisitors and the northern nobles and their thugs was the worse alternative. And the new town was quite pleasant in the low foothills of the Pyrenees and under the watchful eye of Esclarmonde of Foix.

As the new Cathars and the old villagers sat on the ground, they talked and dabbed at the stew with hunks of pita and sipped the wine.

Chloe moved to sit by Zastra.

"You know I must leave and return to Alphonso."

"Yes, mother, I have known that."

"Do you wish to come with me?"

"I had given it some thought, but my place is here with my old village. They need me. I know the herbs and… and…" she started to tear up.

"Yes, dear, I know. You are torn. But these are bad times. We must fulfill the roles we have been given. So I will return to Auch and have Alphonso help our Cathars. What we will do, I have no idea." Chloe signaled to her bodyguards who, like large shepherds, nudged her along her path. She rose and walked with them to the Gascon General Tomric. "General, I think we must return to Auch. What do you think?"

"My men will be ready at first light."

"Well, it is not far, we can give them a decent breakfast."

"As you wish, my lady." Alas, Chloe was not nobility but Tomric and now all the Gacons treated her as such. "We will bed down for the night."

"Leave them a full wagon filled with provisions."

"Of course, and the wine Lord Alphonso sent. There is much of that."

"Leave them some weapons as well. They may not be safe here."

"We have more than enough weapons and horses… from those men we met."

"Yes, leave them all that. And we can travel light back to Auch."

"Very well, my lady." The large contingent found places to spread their cloaks and drew off to the side. More than a few toasts were raised to their success and their return to Auch.

And as the sun rose in the east the next morning, Tomric and his men were ready to escort Chloe back to her new home. They now trotted smartly along the earthen road.

Soon the castle at Auch came into view and, as the train entered the town limits, the soldiers and horsemen peeled off toward the barracks as Chloe and her bodyguards went onto the castle grounds. As her wagon pulled up to the rear, Celine could see her out the window and ran out to meet her. Celine was bursting with the latest tales of gossip and the status of the herb inventory. As Chloe looked at her, she could see more mature lines in her shift. Her breasts had swelled and her hips were fuller. Yes. She must find her a mate soon.

Chloe went to their rooms and fell back on the bed. She waved Celine off so she could take a short nap. She promised Celine a full account of the trip to Limoux and their encounter with the men from the north, but for now – a nap.

News of an Incursion

Chloe once again found the arms of Alphonso and a number of happy days passed as she fell into her old routines – prescribing herbs for the court and gathering them from the forest. It was her calling and one that gave her great satisfaction. No less satisfied were Fulgencia and the rest of the court. Alphonso had now taken to including her in more matters of the court, and they took long walks in the gardens. She and Celine and a few helpers borrowed from the kitchen now tended these gardens which produced spectacular displays of color. Alphonso was now eager to follow the advances of the Count of Toulouse and had opened schools throughout Gascony for imported scholars to enrich his subjects. The court was acquiring volumes from neighboring kingdoms of all manner of studies – mathematics philosophy, poetry and medicine. Yet Alphonso was continually on guard. He regularly received reports from his scouts of the crusade against the Cathars by Dominic Guzman and the Dominicans aided by the northern forces now under Simon de Montfort. So far his own domain had been free from any invasion, but the wide ranging men on the border kept a sharp eye out for any movement on the eastern border. But for now, blessed peace reigned in Gascony.

Chloe and Alphonso walked through the garden which she and Celine had carefully tended and now was alive with blooming things and floral scents. The evening before, it had rained and left the flowers shimmering drops in the late morning sun.

Then the gates burst open and a mud-spattered rider on horse swung the doors open and stomped on the border flowers. "Lord Alphonso, I come from Aulus-les-Bain's. Men had come to slaughter the population. I have just now escaped."

Alphonso rose slowly. "Who were they?"

"There were several monks, many knights on horse and foot soldiers."

"How many?"

"In all, maybe 200."

"When did they come?"

"Several days ago. They may have left by now."

"Why haven't I heard about this earlier?"

"Sire, they ambushed some guards. Then they set up an inquisition. The monks came out to some tables and began to question the townspeople. They seemed to know who the Cathars were. The rest of the townspeople were herded into a perimeter. I escaped just this dawn."

The rider was a pale youth with lank blond hair. He was breathless and trembling but his voice was clear.

"Sire, they kept asking for Chloe, and they wanted to know who had killed their men earlier."

Chloe stepped forward. "So they know."

"I would guess so, my lady."

"Did they ask if the Gascons were among that number?"

"They seemed to think they were from Foix."

Alphonso's brow wrinkled in thought. "So they know of Chloe and believe it was Esclarmonde and the Cathars. Hmm." He turned to Chloe. "We must go down to Aulus and question the villagers."

"Alphonso, it is me they are after, not you. I must protect you and your domain. If they think you are involved, they may invade your borders."

"Yes, Chloe. We must think this over. But first we must see what has happened at Aulus and question the survivors. With that, he spun around and ran to the barracks to find General Tomric.

"Assemble the barracks, alert General Tomric." Turning toward Chloe, he said, "I must protect my border. Go inside and wait my return."

"Please Alphonso, they went for my Cathars and Esclarmonde. I must go with you." He looked at her stricken face and knew she could not be denied. "Very well, hurry and meet us at the gate."

Alphonso rushed to the barracks and found the men assembling. Tomric was barking orders as the men formed into lines of march along the way south, maybe to head off this contingent. Men attended Alphonso now as he strapped on his armor and was handed his mount. Soon he was in the saddle prepared to lead his men. Tomric rode up. "All is ready, Lord Alphonso." Chloe's cart took up the rear, and was soon joined by her two bodyguards.

"En avant," Tomric bellowed and the line spread forward along the road. There were 100 foot soldiers, 50 archers and 100 men on horse. It was a time they had waited for. They had been hearing of the battles to the east in Toulouse and Carcassonne. They knew something would draw them in and they were ready. As they would march due south, they hoped to head off the forces of the northern lords and protect their southern border. It would be a short march, maybe half day before they would reach the old Roman road. There they could determine where these intruders might be. It took no urging for them to keep a fast pace.

Soon, they came to the wide clearing where the road south

met the east-west road. They could see trampled ground in the mud by the roadside and so swung west toward Foix. The horses' and men's' footprints in the mud pointed both east and west. They were late. They had already been passed by a large force going east. The pace quickened as they felt the secure footing of the Roman road under foot. Even Foix could not be far off.

They were at the outskirts of Aulus-les-Bains in short order. Tendrils of dark smoke rose from different points. And then an odor of burnt flesh permeated the air as they drew close. It was a scene of devastation and horror.

Dogs from the villages were wandering around charred bodies that lay strewn about a field. Some of the dogs fought one another over the decaying humans. The bodies had been simply thrown to the edge of the field one on top of another. The bodies were in varying stages of rictus – some with hands praying, mouths uttering silent shrieks.

Chloe's wagon had not yet reached the clearing for the town and had yet to see the carnage. Men motioned for her to stay where she was.

Alphonso and Tomric led the rest of the train forward. There were several posts charred at the bottom with men and women still tied in place. Their bodies too were charred. Not far off was an opening trampled in the weeds where some tables and benches had stood. Off to the far side were torture devices with bodies still on them. On one, there was a serrated saw blade hammered into place upright with the serrated edge facing skyward. Astraddle the saw blade were a male and a female with their hands and feet tied. They were naked and faced each other. On their arms were tied heavy stones to weight them down and force their bodies deeper onto the saw blade. Nearby were limbs torn from torsos and rotting slowly on the ground.

Flocks of birds had now descended on the bodies and were pecking away selectively at the exposed organs.

The men stood in shock and came to a slow halt. The ways of the Visigoths had been brutal but the men, used to seeing bodies bloody and dying from battle wounds had never seen such wanton cruelty.

Tomric turned to Alphonso. "Shall we bring Chloe up to see this?" Alphonso hesitated and stared off into the distance. "I'm afraid she will insist. Go, describe what you saw and ask her." Tomric circled his horse and went to Chloe's wagon.

"My lady. There are many dead, tortured and burned. I am afraid it will upset you very much."

As Alphonso knew, she jumped from her wagon and ran to the scene. As she got closer, she screamed, "Oh, no! It is too much." And she fell to her knees, and her forehead facing the ground and vomited. All stood about her in silence. None knew what to do or say. After several minutes, Chloe slowly rose to standing, wiped her mouth on the sleeve of her shift. "How could this happen?" And she began to pace, speaking out loud. None of the soldiers were Cathars, she was speaking to herself, and her God.

"I am to believe that our body is a shell that contains our soul. Of little importance in this life. Its pleasures are but a detraction from the holy work to be performed. These people are now released from this earth. Yes, that is what I am to believe.

"Yet, for their belief they have suffered great earthly pain. Is this a test from God? Or are we being punished? No. We were good people. Were we a sacrifice? No. God would not have Isaac sacrificed, certainly not us. Is there an answer?

"With these deaths and others in the past and yet to come, our sacred beliefs to bring about the Kingdom of heaven must wait. It cannot die, it is obvious to those who know its mystery.

The sacred feminine must be joined with the masculine. Mercy, compassion, simplicity will come again but not from us. The Pope and the Dominicans have seen to that, this time."

Chloe freshened her face and turned to Alphonso. "My Lord, I know my way now. I must provide a better refuge for my people. You must ask Fulgencia to let my people cross the Pyrenees and find safety in Aragon and beyond."

"Of course, Chloe, if that is what you want."

"I cannot let you go to war on my behalf. I will not ask you to risk the lives of your subjects on a quest of mine alone. I will remain here in hiding. Dominic Guzman has stated my name, and I am doomed if I remain in your domain. I must not be identified with you and Gascony. Leave me my bodyguards for now and some provisions. I will get word to you of where I am."

Alphonso nodded sadly. He must lose his love. She would be in danger if she stayed in Auch and a symbol of defiance to Guzman and Simon de Montfort. He knew the reality. He sighed. "Now we must burn the bodies." Everyone nodded and the men spread out to dig a large trench around the perimeter of the forest.

Chloe sat on a nearby bench and stared off into the middle distance. It was her time to be alone. With so many men digging, a long narrow hole spread along for several hundred feet. It now fell to Chloe to identify each body and record his or her death. She would have to look the charred remains in the face and try to recall what they looked like. So each pair of soldiers carried a corpse past the bench where Chloe sat to record what was a neighbor, a relative. She dreaded the sight of Zastra. With each new corpse, the prospect of looking into Zastra's lifeless eyes grew as the line of soldiers bearing bodies shrunk. In her mind she had tolled the villagers who had come with her to escape Limoux and checked off that number from the list. As they came to the end, it began to appear that there was no Zastra among the dead. Each pair of soldiers unceremoniously had dropped a body into the trench. Confused by the absence of Zastra, Chloe nonetheless rose to her feet and, as a Perfect, now began to recite a prayer for the dead, naming each of her former villagers on the list. She wept and stopped several times. The soldiers too were carried away with emotion and wiped tears from their faces. By now, Alphonso had come and put his arm around Chloe's shoulder as she faltered through the prayer. Done at least, she backed unsteadily to the bench and sat, staring off.

Alphonso turned to Tomric and told him to send most of the contingent back to Auch. He would command a small band as bodyguards. He sat silently by Chloe. The foot soldiers and horsemen nervously formed a loose semi-circle around them and nodded silently.

Several of the women from town who were not Cathars sidled up to the Gascons carrying large bowls, and ladled out lentil soup with chickpeas to the men. One of the ladies hesitantly brought a bowl and spoon for Chloe. She accepted it, took a small swallow and started to cry and shake. The soup was good however. She took a few more sips and took a deep breath and finished the bowl. Thank you, she said as the lady slowly drew back. Chloe took a few more deep sighs and then stood and began to pace absently around the field.

"Lord Alphonso, (she called him this in public) we must speak." As he drew up, "You must return home and protect your subjects and your lands. I must help my people escape. They will cross the Pyrenees into Aragon."

"Yes, Chloe, I see that."

"Please have Fulgencia send someone to vouch for us. She

will know people in Aragon."

"Of course."

"I will go to Esclarmonde. She will help me."

"Yes, of course"

"I do not know where Zastra is. Can we search the woods?"

"Of course." And he turned to Tomric and gestured. Several of the men peeled off into the woods. Chloe paced some more with her hands clutched behind her back.

"Chloe, if you ask, I will send men to seek the death of Simon de Montfort."

"Let me think about that. My blood is too hot just now. I am taught not to kill."

"I understand." She paced more. A thrashing was heard in the brush in the forest. At the edge of the clearing, several ragged and spattered women emerged. Everyone turned and raced to the group.

"Mother, is that you?"

"Yes, Zastra. Come here."

"We heard the Gascon accent and thought it might be you."

Alphonso turned to the women from the village, "May we have more soup please?" The women dashed back to the village.

"Zastra, how did you escape?"

"Some men were dragging us in the forest to rape us. I had kept a knife in my sleeve. Even as we marched here. As he came towards me in the forest, I stabbed him. The other two men were too surprised to react. As the other girl screamed, I lunged at them. I think they are dead in the bushes back there."

Chloe sighed. Tears streaking down her face. She hugged her daughter in a long embrace. The soldiers showed the other girl to a bench and bade her sit. She sat, shivering. They had been in the forest for several days.

"Madame, Zastra, was great." She chattered. "She fed us on

herbs and leaves for three days." She was crying and wiping her nose. She was not over fourteen. She was dirty, there were leaves and dirt in their hair and her shift was stained and filthy.

Soon the women came from the village with another large bowl of soup and clean shifts. "Please, sirs, may we help?"

Chloe thanked the women, "Can these girls bathe?"

"Yes, there is a stream we use over there." She pointed.

"Can they stay here until I send for them? I will go to Foix and arrange for them there."

"Of course, madam."

The girls were lead off to the stream after they had drained and scraped their bowls.

"Alphonso, Zastra will come with me to Foix, the others will stay here. May I keep my two bodyguards?" The men perked up and were happy to hear their names recognized. Before Alphonso could respond, they said, "Of course, we will protect you wherever you go. We wish to join you in Aragon." Alphonso smiled, "Of course, if that is what you want." They nodded and bowed, aware of the impertinence to their Lord.

Alphonso turned to Chloe, "We will also stay as long as you need us."

"No, you must rule your domain. I will go into the village now. I have adequate protection." She nodded at her bodyguards who beamed.

Slowly Alphonso and the other men got their gear together and turned to leave. The women from the village took Chloe to a small cottage in the town.

Alphonso and his men had decided to remain overnight in Aulus and so were sitting around a fire in an open field. The other residents of Aulus had brought several large pots of a fish stew which had boiled cheerfully over the campfires emitting heavy smells of garlic. Alphonso had always traveled with large quantities of his domain's excellent wines, which now the villagers and his men drank in copious quantities. As dark drew over the camp, the townspeople filed back to their homes and the soldiers crawled into their tents in the field. Hearty snores began to fill the camp air. Alphonso and Chloe began a slow stroll along the road into town with Chloe's two bodyguards following behind discretely.

Off in the distance coming from the west, several horsemen came galloping into view and stopped short of Alphonso. Immediately Gerard and Henri spurred their horses to the front and drew their broadswords. The new arrivals consisted of men in the cloaks of Foix over their mail. As Chloe recognized the Foix emblems, she held her hands up to her bodyguards. "Wait, it is from Foix." As she said this, a tall thin rider in a long green cloak emerged from between the men and removed the hood which shrouded the head. It was Esclarmonde seated astraddle a large dark horse.

"Ah, Chloe, we had heard you were here. And who is this fine looking gentleman by your side?"

"Esclarmonde, it is Alphonso. At last, you meet." Alphonso bowed. "Madame, it is a pleasure to meet you."

"Yes, we must talk. Please bring one of your nice bottles of burgundy and join me in one of these houses." Alphonso signaled to Henri and he turned to retrieve a bottle. Esclarmonde turned to one of the townspeople who stood open-mouthed. A quick curtsy and a deep bow were quickly executed.

Esclarmonde asked, "I wonder, good people, if we might borrow one of your houses for a quick conference, Lord Alphonso and I?" Still open-mouthed and stunned, the couple were finally able to gasp out, "Of course, Lady Esclarmonde, it would be an honor."

By now, Henri came with a fresh bottle of burgundy and

handed it to Alphonso. Esclarmonde took Alphonso's arm and escorted him behind the two village people whose house had been borrowed. Over her shoulder, Esclarmonde called to Chloe, "Never fear, my dear, I will not steal him from you."

Chloe turned to Henri and Gerard, "What is happening?" They both shrugged but with sly smiles on their faces. And so, Esclarmonde and Alphonso disappeared into the small hut.

"Once inside and seated at a small table, as Alphonso found two earthenware cups, Esclarmonde began, "Alphonso, I have been waiting for some time to meet you. You have stolen the hearts of one of my favorites, my Chloe."

Alphonso, not as nimble or witty as Esclarmonde, said, "Yes, it is true and she mine. I confess it."

"Tell me, what has happened here, Lord Alphonso"

"Good Madame, I am afraid to tell you that Montfort's men and the Dominicans held an inquisition just over in that field. Some were burned alive, some tortured, all were dead. Somehow, Zastra, Chloe's daughter, escaped by stabbing her abductors and hid in the woods for three days until we arrived. Chloe is still in shock, but has regained her composure."

"I see, my Cathars killed in Aulus, on your land."

"Yes, milady."

"So, we have some things to discuss, you and I. First, we must become allies. As you know, Simon de Montfort and the Dominicans are a force in Languedoc and threaten both of our domains."

"Quite so, milady."

"So we must agree to defend each other. Join together where necessary to keep these forces at bay. In a way, we have a marriage to bind our houses, my beloved Chloe and you."

"I agree, that would be wise. Chloe speaks highly of you and tells me you can be trusted. In truth, my lands are more threatened than yours, so your offer of help is very welcome. And Chloe binds us.”

“Yes, it is so. Now what of Chloe?”

“Good madam, I must admit that I am married to Countess Fulgencia of Aragon and owe her family favorable relations. I cannot divorce her.”

“No… No… No. I do not ask that. Chloe and I are Cathars. We hold the Catholic Church and its sacraments in contempt. We do not honor their rituals or their priests. You may live in peace with Chloe with our blessing if you treat her with respect. She is a Perfect now in our faith.” “I could do nothing less, milady.”

“I believe we are on a first name basis now. Call me Esclarmonde.” “Ah, yes. The crystal moon. I descend from the Visigoths as do you. But Chloe feels she must move to Aragon to help her fellow Cathars find refuge. I am heartsick that she will leave me.”

“Alphonso, what were her plans for this? She does not know the safe passage through the Pyrenees and has no allies in Aragon.”

“I agree. She was going to confer with Fulgencia and have some of her compatriots help her.”

“Hmm. I don’t like this. This Fulgencia is not a Cathar, and may not be a good ally for Chloe. She has much to gain by Chloe’s disappearance especially in Aragon territory.”

“What do you mean?”

“She has no children by you, am I correct?”

“Yes.”

“So her eldest, your stepson Osric may have a claim to the throne on your death.”

“God forbid.”

“She is also still able to bear you an heir. Even if it is not your child.”

"It is possible."

"With Chloe sharing your bed, she is an obstacle to this."

"Yes, I see that."

"Moreover, Fulgencia is not a Cathar and does not have their interests at heart. Why should she save them?

"She is friendly now with Chloe, who supplies her with special herbs to keep her lover potent in the bed chamber."

"But, from what I hear, she is a selfish, vain person much into luxury and foolish fripperies. She may be manipulated by others.

Maybe, Dominic Guzman and the Pope."

"Hmm. I hear what you say."

"I am a Cathar. I am dedicated to my people. I will help them seek refuge in my case. With your protection along my borders and to my north, Foix can become a refuge and a passage to Aragon over the Pyrenees. I know the terrain well and have good people in Aragon to help me."

"Yes, I see that."

"Most of all, I wish Chloe to stay near me and with you in Gascony. I want to train her for these missions of the Cathars."

"You make an interesting offer. One I cannot refuse."

"But you must help settle some of my Cathars in your lands."

"I see no objection to that. Chloe has taught me much of your ways. Your people would be most welcome."

"We have many points of agreement then. I am pleased to see you have grown into such a wise ruler. I had seen you when you were just a boy at your wedding years back. If I may say so, it was not a good match. But I have another point to discuss. This may be difficult."

"Please, I am open to suggestions."

"What about Simon de Montfort and this Dominic Guzman. What is to be done with them?"

"I am sorry, Esclarmonde, but I do not wish to risk my domain in a war with these people. So far they see me as uninvolved. I would like to keep it that way."

"I did not mean open confrontation. I can see such would be a losing proposition."

"What do you suggest? I might add that Chloe is opposed to war or killing."

"Yes, she is a good Cathar Perfect. I am not so pure. I have a domain to protect too and many of my subjects. I suggest a covert assassination."

"I too would like to do something. That sounds interesting. What would you do?"

"We would get several people close to Montfort. When it can be done, one of my men would bring him down."

"Ah, I see. We must be careful. Most of my men speak with a heavy Gascon accent, but they are good Christians and will pass any inquisition."

"Most of my people are Cathars and will not know the proper answers."

"We must find someone who fits – a good Christian, with an accent of Languedoc, but loyal to us."

"Yes. Let us cull through our best people to see who meets these criterion. Let us meet in a week, here at Aulus."

"Agreed. But we must not tell Chloe. She will not countenance an assassination."

"Yes. Agreed. Now, we must call in Chloe and tell her of our plans."

Alphonso took another earthenware cup from the shelf while Esclarmonde whispered to her guard to bring in Chloe.

She came through the threshold in awe of the two rulers. In her mind, she was just a simple commoner, but could feel the sense of power and command in the room. She gulped at the cup of wine Alphonso offered and sat timidly where Alphonso directed. What could all this mean?

Alphonso spoke first. "Chloe, I cannot bear to have you leave on your mission to save the Cathars. But we have more important concerns."

Chloe moved stiffly forward, still in shock over seeing the deaths of her beloved villagers. "Chloe, are you alright?"

"Yes, Alphonso, I must be so. I have been called upon."

"Good," said Esclarmonde. "There is much to do. I have reviewed your plans to save the Cathars by taking them over the Pyrenees to Aragon. My dear, it is not well thought out."

"How so, milady?"

"You do not know the Pyrenees and you have no allies in Aragon."

"But I have asked if Fulgencia will help me."

"Again, not well thought out. She is a vain foolish woman, interested only in her pleasures. She has no love for the Cathars. She can be easily manipulated. With you in Aragon, she will regain her prestige and try to bear Alphonso an heir. She is a Catholic and easily turned by the Pope, Guzman or Montfort. We must avoid the risk."

"What shall we do?"

"I will shepherd our flock of Cathars through Foix and the Pyrenees. I and my people are Cathars, know the routes and have many allies in Aragon. You must stay in Gascony and help settle Cathars there, discretely of course."

"Yes, I see that. It is your will then, milady?"

"Yes, most certainly. You will send me messages frequently and I you. You must come to Foix often to confer."

"I understand, milady."

"And Chloe, if it is not too much to ask, I would like to take Zastra into my court. When you come back next, may I introduce her into Foix?"

"Good milady, she is my heart and soul. When I thought she might be among the dead here, I thought to die myself."

"Of course, but she has shown her strength of will and character. She wants to be a Perfect as you. I can help her along the way."

"My dear Esclarmonde, may I discuss this with her. I can see the many advantages she will find in Foix. It is a difficult decision."

"Of course, my dear. I understand."

"And you must keep my good ally, Count Alphonso of Gascony, happy or he will mope around, having lost you." Chloe turned to Alphonso now and grabbed his hand. "It that your command, milady?" she smiled.

"Yes, it most certainly is."

"I have no choice but to obey the Esclarmonde." He blushed in the company of these women.

"Now, go in peace. We will set up lines of communication and direct our Cathar refugees. Go in peace."

"Chloe and Alphonso bowed and left. They walked back to the field, with Alphonso's arm around Chloe for all to see.

The following morning, Alphonso and Chloe and the rest took the road north to Auch. Chloe stared into the middle distance; much had happened in the past few days. There was much to think about.

Back in Auch

Now, back in Auch, Chloe was joined by Zastra and Celine as they wandered in the woods and fields gathering herbs and specimens for the apothecary. Chloe was mostly quiet as she mourned and turned over the events of the recent past, breaking her concentration only to explain the varieties and cures to her companions. Henri and Gerard kept a discrete distance and occasionally circled the perimeter to look for anything suspicious; these were perilous times and Chloe was now a known quantity to the Dominicans.

Alphonso, along with General Tomric culled through the soldiers under their command for a few likely spies to infiltrate the Dominicans or Montfort's troops. While the Dominicans were well disciplined and looked to Guzman for direction to be passed down to the wandering monk inquisitions, Montfort's troops were disorganized, underdisciplined and often drunk and unruly. These men had been freed from the drudgery of serfdom and now enjoyed the manly comradery. When unoccupied they lingered in taverns or sat around campfires passing jugs of sweet wine. They had little training as soldiers, nor did Montfort try to instill it. Their main attack was a headlong rush brandishing weapons, broadswords, maces, or hammers and yet they met with success, they were rarely met with resistance, the usual practice was to mass around the Dominicans as they entered unfortified towns and confronted unarmed villagers.

While the Dominicans conducted their minimal interrogation before torture or burning suspected Cathars, the guard duty once over, lead to rampages of rape and pillaging. Men collected their booty and returned to camp for celebratory inebriation.

It would not be difficult for a few of the men of Foix or Gascony to mingle in with these men. They had come from many northern areas, had not known each other before this so-called crusade, and new recruits arrived on a daily basis.

Esclarmonde and Alphonso were due to meet shortly and send a contingent to the ranks of Montfort. They sorted through their men to find those who could answer the Catholic catechism and did not have a Gascon accent..

In 10 days' time, Tomric conducted his six men selected from his ranks to be trained at Aulus. They left Auch and took the earthen trails through the forest to meet their counterparts from Foix. Once in Aulus, they laid out their tents and set a campfire. By nightfall, a number of riders from Foix came into Aulus. They were led by a young officer, Etienne by name and as they came up, Tomric came out to meet them. But then stood open-mouthed as the seven riders came near.

"But… you have brought me women. What is the meaning of this?"

"Good General Tomric, it was at Esclarmonde's suggestion. We Cathars consider women equal to men. She also thought they could be better to infiltrate Montfort's ranks."

"But… why?"

"As she explained to me, men – especially Catholic men – do not hold women in high regard; in fact, they are almost invisible unless they are young and pretty. And they are not questioned closely in the inquisitions. They easily plead ignorance so they are safer than their male counterparts."

"But can they defend themselves?"

"You be the judge of that. Ladies, please dismount." Three women in their thirties slid off their donkeys. They were indeed of sturdy Visigothic stock, broad shouldered and wide-hipped, and past marriageable age. "May I introduce Bertha, Gertrude and Frieda."

The first training consisted of close quarters self-defense. Tomric wished to test these women since the men had already been trained in combat. The women were alternately armed with wooden short swords, or daggers and attacked from various angles. These women had already spent many years working hard in the fields and were quite muscular. With some time, they learned the techniques of both the Gascons and those from Foix.

After a few days, some of the war machines rumbled down the road from Foix. Catapults, arbalests, mangonels and trebuchets were arrayed out in a field outside of town. Large boulders were strewn behind them. These machines now in common use in warfare could hurl large rocks or flaming bundles over city walls and cause great damage. Most of the men had already been trained in this sort of artillery, but they went through the firing sessions aimed at targets down range against the woods. The women sat on a few scattered logs and cheered the men on as they grew more proficient at the machines and came closer to the targets.

Soon, Frieda came up to Etienne, officer in charge of the Foix contingent. "Our turn," she demanded.

"But why, you will never use them."

"It looks like fun and we think we can do it." Etienne timidly glanced over to Tomric who stood hands on hips. "What do these women want now?" The women gave an awkward curtsy.

Tomric looked skyward. "Can you defend yourselves?"

Bertha stepped forward. "Sire," she said in the Visigothic

accent, "you have never been a peasant. You do not understand how women are treated. We are often attacked or harassed. So we learn." Slowly she drew a dagger from inside the sleeve of her shift and made a slashing motion. "We have kept our virginity when we were young only by our willingness to fight, especially drunken and clumsy men."

Frieda, too, stepped forward and drew up the skirt of her shift to reveal a dagger strapped to her calf.

"Alright, alright. Let's see how you do in training. Bed down for the night and we'll start at first light."

The women from Foix settled in together and unrolled their tent.

Soon, the entire party was standing around the campfire eating a stew from their bowls and drinking the ever present wine of Bordeaux the Gascons had brought with them.

At dawn, the women were up setting out breakfast of yogurt and fruit. The men rubbing their eyes and scratching were pleased to see the spread laid out. The women were demonstrating their prowess learned from early childhood in preparing food. They were to be the women who prepared meals for Montfort's men. Tomric grunted satisfaction – at least they had a serviceable function.

"They want to try the machines."

"They can't even lift the rocks." Bertha and Gertrude needing no further encouragement, went over to a nearby pile, each lifted a rock and carried it to the trebuchet.

"Now what?" demanded Bertha.

"Alright. Let's see what you can do."

Having watched the men do this most of the prior two days, the women hefted the rocks into place and pulled on the arming levers. When stretched to its tightest, they turned toward Tomric. "Your command, sir?"

Tomric bellowed out, "Fire," and Gertrude hit the lever with a small hammer and the rock thundered down the range. All three women turned to Tomric. "May we do another?"

Tomric duly impressed said, "Alright, let's try the mangonel." This device – somewhat smaller – required more strength to set the torsion. Two of the women pulled back the lever while one loaded another rock into the sleeve. Again, they turned toward Tomric, "Fire," he bellowed. The mangonel sprang into action and competently flung the rock towards the woods. It landed close to the hay bale used as a target.

From then on, the women were included in making the adjustments necessary to gauge the distance of the machines, much to the delight of the men who now felt they had to compete with the women.

Soon the women were included in the broadswords and archery. They clearly enjoyed the new ventures.

During each rest period and at lunch, a young man sent out by Esclarmonde, came out to the gathering to quiz them on the Catholic catechism so they could confound the Dominican friars. They even knelt and took communion using the Frankish style.

But the women had additional weapons at their disposal. Esclarmonde's apothecaries had concocted a variety of poisons and potions to disarm and disable. Most could cause weeks of sickness, dysentery, hearing loss and weakness in the joints. Small discrete packets were placed in the women's traveling packs.

Then, the secret signs. A series of written symbols and hand signs were put into the vocabulary of the group to be learned. Every few days a messenger would seek them out and get reports on the situation. The messenger, now down from Auch, was introduced all around as they practiced the hand signals.

After several weeks, Tomric was beginning to feel more confident in the enterprise. He sent back the messenger, to be named Claude, to Alphonso saying he was ready. Etienne sent one of the men back to Esclarmonde with the same message. Each commander was given the authority to proceed.

So the group mounted up, taking the road toward Toulouse and then were directed to where Montfort had assembled his troops. On this information the men and women split off from one another and prepared to amble into the army from the north. The women traveled together.

Foix Men to Camp

Carefully, the men and women drew up to the ranks of the Montfort troops sprawled around the exterior of Toulouse. A siege had been going on for a week now. In the Montfort camp, there was little activity. Men lounged about for the most part drinking, playing dice and card games, occasionally arguing. As the men from Foix and Auch ambled up, they asked to see the closest commander to see if they might be needed. Sometimes, they were refused, other times they were welcomed. It depended on the money and food available for that commander. Since they were not all trained and marching under the direct command of one leader, each commander could make his own decisions. It was not long before all the men and women were situated somewhere across the siege line.

At sporadic intervals, the archers would send volleys of fiery arrows over the walls into town. The arbalests or catapults would launch a barrage of rocks. Otherwise, the actual foot soldiers had little to do unless a skirmish might emerge from the gate and attack a group nearby. Mostly it was boredom. Wait and hope the residents inside would run out of food or water, while the siege party sat in the mud and foraged the nearby fauna for food.

The Foix women had been placed in the kitchen staff in the rear of battle line. They had been well supplied with herbs to be placed in the large bowls of stew served at supper to the men. From Esclarmonde's formulary came a variety of ingredients to cause hallucinations, dysentery, vomiting and other discomforts to chip away at the morale of the men. Jars of condensed ipecac were surreptitiously poured into the cauldrons boiling with stew. Lore from the desert Muslim tribes had been searched and yielded lists of natural plants that caused hallucinations. As the women wandered more about the other kitchen areas and became friendly with the other women they felt more at ease gaining access to the boiling stewpots. Claude on his visits to get reports was able to re-supply these potions. Soon many of the soldiers had been subjected to these infusions. This did not help their morale as days after days of boredom dulled their spirits.

Often, when large armies are assembled and are in active attack mode, men are, in the confusion of battle, known to inflect injury and death on their own men. The men from Auch and Foix were able, during fusillades of fiery arrows and large rocks, to direct fire at the adjacent companies and across to the other side of the siege formation. With all the disorganization among this hastily assembled fighting force, the lack of any discipline made the discovery of the source of these apparently misguided barrages impossible. Yet scores of their own men lay dead or severely wounded in the ranks when it did not appear that any answering barrages had come from behind the city walls.

The command staff rarely mingled with the men. The camp became a malodorous swamp, and the men themselves were often drunk and capable of any mischief. Nonetheless, there were regular inspections with Montfort and his retinue in sparkling uniforms and horse caparisoned in brilliant colors representing the noble houses their riders came from. With the men at some form of military attention, Simon de Montfort would walk his horse imperiously down the lines and receive the salute of a commander. Soon this inspection tour began to occur at 10:00 a.m. on Mondays, Wednesdays and Fridays to inspire the men. It also became a time for the fiery arrows and massive barrages of rocks to be flung over the lines of the men as a rallying cry. The men would alternately stomp their right foot and bang their weapons on the ground with a deep grunt, as trumpets and tubas blared out march rhythms. In this way, the long wait for the end of drudgery would seem less so.

The women of Foix now wandered around camp, known to many, whom they would cheerfully insult as they fended off crude offers to be mounted. Since they travelled together and were sturdy and just as crude as the men, little came of the male offers which had now reached the stage of ritual rather than actual solicitation.

The women were able to quietly commandeer several unoccupied mangonels which they quietly loaded with a few massive stones and stretched the lever to maximum tension. As the barrage of arrows and rocks flew overhead to the tune of marching trumpets and tubas, Frieda quietly struck each holding pin with a small hammer sending three large stones over the heads of the men at attention down range at the brilliantly dressed entourage of Simon de Montfort. She scurried away back to the kitchen tent where her two compatriots watched in silence. Miraculously, a large rock struck Montfort directly on the forehead and knocked him from his horse. Blood flowed from his scalp and drooled from the sides of his mouth as he attempted to rise on his elbow. But then, he fell back, inert at his side while generals rushed to his body, shouting for a stretcher.

The women quietly stole glances at each other and drew back among the other women in the kitchen tent. The tubas ceased and the camp fell quiet. The rumors flew around camp. With 10,000 pairs of eyes, no two could agree. It was definitely a stone hurled with some force, but it struck him in front on his forehead knocking his ornate helmet backwards. But no one could describe the direction or the trajectory. Some claimed to have seen a woman near the machines, but none could say for sure. Over the weeks, the final word became that a woman had thrown a rock at Montfort from behind the besieged city wall.

The funeral procession took him back to his home castle, and so he was buried not near the front where the death of their prestigious commander would have depressed morale.

It did not take long for the men from Foix to realize what Frieda had done and what the rumors might say. Whether true or not, the rage of the soldiers about the death of their commander could alight on anyone. No one yet had implicated Frieda's mangonel, so now was an excellent time to spirit Frieda and her companions away and back to Foix. The quickest route lead to Auch and so, at dusk, Frieda, Bertha and Gertrude astride donkeys and surrounded by their bodyguards from Foix stole into the night and rode west. They were greeted at the outskirts of Auch by a patrol. When they asked for Alphonso, and mentioned the name of Chloe in their explanation, they were shepherded to a stable near the castle for the night and kept under careful guard.

The next morning as the women splashed water on their faces at the trough and pulled straw from their hair, Chloe and Celine ran up to the barn door. "Frieda, Bertha, Gertrude, what has happened, why are you here?"

Bertha, the bigger and stronger, stepped forward and clasped Frieda by the shoulder pulling her forward. "Milady, Frieda here has hit Simon de Montfort with a rock from a mongonel. He is dead." Frieda bowed her head shyly.

Then, several soldiers and Tomric came to the barn door. "Ladies," he began.

Chloe burst in, "General Tomric, Frieda here has hit Simon de Montfort with a rock from a mongonel."

"What…" he gasped, "What."

"Yes, it is true, General Tomric. I saw it. He lay on the ground with blood coming out of his head and mouth," and Bertha, still clasping Frieda proudly.

"Then, we must celebrate her."

"But quietly, General Tomric," said Chloe. "They may not know she is from Foix. We must keep her identity secret and have Claude spread rumors."

"Yes… Yes… I agree. So, ladies, when you wanted to play with the war machines, I never imagined…"

"Thank you, General."

That night at supper, Alphonso rose to give a toast, but carefully explained the need for secrecy. He extolled the bravery of the Foix women and especially Frieda. The men cheered and pushed Frieda to the front.

"Have you anything to say, my dear?" asked Alphonso.

She curtsied, and staring at her feet, said, "Good my lord, I take little joy in this. I am a Cathar and I do not believe in killing, but I am forced to protect our people." She now had tears in her eyes. "This body is but a shell for my soul. My death would only release my soul."

This sobering thought chilled the assembly for but a moment. Alphonso raised his cup, "Gentlemen and ladies, we still have seen an act of heroism. And a great advance in the defense of our Cathar brethren. While very modest, this brave woman must be toasted. All hail!" the excellent Bordeaux wine was raised around the room and "All hail" was echoed several times. Frieda went back to her seat on the bench next to Bertha and

Gertrude who stroked her back and she shuddered between them.

And so it was that the great Simon Montfort was struck and killed by a rock hurled by a woman at the siege of Toulouse. He would receive no lands, no riches from this victory in what was a slaughter of an entire religion dedicated to peace and purity. At his death, he held lands in England and France from his own achievements, but mostly from massive inheritances from many high born relatives. Even though he had returned exhausted from an embarrassing crusade which was to be directed at the Muslims but actually ended in the sacking and destruction of the Western Holy Roman Empire which had survived over a thousand years. Henceforth, the greedy and corrupt Ottoman Empire would survive and rule the lands of Turkey and the Muslim lands to the East.

Now King Philippe – self-styled Auguste – of France would accede with little effort to the rich lands of southern France, soon to be rid of the Cathars.

The northern lords continued to pursue the war of eradication of the Cathars, and town after town was captured and often destroyed. The favorites of the Pope were entrenched in the new churches throughout southern France and continued to practice simony and, for a large fee, grant forgiveness of sins – confessed and unconfessed – and paid-for admission to heaven in the afterlife. The rich culture fathered by Count Raymond in Toulouse slowly began to disappear as the severity of the church inquisition began procedures to banish ideas inimical to church doctrine in the arts and sciences. The religion in adoration of the Shekinah – the holy feminine – would have to wait for its joinder with the masculine god. Slow ignorance and superstition would sweep over the land.

It was the year 1885 when Pere Berenger Sauniere pulled his battered trunk and suitcase off the wagon at Rennes-le-Chateau. This was his first assignment as the resident priest of the Church of Ste. Mary Magdalene. He had served as an assistant for 10 years at other churches, but now he would be the sole priest. It was a warm day in summer in Languedoc, and dust swirled as the wagon pulled away, leaving him in the middle of this sleepy town after the long climb up the steep hill. His salary would be 900 francs a year, hardly enough to live on, but he could earn another franc for each mass he said, but since he could only say three masses a day, his prospects were grim. Nonetheless, he was now on his own in his own church. He couldn't complain for this is what he had sought.

The church itself was on top of a steep hill up a road which was at one time partially paved, but now over the years, was pocked and rutted. It was dedicated to Mary Magdalene, whom, people in the area still believed, had settled in the area with her beloved Jesus and in her belly, her daughter Sarah. It was still murmured that she and her daughter after her had preached throughout the area, until Mary had chosen to live in a cave and end her days in prayer. This rumor was only murmured because it was part of the Cathar legend and the Cathars had been killed off by the Inquisition lead by Dominic Guzman, St. Dominic. It was also murmured that many of the Cathars had survived by going into hiding or going through false conversion to the Orthodox Roman Catholic faith. Perhaps some of these Cathars had descendants who still espoused some of the Cathar faith in this very area of Languedoc. It was rumored that there were still secret Cathars in this area. The church itself had many mysterious symbols. At the alter, St. Joseph was one of the principal statues, holding the baby Jesus. Why Joseph should be venerated was a mystery. Throughout, Mary Magdalene was venerated. The initials JSM were in a few key spots, it was rumored that this stood for Jesus, Sarah, Mary. The Magdalene's daughter was worshipped as a saint in Languedoc as well as Mary herself. The most striking feature was a scary plaster sculpture of a devil, Asmodeus, at the entrance. Above him was a plaster sculpture of angels. The devil was not part of Orthodox Christian theology, but the Cathars believed in the duality of good and evil, incarnate in the devil in many early Cathar tales. A sculpture of Jesus being baptized by John the Baptist is opposite the devil. But, to Pere Sauniere, this was only some old wives tale, as he slowly climbed the hill to his new church. But it was hardly new. Like the road on which he now climbed, the church was also ancient and neglected. As he stopped often to rest going up the hill, the ravages of the church became more and more visible.

At last, he was able to go into the nave of the church, into the cool, but dim interior. He rested in the last of the pews and wiped his brow. As he recovered from his climb, he could see the images and carvings of Ste. Mary Magdalene, and they were astounding. There were none of the accepted, standardized images of the saints, and gothic architecture of the many country churches he had seen. These were odd symbols, odd figures, and esoteric carvings here and there. Yes, he had heard the church was odd, but not something like this. He walked around the church staring at these fixtures. What could they mean? As he made his way around the walls, a voice came from the entrance behind him.

"Ah, Pere Sauniere, it must be you." He turned and in the

doorway stood a pleasant plump woman in a blue dress and an apron.

"Yes, Madame, and who are you?" He bowed.

"I am Marie, Marie Denauraud. I am the housekeeper of the church and the rectory. I have been told you were coming." She added, "It is not madame, it is mademoiselle."

"It is nice to meet you. I find this church to have many strange symbols and images on the walls. Please sit and tell me what you know about them."

She sat in the last pew, and settled herself in. "Pere Sauniere, this area is indeed a strange one. We have many tales to tell, and this very church has many secrets. As you can tell, it is dedicated to Ste. Mary Magdalene, but it is built over an old Roman one dedicated to Venus in Roman days. Some say people still worship the feminine god. Have you heard of this?"

"Only briefly in my seminary days."

"The Cathars too worshipped a feminine god and were settled in this area."

Marie stared intently at Pere Sauniere as she said this. Would he be shocked? No. His response was benign.

"Well, Marie, people who seek God seek him in many ways." Ah, he was an enlightened priest. "For now, can you show me around, so I can get settled? I will have my first mass this Sunday, and I will have to prepare."

"Yes, Father." She rose and led him out the door to the rectory.

Like the church, the rectory was old and dusty, much in need of repair. The kitchen was ancient, but it was serviceable. He laid his trunk on the bedroom floor and paced about. "Thank you, Marie."

"Oh no, Father, I will have to dust and mop. I will be back soon." She scurried out, and returned with a mop and a bucket of water from the well outside. She busied herself now in the few rooms of the rectory while Pere Sauniere strolled about the church grounds.

At Sunday mass, only a few stragglers shuggled up the hill to hear Pere Sauniere and receive communion, mostly older women. As the weeks passed, Pere Sauniere felt discouraged and although he tried to present better themes for his sermon, the same few were all that came.

At first, he tried to walk about the town and meet his parishioners, but they were polite but reluctant to speak to him. After more than a few lukewarm responses, he turned to Marie. "I'm sorry, Marie, but the town does not seem to warm up to me. I have been successful before. Can you help me?"

"I'm afraid so. If you remember your history, the Pope declared a crusade against the Cathars in Languedoc, and sent St. Dominic out on an Inquisition to root out heresy. Many people were killed, tortured and lost their lands which the French king from the north took over."

"But that was over 700 years ago."

"Yes. They still fear and hate the pope and Rome. Most of these people have lived on these lands for centuries. That distrust remains."

"I have heard they look to Mary Magdalene and her daughter as saints. How do they feel about them?"

"Just as you said. While some believe Mary landed here with Jesus and began to preach, not everyone does, but many revere her as a symbol of Jesus' love."

"So if I preach about Mary Magdalene, people may respond."
"They may not trust you. The church still says she was a prostitute.

Would you listen to such a person?"

"Do they believe in what I hear is the feminine god?"

"It is hard to say."

"I can't do worse than I am now."

Pere Sauniere tried vainly to refer to Mary Magdalene as a message of God's forgiveness for those who repent. The townspeople never liked the depiction of Mary Magdalene as a whore and ignored his sermons. Also, none of the townspeople spoke Latin, especially church Latin and so his masses were meaningless. He did receive a few requests for masses by several charitable donors who did not actually attend the masses, but these one franc receipts were limited.

So it was that he sat smoking his pipe in the cool fall day with his feet up on a bench as he contemplated what this message from God might be. Marie, his housekeeper, with whom he was now quite friendly since he had few friends in the town, came to sit.

"You know Father, this area is very strange and has much to learn from years past. It was not always just a forgotten village."

"What do you mean?"

"As you know the Cathars lived in this area for many years until the Pope and St. Dominic led an Inquisition against them."

"I'm not interested in some long lost belief; the Pope said it was a heresy. Who am I to learn about something that was killed off 700 years ago?"

"There is talk that the Cathars hid away their treasures as they fled the area or were killed off."

"Hmm. Treasure, you say." Pere Sauniere was now very much on edge.

"Yes. And Pere Sauniere, this was a Cathar church in its day. All those symbols you speak of were Cathar symbols. Maybe, they left a clue as to their hidden treasure."

Pere Sauniere who had fallen into a state of depression as to his inability to preach to the town, now perked up. Perhaps a new mission had been given to him. Hmm. Cathar treasure.

He lurched to his feet and began to review his church. Marie sat in the back pew, happy to see the Pere so animated at last.

Pere, just lightly burdened with parishioners, had many hours in the day to fill. He began an exhaustive research of the Cathars on trips to Narbonne, Toulouse and Carcassonne, but, as the loser in the Pope's crusade, little had been recorded. So again he sat smoking his pipe and stewing. The church was deteriorating and that depressed him as well. There was a leak in the roof, the floor boards were warping, the paint was peeling, and the place smelled musty. Marie did her best but to no avail.

By now, Marie had moved into Pere Sauniere's bed and could feel his unhappiness. "Berenger, (no longer Pere) have you learned anything from the Cathar history?"

"I can't say very much," he mumbled gloomily staring at the ceiling.

"You know they were an educated people, but they kept to themselves."

"Marie, are you sympathetic to these Cathars?"

"Yes, of course, Berenger. They were kind and gentle, and lived holy lives."

"I must say, Marie, you often sound like a Cathar yourself."

For some time, Marie was quiet. Dare she say her thoughts? Yes. Berenger was a reasonable man. "Berenger, my ancestors were Cathars I am afraid. And, I must admit I believe in much of what they preached."

"Do you tend my services? Are there still some locals who need to share their beliefs?"

Again, silence. "Yes, there are some. Am I causing trouble by telling you? Must you tell the bishop?"

"No, Marie. Your little group sounds harmless. While their beliefs may differ from what I was taught I must say they are intriguing. They do sound a bit like Jesus himself in the gospels. Do they pray here locally?"

"Yes. There is a cave where they meet. Near Mont Segur near where they were slaughtered in the last battle."

"Marie, I must ask, can you show me? I swear not to reveal its location."

"Yes, Berenger. It is not far, maybe a day's ride."

The next morning, Pere Sauniere and Marie road out on the cart for Mont Segur. Marie had prepared a breakfast of yogurt and strawberries which they ate as they rode. About midmorning they stopped at a small roadside inn. They stopped halfway at Purvert where they could see rugged foothills ahead. A woman with a stand beside the road sold them cheese and some hard sausage which they ate in the shade at the edge of town. The donkey was given some water at the town as well, and had spent some time grazing on the weeds by the roadside. Once again they got into the cart, clucked to the donkey. Soon they could see the sad remains of Mont Segur where the Cathars mounted their last stand before being slaughtered.

They passed Mont Segur and rolled down a narrow road which was lightly covered with weeds.

""Here, Berenger, stay here." He tied the donkey to a tree by the roadside and walked up a narrow path. As they came to a large rock outcropping, Marie pointed to a clump of underbrush and waded through it. Just past the bushes, there was a small entrance to a cave with piles of scree obstructing the entrance. Marie started to remove a few rocks in the path and entered the cave. When Berenger followed, the cave widened out into a cavern. On the floor of the cavern were several benches in a circle. The walls were daubed with strange symbols as they had seen in Ste. Mary Magdalene.

"Here, Berenger, here is where we meet." And she knelt

and began to pray quietly. He looked around and could not decipher the symbols. They were not anything Christian he was aware of. He wandered around the interior looking for nooks or movable rocks. Nothing. It was what it seemed. An old cavern with a floor of light rubble. He too knelt to see if he could absorb some of the presence in the room. He felt nothing. Marie rose and looked at Berenger.

"Anything?"

"No. I'm afraid not.

That day, Pere Sauniere and Marie returned up the steep hill to Rennes-le-Chateau. For days, Sauniere sat in the pew in the back row of the church in studious reverie. Something was here, but what? The tales of the Cathars and their treasure were everywhere. Could it still be near here? He jumped up quickly and took a spade from the tool shed by the cemetery. He began digging among the tombs. Then, he scrutinized the whole church, hammering at bricks, raising pieces of stone flooring. After days, he came to the pulpit and began to rap lightly. Suddenly, a panel fell off revealing a small enclosure with a scrap of paper. Rudely drawn it was a map which seemed to show the cavern he and Marie had been to earlier. From the cavern, there was a line going up a hill with a fire circle at its top. Along the way up the hill was another small cave depicted with several wooden chests drawn beside it. At the bottom of the map was a symbol for a moon. What could this mean? A treasure? More Cathar relics? What?

"Marie, Marie!" he called. "Come, we must go!"

"Go where, Berenger?"

"Back to that cavern with the Cathar symbols."

She rushed to assemble some food for the journey while he readied the cart and put the tracings on the donkey. Soon they were off on the road back to the cavern.

Once again they stopped near the cavern and climbed up to the old Cathar meeting place, leaving Marie to sit on one of the benches there. He pulled out the scrap of paper he had found in the opening of the pulpit and traced his way further up the hill. Pushing through ferns and bushes, he could make out a small boulder and behind it a narrow opening. He tried to move the boulder but it was by now firmly wedged into the ground. Yet he could stretch his hand over the boulder and feel… feel, yes feel a wooden chest. He could pull up the lid and further feel a bag of what seemed to be coins and a circular leather piece. He was able to fish these out over the boulder, and sat back, opening the bag of coins. There were piles of gold… yes, real gold coins with markings on them he did not recognize. He unwrapped the leather piece and could see parchments with writing which looked somehow Arabic. He rewrapped the leather piece and carried it and the pouch of coins back to Marie.

"Come, Marie, I have much to do." He showed her the bag of coins and the leather piece.

Berenger knew that his life would change forever; But waves of caution swept over him. Yes, he had found treasure but he must keep it a secret. He must find a way to cash the coins, and he must show these writings to someone to interpret. But who? Who could he trust?

"Marie, we must keep this a secret. But no one can know what we have found. And these writings, I don't know what to do with them. I will bring them home and study them."

"Yes, Berenger, I agree. This is very good fortune, but dangerous. Only we can know where this chest is."

They carried their new found items back their donkey and rode home, looking over their shoulders at every turn.

Pere Sauniere shortly thereafter left with his new found treasure for Paris. He would take the coins to a numismatist to determine their value, and the documents to the University to see what they were and have them translated.

It was now 1947. Pere Sauniere had died in 1917 depressed and embittered. M. Corbu had heard of his travels and wished to buy what remained of his estate from Marie Dé Narnaud. Marie Dé Narnaud welcomed Noel Corbu into the small parlor. "Monsieur Corbu, I was surprised to hear you are interested in Berenger after all these years. He died in, let me see, 1917, yes some 30 years ago. You asked me many details about his life but I must tell you he was very secretive. I can tell you what I know."

"Thank you, Madame."

"I'm sorry it is mademoiselle, we were never married."

"But he left you his estate."

"Quite so, we were indeed close." As M. Corbu looked around the room, the surroundings were hardly lavish, even in spots somewhat shabby.

"Well, Mlle. Dé Narnaud…"

"Call me Marie, everyone does."

"Very well, Marie, what can you tell me about this vast fortune which Pere Sauniere is accused of having. As you know, I am interested in purchasing his estate."

"As I told you before, Berenger had heard of the supposed Cathar treasure. As you know, the last massacre of the Cathars occurred at Mont Segur, not 40 miles from here and it was rumored that they had hidden or buried some of their valuables in this area. Well, poor Berenger had not been successful reviving an interest in Ste Mary Magdalene over in Rennes-le-Chateau, and, being his first assignment for his own church, he was depressed. He went home to visit his family in Limoux and returned refreshed. I am not sure what he may have found, but this Ste. Marie Magdalene was believed to be a Cathar church in its day. Maybe he heard some old stories about the Cathars.

So he began to search the interior of the church, among the old graves in the graveyard, all over. We didn't find much, and he had trouble living on the small salary he received as a priest.

"So he began to advertise to sell masses. In those days, people would send you one franc if you said a mass for them. Some people wanted to remember dead relatives, bless newborns, commemorate first communions, new businesses. So he made some money saying these masses. I might add to very few people. You could only say three masses a day, and you weren't supposed to double up. And the church called it a crime if you took the money and didn't say the mass. So he survived on his 900 francs a year salary and some money for the masses.

"Then, one day, he came in all excited. A wood panel had come loose from the pulpit, he said. So we rented a cart and went to a place near Mont Segur. He seemed to be following some directions so we stopped after a ride of two days. He wandered around some brush until he found an old path up a hill. We then came to a cave where it looked like there had been a meeting place with symbols on the walls of some kind. I had showed it to him before but nothing came of it then. Berenger kept saying 'uh-huh' as if he recognized the symbols. Some were like those on the walls of Ste. Mary Magdalene. He explained some of this to me, but I didn't understand it at all.

"Anyway, he left the cavern and went up a narrow path to another small cave. There, he said he found a chest, which he couldn't pull out of the cave, but Berenger was able to pry open the lid and reach his hand in. He pulled out a bag of coins and a leather sheath with some parchments in side. The parchments had something that looked like Arabic on it. So we took these back to Rennes-le-Chateau. What happened after that I am not sure of, since he kept it to himself.

"I know he took the train to Paris with the coins and the book. He told me the writing in the book was ancient and looked like Arabic. Anyway, he came back from Paris with lots of money and a bank account. He left the sheath of parchments with some scholars at the University."

M. Corbu could hardly contain himself, this sounded like a great find Sauniere had made. "So what happened next?"

"With the money he brought home from Paris, he had the church completely refurbished. He ordered some sculptures from a catalog, and had the roof and the floor repaired. I know he spent 12,000 francs on that. And then he built a home for old people that cost 20,000 francs. He was a good man and he wanted a parish he could be proud of. For some reason he also built the tower you see over there – he called it Magdala after Mary Magdalene and it was his library.

"But then he was summoned by the Bishop of Carcassonne and he told me some senior priests from Rome started asking him some questions. After that he was scared. He said he refused to answer their questions and they threatened him. He never told me what they were asking him, but it was about the coins or the parchment.

"It later came out that they wanted to know where he got all this money to spend on his church. When he wouldn't answer, they demanded to see his books and records. He again refused. We spent the next few years in fear. Eventually, they decided all this money came from selling masses – taking peoples' money and not saying the mass.

"After he had been threatened and interrogated by the Roman priests and the Bishop of Carcassonne, he was scared and depressed. Apparently what he found was dangerous. All the money he had now, he could not use. The parchments he had taken to Paris had found their way to Rome. They were, so they said, dangerous. So he was followed for some hint about his hidden money or the parchments.

"The first time he just refused to appear so the church sent some men around who seemed to be threatening him. So he appeared, and the bishop decided he was 'trafficking in masses' – taking money to say mass for people but not saying it. They decided he had taken in 130,000 francs and demanded he return it. Since he didn't have the money they required him to go to a monastery to repent. Eventually he just became a 'free priest.' He had no church or appointment by the church. He was very depressed. I saw him just shrink from the world. He died during the first World War – a sad and broken man."

"But what of the chest, the coins, what happened to them?"

"In his Will, he left his estate to me, but I couldn't find anything.

I think he lost access to his funds during the war."

"But what about this cave? Where is it?"

"He was looking at some kind of map which he said had been hidden in the pulpit of the church, but I don't know where he kept it. He often disappeared for a few days and came back with more coins. He said he found more parchments and codexes. He may have sold these or given them to a secretive organization. A lot of strange men were coming to see him.

"In any event, he took some money to a bank and left it in trust for me."

"But, Marie, what about the map he found?"

"M. Corbu, I am afraid. I fear the same men who scared Berenger so many years ago."

"But these things he found. It sounds like there were more in the chest. Where is this cave?"

"M. Corbu. I am a simple woman. I fear the church. I will leave you a letter when I have died. It will show you where Berenger found the chest."

"Please, Marie, it is very important."

"M. Corbu, I know. As I said, when I die."

Marie Dé Narmaud died in 1958. No letter detailing the location of the chest in the cave was found among her things.

Sister Smile

A hit song miraculously burst into the record charts in 1963. A Belgian nun, known as Soeur Sourire ("Sister Smile") became the Singing Nun with the hypnotic folk song "Dominique" about St. Dominic, Dominic Guzman. The nun, Jeanine Deckers, played guitar and sang with several other nuns of the Dominican Order in tight harmony. The song lyrics appear below:

Dominique, nique, nique, over the land he plods
And sings a little song
Never asking for reward
He just talks about the Lord
He just talks about the Lord

At a time when Johnny Lackland
Over England was the King
Dominique was in the backland
Fighting sin like anything

Now a heretic, one day
Among the thorns forced him to crawl
Dominique with just one prayer
Made him hear the good Lord's call
Without horse or fancy wagon
He crossed Europe up and down

Poverty was his companion
As he walked from town to town

To bring back the straying liars
And the lost sheep to the fold
He brought forth the Preaching Friars Heaven's soldier's,
brave and bold

One day, in the budding Order
There was nothing left to eat
Suddenly two angels walked in
With a loaf of bread and meat
Grant us now, oh Dominique
The grace of love and simple mirth
That we all may help to quicken
Godly life and truth on earth

Dominique, nique, nique s'en allait tout simplement
Routier pauvre et chantant
En tous chemins, en tous lieux, il ne parle que du bon Dieu

Il ne parle que du bon Dieu
A l'e poque ou Jean-sans-Terre de' Angleterre etait Roi
Dominique, notre Pere, combattit les Albigeois
Repeat first 4 lines: Chorus
> *Ni chameau, ni diligence il parcout l'Europe a pied*
> *Scandinavie ou Provence dans la sainte pauvrete*

> *Refrain*

> *Enflamma de toute ecole filles et garcons pleins d'ardeur*
> *Et pour semer la Parole inventa les Freres-Precheurs*

Refrain

Chez Dominique et ses freres le pain s'en vint a manquer
Et deux anges se presenterent portant de grands pains dores

Refrain

Dominique vit en reve les precheurs du monde entier
Sous le manteau de la Vierge en grand nombre rassembles

Refrain

Dominique, mon bon Pere, garde-nous simples et gais
Pour annoncer a nos freres la Vie et la Verite

RefrainWriter/s: SOEUR SOURIRE, NOEL REGNEY
Publisher: Sony/ATV Music Publishing LLC, Warner/Chappell Music, Inc.

It held the United States and Europe in thrall for weeks.

As happens with one time hit records, the Philips record company and the producer got the lions share (95% it is said) of the profits of the 2 million records sold. Ms. Deckers fared poorly after that.

In an undisclosed dispute of an unknown but allegedly theological nature, Ms. Deckers was dismissed from her Order. Since the record company had received almost all the profits, and Sister Sourire's abbey got the rest, she received little for her sensational hit. Yet Belgian tax authorities pursued her relentlessly for the taxes due on the song's profits although they had been paid to the nunnery.

Thereafter, the record company and the Order refused to let her use the name "Soeur Sourire" or "Sister Smile." As a result,

Ms. Deckers' later attempts to pursue a singing career – or issue a second record met with failure. Neither the record company nor the abbey contributed to her tax debt.

After leaving the Order, Ms. Deckers entered into a long term relationship with Anne Pecher that lasted 20 years. In 1985, they both committed suicide.

www.ingramcontent.com/pod-product-compliance
Lightning Source LLC
Chambersburg PA
CBHW030349200726

48286CB00013B/610